ZAHIRA

ZAHIRA

and the Riddle of the White Star

Abdullah Kirk

To order additional copies of this book, contact:
Xlibris Corporation
1-888-795-4274
www.Xlibris.com
Orders@Xlibris.com
106412

Contents

Dedicated to the persecuted and afflicted, but through perseverance maintain their faith and conviction to succeed in this life .... for the reward of the next.

IN THE BEGINNING

The Conundrum of the White and Blackstars

Antiquities of Aegon:

Astral aliens, twin brothers, but each a leader of opposing nations from a distant celestial universe, engaged each other in combat over the ancient Koryan, a fluctuating sphere containing vast amounts of cosmic energy. Their monumental battle opened a dimensional portal that flung them from their universe into ours. One brother was chosen by the light and the other by darkness, thus the names 'the White and Blackstar' as perceived by the primitive humans of the day.

Fimaya Period—Black Period:

(From mans start of the building of nations and kingdoms. The start of Emperor and ancestor worship, the weak are conquered and subjugated while the strong prosper. Dates unknown)

Passing through our galaxy the alien's astral forms inadvertently merged but once hitting earth's atmosphere, it caused a rift between the two forces. When observed by the primitive ancient humans of that age the cataclysm resembled small stars emanating large amounts of light plummeting to the earth.

The result of the crash was mutagenic changes in a few select humans and beasts that were in the various lands of the earth.

The aliens were unable to survive on earth in their alien forms, thus they searched for bodies to share symbiotic relationships. Once merging with these humans the union affected the DNA of their hosts.

The being of light found the body of the righteous general Zada and the Azmarian people.

Whereas the creature of darkness joined with the brash Akin, Zada's cousin.

Others were affected on a lesser degree by means of residual dust that came from the division of the two alien beings. This new species of humankind struck terror in the hearts of man. Many chose to play gods over their fellow, while others use their power for evil and dishonest gain. But there were those that chose the path of righteousness, following the ideology of their predecessor, the Whitestar in the person of Zada.

Amidst this turmoil, hidden away deep in the mountains of modern day Morocco, in the great continent of North Africa, laid 'the Koryan', which was lost in the conflict between the two.

Darkness and death came to earth that day. The power of the Koryan is the only hope that will bring an end to the war between the White and the Blackstar.

Due to the Whitestars weakened state, the Blackstar grew to be more powerful eventually annihilating Zada and his Azmarian inheritors, seeking complete control over the world of mankind.

PROLOGUE

During Fimaya, the first age of our planet (as recorded by the Azmarians), Azmaria, the realm of light, was enslaved to a coalition of neighboring kingdoms, north, east, and south of its borders. However, over time, many of these kingdoms broke away from the coalition and gained their autonomy.

The strongest of that coalition, the land of Punt, under Emperor Po'dela, kept its grasp on Azmaria because the land was rich in resources.

Emperor Po'dela was a vile and sadistic ruler and encouraged his subjects to engage in vile and sadistic practices. But despite such practices, the people of Azmaria remained pure and separate from such loathsome ways. This repulsed Emperor Po'dela.

The incensed Emperor dealt harshly with the people of Azmaria; enslaving many of Azmaria's sons and daughters. All attempted rebellions were met with severe punishment, from the gouging of their eyes, to the removal of their genitals, to serve as lessons for all would be insurgents.

Finally, after over eighty years of oppression, a change for the better in Azmaria's future came in the persons of Zada and Akin.

An army of ten thousand able-bodied Azmarian warriors assembled under Zada and Akin; and with this powerful juggernaut, they broke through Po'dela's overwhelming defenses. Po'dela was unable to stand against their determined zeal.

The takeover was so astounding that before Po'dela's death, it was recorded that he uttered, "Not by the hand of your leaders have I and my people fallen . . . but only by a god could such a feat be afforded you;" and so came an end to Po'dela's eighty year reign of tyranny.

For many years, Azmaria enjoyed peace and prosperity under the hands of Zada and Akin. They were wise and resourceful rulers. But beneath the veil of tranquility there was a gloom waiting to emerge. The scene of Azmaria took a dramatic change, and this time, her pains of distress came from within.

It was during the start of the second age (called Koyimai in the Azmarian language). Internal complications caused Zada and Akin to divide Azmaria into two kingdoms, the North and the South. This division eventually brought about much turmoil and confusion amongst the people. But despite the division and confusion, the people did remain one, until the day of the great star. With its arrival came a momentous battle between Zada and Akin, the White and Blackstars, with the dark forces of Akin eventually obliterating Zada and his virtuous forces.

After the merciless massacre, Akin, now Rathamun, and his horde of dark soldiers began to pillage Azmaria, marking an end to the possessors of the Whitestar. This is then when Rathamun self proclaims himself as a god. Yet, despite this poignant day, a ray of hope sparkled amongst the genocide.

A child was born to Zada and before his going into battle to face his inevitable death; the infant was left in the care of a nomadic tribespeople. Only an infant, she would later remember the people she once belonged to.

However, it was written that once of age she would face her greatest challenge, a challenge that her extinct people failed to surmount, but one that she was destined to undertake . . . the destruction of Rathamun and the Blackstar. Due to the words of this prophecy, Rathamun started his search for the estranged infant. Throughout the entire continent he dispatched minions who sought diligently for the infant, seeking to destroy her. However, she managed to remain hidden, for awhile. Where is she now? The future has not yet been revealed and the story has not yet been told . . . until now.

CHAPTER 1

'That which is told is Provisional, but that which is written is Eternal'

In an antiquated era, from an unsung time, when man declared rule over earths lands and when empires laid strewed like seeds tossed over a barren field by an unsteady hand. It was an age of Kings, oppression and the paranormal folk. Unto this era spawned the Knights of the crescent moon, warriors born of different lands, different times, but all upon the same day and kin by spirit, when the moon crescent and the phenomenon that inadvertently formed during such nights. Thus is the saga of one such warrior, Zahira, a female born to this age of despair. It is she that walked the soil when darkness encroached onto the earth and it is she that will be pelted with the task of bringing order to a Black land.

The Days of Misery

The sun shines brightly in the sky over Naldamak. There on the fringes of that city is the peaceful land of Beshari, a Bedouin tribe that has lived mainly in and around the hills of Kush for over a thousand years.

This mountainous, semi-desert region lay parallel to the coast of the Al Qalzam Sea from northeastern Kush through southeastern Nubia. They are of mixed Kushitic blood, a pastoral people that remain free from the world that surrounds them.

"We are to journey to Tan'a tomorrow and pay homage to our ancestors and the gods of my fathers," explain Romana.

Romana is a servant of the high chief in the Beshari tribe, his most valued. She is beautiful in appearance, possessing caramel color skin kissed by the sun's rays, round deep brown eyes and long straight ebony hair underneath a black shroud. She, like all the women her age, wears a large array of face and hand jewelry. On her face are earrings from the top of her ear the helix down to the bottom of the lobe. She also wears a distinctive nose ring and beads around her neck. Her distinctive dress proclaims her position over the other servant women.

"Why must we go tomorrow mama," Zahira ask with a slight sound of irritation in her voice.

"Stop complaining! We go through this all the time," sigh Romana, who herself is flustered over preparation, "Twice a year we go to show our loyalty, you know this Zahira but yet you complain . . . always complaining."

"Ahhh mama, I am tired," Zahira replies with an unenthusiastic sigh.

Finally Romana momentarily stops her frantic preparations and patiently kneels down to Zahira's level, looking into her wide chestnut colored eyes she tenderly explains, "Come, come now, it will be fine. Just eight days and we will be there with many other women of various tribes. There will be much to do and much to see, your friends from last year will be there, and I promise you, I will get you that bracelet you so wanted last year. When you are older, my dear, you will come to learn and cherish this event."

"Ok mama, im sorry," Zahira reply after lowering her head in regret.

"No need to be sorry my love, i understand how you feel more then you can imagine," Smiles Romana.

The two then turn to complete their packing and perform the chores to be done before leaving. Drawing water and milking the camels. After some time they take a brief break from the intense heat of the sun inside their well crafted tent. The Beshari tent is textile decorated in beautiful colors. Its construction is weaved from goats' hair. In the heat of the sun the outside of the tent is very hot to the touch while the inside remains cool.

Spawned from the extinct Azmarians, but brought to and cared for by the Beshari at the age of five, Zahira is indeed a beautiful child in appearance. She possess odd long starkly-white bushy hair, full lips, and her complexion the color of amber all trademarks of her extinct people. Being very quiet and shy, Zahira rarely leaves Romana's side, now at the age of ten.

Their trip to Tan'a is a days journey east through a semi desert terrain. It is a vibrant town with crowds of merchants and camel travelers from the most distant parts of the north, west and east. Slave trade is big business here along with the sell of spices, herbs and fragrances. In the midst of the lively community stand decorated tents with gold, silver and expensive textile scattered about dedicated to the various tribal gods of the peoples. The women meet bringing gifts and supplication in reverence to their ancestors or gods. They dress their shrines with gold and silver, sing songs of sorrow or good health, asking for favors while walking around the shrines, yelling out, rolling their tongues inside their mouth in jubilation.

The ceremony last for over three days, on this visit the women are joyful during the occasion and lavishes in each others company, exchanging much gossip and personal concerns. On the last day of the ceremony the Beshari women bid each other emotional farewells and head back to their respective tribes. Romana and Zahira gather their things joining the others and start on their full day's journey back home.

While traveling they pass a large dense forest facing south of their pathway.

"Every time we pass it I get chills mama." States Zahira nervously, "Even when it is daytime. It's so close to home mama."

"Don't be afraid of it Zahira, just remember never to go into that forest. There are many stories surrounding it. They say the gods protect it and only the men can go in there during certain times of the year and hunt for the tribe, during the safe season."

The forest is called Ajulag, the forest of mystery. Many tale's surround these woods at night time, thus a place where the Beshari carries much respect for.

On arriving back the women quickly go to their respective tents and pick back up on their daily duties. Romana and Zahira likewise do the same, but before reaching their tent the two are intercepted by unruly boys who have frequently harassed Zahira in the past.

"There she goes," scream one of the boys name Hamas, "the mute!"

They form a circle around Romana and Zahira, dancing, laughing, and singing, "The fatherless girl, the fatherless girl . . ."

This they sing continuously while Romana attempts to shoo them away hastily screaming, "Go back to your fathers you worthless little dogs!"

Suddenly Hamas father, who is nearby conducting business with two other men, catch ear to Romana's insult and runs over to confront her, he shouts, "Who did you call a little dog?"

Romana cries out,

"The boys are taunting us, including your son who is the ring leader. They will not allow us to pass. We only wish to go to our tent. We are the *only* ones they jeer like this."

The man grows angry and yells, "I don't see your face much who's your owner?"

This irritates Romana greatly for she has a bit of a rebellious streak in her, but she knows not to speak out of place to him for this is punishable by Beshari law, so calmly Romana answers with a soft tense voice saying, "I remember you, you are new here, visiting from our brother tribe . . . in that case, you should know my master is Chief Elnak,"

With a look of surprise about his face he states, "Chief Elnak . . . then you should know better. I'm sure he taught you better manners then this."

The man rushes to Chief Elnaks large tent, leaving the boys to further harass Romana and Zahira. One of the boys throw a rock at Zahira, but it misses and hits Romana in the head from behind, drawing blood. She frantically screams at them finally running them off.

Romana reachs inside her veil feeling the back of her head. On seeing her blood-covered hand she grindes her teeth in ire quickly takes Zahira's hand and rush to their tent.

Despite the pain Romana does not shed a tear. Her first priority is always the welfare of Zahira. So she sits on the tent floor and after grabbing her loom starts to work the loom.

Zahira gazes at Romana with a look of concern, finally asking, "Are you ok mama?" Romana remains silent rocking back and forward working her loom.

Zahira cries aloud saying, "Why are they like this with us?"

Finally breaking her silence Romana reply, "Because they fear what we can become."

Shortly thereafter, Elnak barges into Romana's tent, with the boy's father. All in the tribe submit to the authority of notably Chief Elnak. Only Tafari, high leader/priest comes second in command.

Agitated and upset, Elnak ask Romana, "What is this I hear Romana, that you called this man's son a dog."

Elnaks irritation is taking into consideration pressing problems within the elder ranks and Romana's past rebellious actions, his patience has grown thin.

"My apologies lord Elnak, but I believe you heard only one part of the story." She answers softly still working her loom and never making eye contact with him.

Elnak then leans sideways and notices a speck of blood on the back of Romana's head scarf. Confused and shocked after seeing that he ask,

"Why are you bleeding Romana?"

Romana remains silent this time turning her head right and left grinding her teeth bitterly.

Again he asks but this time far more sternly, "Are you deaf woman. I asked you 'why are you bleeding?'"

Romana looks up into the eyes of the boy's father who stare intently at her as if daring her to reveal the real reason she is bleeding. She then turns to Elnak and ask,

"My lord . . . you mean he didn't tell you?"

Elnak turns to the man looking at him, waiting on an answer. The man quickly replies,

"I thought I saw her fall . . . did you fall Romana?"

Romana looks at him with a stare of death, but surprisingly she turns to Elnak and answers saying,

"I fell my lord. I fell on a stone when I was coming back from worship."

Shaking his head, denoting his shameful displeasure, Elnak calmly states, "Apologize to this man for disgracing his son before all the tribe."

Romana reluctantly apologizes but lowers her head in antipathy.

Elnak then declares, "All is well, she has learned from this ordeal." Elnak then turns to Romana and demands, "Tend to that wound. You don't want to make a mess of things here." He then motions with his hand to the man whose name is Adul saying, "Let us go."

But before leaving out with Adul, he turns to Romana and whispers,

"What is wrong with you, he is a guest amongst us, why must you continue to cause trouble? What you've done has not only shamed me but also indebted me to pay this man for his troubles."

Romana looks up at Elnak and after sighing she reply, "What is the trouble my lord, is it really me or our bias laws, please you tell me?"

With that, frustrated he leaves the tent.

Later, Elnak proceeds to his tent to prepare for a meeting with the elders of the tribe. Adul visits the tent of Elnak and makes a request to enter. On being allowed entrance he asks, "Excuse me, my lord Elnak, can we speak together?"

Busy gathering scrolls placing them in his bag and sensing Adul's reason for wanting to speak with him, Elnak hastily reply, "I am quite busy now Adul, as you might see. Quickly, what is your request?"

After a brief pause, nervously pacing back and forth, Adul hesitantly ask, "Ok, I am going to make this as simple as possible . . . I wish Romana's hand in marriage."

Elnak abruptly pauses what he is doing with a look of shock on his face and slowly turns to face Adul and reply. "You wish to marry my maidservant Romana, my most favorite and loyal?"

"Yes my lord Elnak. You have many maidservants and since the death of my wife a few years ago, my boy and I have not had the benefit of a woman in our home, being here amongst your tribe and away from mine have left me lonely. My son needs a mother's attention. We are cousins by tribe, show compassion this day . . . this is all I ask for, that is, what is owed to me."

The tribe is the main unit with each tribe consisting of groups of kindred clans with leading male figures. Adul uses his closer relation to Elnak to smooth over his request and also his awareness of an owed debt hovers as well.

"A mother or a slave?" sarcastically asks Elnak.

Adul, however, remain respectfully silent with his head down feeling a bit embarrassed.

Finally after a long uncomfortable pause Elnak states, "Then produce a dowry and come back to me that I may think upon your request and offer."

Elnak cares deeply for Romana's welfare, at least for his own means, and does not want to see her in the hands of just any man despite the owed debt, but her clever mouth unnerves him most times. Thus, he asks for an enormous dowry from Adul, knowing Adul is poor, but testing his sincerity.

"But my lord, I am a poor man. All I wish is for a good woman to care for me and my son. I will do right by her and love her dearly. I implore you."

Elnak strokes his thick beard thinking heavily over Adul's request.

Adul then adds, "I shall service your flocks and your fields for one year without payment."

Elnak takes a seat on a large chest in the corner of his tent pondering over Aduls request. Finally after some time of intense thought, out of pity faor both Adul and his son, Elnak speaks, "Very well. But you shall service me not for two years, but four. Four years you are to tend my flocks and my property. Just how you wished for a servant for yourself, so shall you be a servant to me. For four years your worth will be tested."

Adul smiles, however he adds to his request, "What of the little girl that she cares for?"

Already frustrated and running late for his meeting with the elders, Elnak quickly answers while rushing out, "Consider her a gift."

It is a common practice amongst the Beshari men to mistreat their women. These times are indeed troubling for the women of Beshari society for they bare little rights. These are the days of old, and even though such abusive practices are engrained in the hearts of men, the uncertainties of a shy little girl would mark the beginning of a perilous journey that will challenge man's pride.

CHAPTER 2

The Misguided Antics of Boys

Two years pass and Zahira is now twelve years of age. Now living with Adul and his son Hamas, the transition to their home was a disparaging time in Romana's life, however, Adul is rarely home but Romana and Zahira must contend with the childish foolishness of his son Hamas.

One day while sitting in Adul's tent with Romana, accompanying her as she crochete, Hamas comes in and plops down beside Zahira.

"You look pretty today," he comments while playing in her hair.

"Hamas," Romana firmly states, "your father told you not to come in here while we are here, alone."

"I do what I wish. I am here to see Zahira, not you." He childishly retorts. He continues to play in her hair and starts to poke her in the side with his finger all the while Zahira continues to ignore his antics, drawing closer to Romana. Romana continues fussing at him, attempting to shield Zahira from his constant prodding.

Suddenly, in a state of frustration, Hamas slaps Zahira hard on her cheek and then spits in her face. Romana can take no more of this abuse; she leaps up and grabs him by the collar of his robe,

"Boy . . . I don't care who you think you are, but if you do that again I will personally flog your backside twenty times."

Freightened Hamas forcibly pulls away from Romana's grip and runs out the tent yelling,

"You dog, both of you . . . dogs."

Tears run down Zahira's cheeks while hitting the tent floor with her fists in anger. Romana embraces Zahira tightly into her arms, rocking back and forth, singing a soft song.

"Hush now . . . dont fear the evil that reside . . . you are indeed the jewel of the dessert, the flower that blossoms in the harsh weather . . ."

These words roll off Romana's lips as she pulls Zahira even tighter to her while rocking back and forth. Eventually Zahira's tears cease and is replaced with a soft chuckle.

"Is my singing that horrible that it makes you laugh," Romana ask as she too joins in the laughter.

"No," Zahira reply. "Your voice is beautiful, mama."

"So beautiful that you are tickled by its melody eh," Romana laughs.

Zahira laughs saying, "Hamas ran out of here so fast, I thought he was going to pee on the floor."

The two burst into laughter and finish singing together.

Later that day three of Zahira's friends visits her tent and invites her to go with them to the lake of Tobal. The lake of Tobal is a large lake, which in effect is an extension of the Al Qalzam waters. It is man made and has been used for many years by the residencse. Men and women of the Beshari were never allowed to accompany one another at this pool, based on Beshari law. Eventually it became a pool strictly used by the women of various tribes, negating the use from the men.

"Zahira, Zahira," anxiously calls Tejima running into the tent. "We are going to the lake. Please Romana, may Zahira come with us . . . Pleeeeeease?"

Zahira smiles hardily and looks at Romana anxiously awaiting her approval.

Romana returns the smile and answers Tejima saying, "Yes she may."

Zahira quickly leaps up and begin to rejoice with Tejima.

The two start to run out to meet the other girls when Romana sternly states, "Go straight there, stop nowhere else, and do not be gone too long. Be back before sunset . . . and most important, stay together."

Zahira fails to reply based on her excitement.

"Do you hear me? Come back before sunset and do not go anywhere else. Stay on the path and together!"

Romana states but even more sternly this time. Zahira runs over to Romana and bows gently kissing her on the cheek. "Yes mama. Thank you." Romana gives Zahira a tight hug that seems to last for hours. Finally, she releases her and watches the two girls run off playing and singing. Salasa, a close friend of Zahira, shyly wait outside.

Tejima is the eldest of the girls and the lake is not that far away, but still Romana is concerned. However, she realizes that Zahira needs this association.

The girls run and play joyfully on their way to the pool. Tejima, being more assertive, takes the lead as she skips about flamboyantly ahead of the girls every so often looking back and dominating the conversation with jokes and jeers about the boys from their tribe.

On arriving at the pool, the girls quickly run as hard as they can, with each one leaping into the cool water with a big splash. They swim and enjoy each other's company, playing games and splashing water onto each other. Other women from neighboring villages also are there at the pool with their daughters. They sit beneath shaded trees, enjoying the warm sun against the cool sand. Unbeknownst to them, Hamas along with his friend Taval watch from a large Acacia tree as Tejima, Salasa, and Zahira play in the lake. Although tempted to reveal themselves, the boys think long and hard about the consequences of their actions and remain hidden unseen.

Salasa, Tejima, and Zahira splash through the water, which is quite refreshing due to the warm rays of the bright sun.

As the sun starts to set the girls start to make their way out of the pool. They dry off and hurridly start on their way back home.

"Can you believe that," Tejima shouts out, "That idiot Hamas tried to touch me yesterday."

"What do you mean?" Salasa ask.

"You know," laughs Tejima, "what all boys want. They are so bad."

"Ohhh," Salasa smirks with her face turning flushed red. "So what did you do?"

"I pushed him down and ran like a Jackal."

The girls laugh hardily and continue their jovial antics as they near home. Zahira, on the other hand begins to worry, for an uncanny feeling that they are not alone creeps through her body. Suddenly from behind some bushes just ahead of the girls, Hamas and Taval leap onto the path in front of them, "RARRR!" The boys scream frightening the girls. The girls grab hold of one another, screaming at the top of their voices before realizing who their pursuers are.

The boys laugh hysterically. "We got you," Hamas jeers. "I bet you soiled yourself!"

Hamas infatuation with Tejima is not a secret, though he attempts to keep his feelings quiet. However, the feelings are not mutual.

"You are not supposed to be here, this lake is off limits to you boys!" Tejima shouts in anger.

"Shhhh," Hamas whispers, "not to loud, besides, we are not at the lake. Tobal is behind you. But I did enjoy watching you . . . from the tree."

Disgusted, Tejima grabs hold of Salasa's hand. Salasa in turn grabs hold to Zahira's and they run past the boys as fast as they can.

This aggravates Hamas who yells, "Where you running to? We are not finished here!"

But the girls pay no heed to his calls. They run long and hard, leaping over every crack in the road and stumbling through the long grass beside the pathway as they search for a shortcut to get to their homes faster.

Zahira turns to gage the location of the boys, only to see that they are gaining on them. Frightened, Zahira lose her footing and falls into a puddle of mud causing her to break free from Salasa's grip.

Salasa screams for Tejima to release her hand so she can help Zahira, but Tejima ignores her pleas and answers Salasa saying, "Are you crazy? If I stop Hamas will catch us! Who knows what he's scheming this time!"

Unable to break free from Tejima's grip, Salasa cries out to Zahira, "Get up! Get up!" But every time she attempts to rise she slips right back into the mud.

Finally, the boys catch up to Zahira who is still struggling in the mud. Taval grabs her by the arm and yanks her up out of the mud. Hamas yells out to Tejima and Salasa who are still ahead running, "I will get you Tejima, you watch!"

Frustrated he turns around and punches Zahira in her side. Taval releases her and she falls back into the mud screaming while holding tightly to her aching side.

Again he turns towards the fleeing girls and yells, "You stupid girls! Now she will pay the price double!"

Taval laughs and scornfully mocks Zahira.

"Look at her . . . with all that mud on her she looks even skinnier, you aren't all that cute now . . . hahaha."

Showing off, Hamas grabs hold of Zahira's long plush hair and pulls upwards, forcing her to stand again, despite her apparent greif and pain.

"What do you have to say for your friends, huh," he shouts while Taval continues laughing deliriously.

Zahira does not say a word, but remain folded over staring at him with tear soaked eyes. Suddenly his nerves start to shake, for while looking into her eyes he can faintly see a strange white glow emanating. Dismissing what he sees to be his imagination, he shakes his head so as to clear his mind and states crossly,

"Who do you think you are looking at girl?"

He then smacks her face with his other hand and pushes her back into the mud.

Taval laugh, "Look at her. Hold her up! I want to see what she looks like."

Hamas reaches down and lifts her face from the mud.

"She looks like a monkey," Taval mockingly screams.

After releasing her Hamas rises back up, leaving Zahira in the mud. He then looks down at her and spits on the back of her head with Taval doing the same.

"Now go tell this to to your nanny Romana, you fatherless dog."

After that the two boys run away leaving Zahira their alone. Hamas remains a bit unsure as to what he thought he saw in Zahira's eyes, but he says nothing to Taval or anyone else.

It is now night time and Zahira lay's in the mud giving way to tears. She is embarrassed and ashamed, not wanting to return home in her condition. She merely curls up into a fetal position in the mud not caring as to what happened at this point.

She continues laying there in the mud until the whole mud puddle dries up. Her intensive tears cried are now white streaks decorating her dried crusty cheeks. She can hardly catch her breath as her breathing rattles and shivers with every inhalation made.

After some time of laying there she soon can hear faint calls from Romana in the distance. However, Zahira remains silent, still worried over her experience.

When Romana, accompanied by Salasa, finally locates Zahira she is sitting up in the dry dirt with her legs and arms folded up under her as she rocks back and forth. Romana quickly runs over to her, falls to the ground and embraces her tightly with tears flowing.

"What happened to you," Romana ask in a frantic voice while pealing the dried mud from her face.

Zahira keeps silent merely staring into the sky.

"It was Hamas and Taval! They did this," Salasa blurts out.

Romana, with the assistance of two other women, slowly pick Zahira up and carries her back to their tent.

On arriving, Romana takes Zahira into the tent and strips off her dirty clothes. A large basin of water is brought into the tent by four other women. Romana helps Zahira to step into the basin. They then submerge her entire body into the water. Romana starts to wash Zahira's body and clean the mud from her hair and face. During the entire process, Zahira can only remain quiet as if still in a state of shock.

Pained by the ordeal Zahira experienced, Romana gently strokes her hair with a brush as she sing a song, hoping to sooth her pain.

Finally after some time Romana asks her once again, but in a calmer tone, "What happened sweetheart?"

But Zahira still refuses to speak, but in her eyes Romana can see the resentment swelling. Romana thinks to herself, "Perhaps now is not the right time to continue prodding her."

After bathing her thoroughly, Romana then dries her off, puts on her sleeping gown and prepare her for bed.

When the other women finally leave the tent, Romana tucks Zahira into her cot. She tenderly kisses her cheek and lay down beside her. Soon they are both fast asleep.

CHAPTER 3

The Calling

The evening is quiet and peaceful. All in the village have retired for the night. A refreshing cool breeze blow outside and the countless stars shine brilliantly in the night sky. The thin crescent moon hangs in the sky; a day after the new moon.

Zahira soon awake, unable to sleep due to the pain she still feel in her side from Hamas' punch. She quietly rises from her cot so as not to wake Romana. She then quietly creeps over to the tent opening and peeks outside. Looking out south of her tent she can see the silhouette trees in the distance of the Ajulag forest against the night sky.

The sight of the forest causes a chill to rush down her spine making her step back into the tent. On entering back into the tent she can hear a faint whisper of a woman say, "Where are you going? Please, come and visit with me tonight."

Astonished, Zahira hastily turns back to the entrance of the tent opening. She quickly pulls back the tent flap and peeks outside once again, searching for the strange imperceptible woman.

Again the voice urges with a whisper, "Zahira come and stay with me tonight."

With her overwhelming curiosity getting the best over her, Zahira quietly steps outside the tent and leave into the darkness. She courageously follows the soft chants whispered in her ear. Its tone is so alluring that she is unable to resist.

After walking aimlessly in the dark for some time, she is lead directly in front of the Ajulah forest. At that moment she abruptly stops in her tracks. The forest is dark and eerie with a heavy skirt of mist hovering at its floor. This sight now causes Zahira to second guess the circumstances. She slowly turns around to head back home for fear have now began to seize her, but she is reassured by the voice,

"Please, do not be afraid of what is before you. No harm shall befall you my dear."

Zahira slowly approach the forest once again. She pauses for a moment, longingly looking back toward the village with Romana pasted to her mind, but unable to dismiss her curiosity, she takes off running deep into the dark enigmatic forest.

She runs long and hard, leaping over shrubs, scraping through the dense bushes, and evading the towering trees. She finally come to an opening in the forest, a large space of tall grass and long vines devoid of trees and bushes.

She stops for a moment to catch her breath when suddenly the ground starts to tremble. Its thunderous roar emanate throughout the forest. The grass in the vicinity begins to blow fiercely back and forth with an unnatural chill blowing past her body.

She backs away looking in all directions for shelter.

The clouds turn dark gray and an unsettling faint voice is heard speaking across the wind. The words uttered this time are not ascertainable, for the speech is slurred and distant. Suddenly, just ten feet ahead of Zahira, the ground ruptures and forms a large lump of earth that grows and churns swiftly. From the forming mound a large chair forms from the soil and grass, growing taller and taller until reaching a height of at least seven feet and taking the shape of an elaborate earthy throne. There it sits before Zahira, lavished in the vegetation of the earth.

After a brief moment of peace, the ground shakes again and the earth forms into another object, but this time the shape is the form of a living woman made of grass, flowers and vines sitting on the large throne. From out of the darkness emerge two imposing Lions who position themselves on each side of the throne. One possess a coat black as night, the other is stark white. Their eyes glisten as the sun and their teeth shine like polished steal.

After the completion of the ordeal, the clear soft voice of the woman call out from the throne asking, "Why were you weeping, Zahira? Do not weep any longer."

Zahira is already horrified over the experience, not knowing if it is real or just a dream. She stumbles backwards falling to the ground. She then pushes back with her feet until her back hit against a large tree. Her eyes are wide open and she tremble with fear as the forest woman sit upon the chair with a beam of light shooting from the sky around her and the lions.

The strange woman tilts her head sideways, ascertaining Zahira's fear.

"Do not be terrified," she express in a comforting tone, "for you are smiled upon this day . . . by powers unprecedented by any man."

Zahira remains silent, flabbergasted over what seems to be an apparition.

The woman continues saying, "Zahira, I have heard your pain and my heart aches. You need not say a word; just listen . . . for after tonight, your rise to ascension will indeed begin."

The lady of the forest then extends her hand to Zahira saying, "Come and hear what lies before you."

Zahira reluctantly approach the throne and holds the hand of the strange woman. Her hand is surprisingly warm to the touch. The woman then says,

"You are indeed most gifted amongst all girls. You are the last of a great people and will bring peace to these lands. Your path has been laid out for you, and before it is disrupted changes will be administered in your tribe. It is you, from a long line of knights that were born during the crescent moon on a fixed day and fixed time to bring retribution to evil and to bring back the balance between the White and Blackstar. Your caretaker Adul will die, for he and his son have dealt harshly with you. His continued existence will interfere with your ascension. But do not fret, for you and Romana will come under the care of the compassionate Tafari. Then and only then will your journey begin."

Perplexed, Zahira apprehensively ask, "Who are you . . . are you one of our gods?"

The woman rears her head back and delivers a hunting laugh that echoes loudly throughout the entire forest.

"No, not even by the farthest stretch of your imagination, for there is only one true source of creation and none can match unto him. He it is that has created and sustained all life and it is that one alone that all tribute is due."

"Only one?" ask Zahira with a sense of distress and confusion, for she was taught that there are many gods controlling the universe.

"Yes my dear, only one, for if there were many there would be constant conflict throughout the universal constellations and life would boil with contempt, but as such, there is not. This too your people the Azmarians believed and understood as well. Their example and faith has paved the way for much enlightenment. As for me, I am not of this world, but only a foreigner from another cosmos and subject to the pains of death as you. I and those that dwell here like me have been lost here for millennia. However, this too is our home now, and there are forces of both good and evil at work. I am that force that resides with righteousness and within you is the same power that gives me life. Do not concern yourself with this . . . for these things you shall learn in time as you mature."

"What does all this mean?" Zahira ask.

"You will see dear one. After you have reached your destination, I will no longer be able to assist you. Your path will be for you to mark. Do remember the grander scheme of things, and turn neither to the right nor to the left. Now, I shall tell you no more, for your ears are still young, but go now and take comfort, for there is more to come regarding you Zahira."

After that, the woman releases Zahira's hand and absorb back into the earth from which she came, as well as the throne she sat upon. The lions turn and leave back into the dense forest, soon vanishing from Zahira's site, leaving her standing their mystified.

Zahira rubs her eyes rigorously trying to ascertain if she was dreaming or not. Finally, she turns and run back home still unsure of her experience.

As she enters her tent she looks over at Romana, who is still fast asleep. She slowly sits on her cot, careful not to awaken Romana. She then eases under her blanket and lay her head on her pillow. While laying there she stares vacantly at the ceiling of the tent with a big smile, soon drifting off to sleep.

CHAPTER 4

The Plot

The next morning Zahira is awaken to Romana's urgent tug.

"Zahira, Zahira. Wake up child! Are you going to sleep all day?"

Zahira's eye lids flutter as she awakens from the deep sleep that embraced her. She turns to look into Romana's eyes, seeing a look of concern in them,

"Are you ill, child? What has come over you? You have been sleep for a long time now."

Zahira slowly sits up and looks around the tent.

"Where am I," she asks rubbing her eyes.

"Girl, what is wrong with you? And we really need to talk about what happened to you the other day, with you and those boys."

"I am fine mama." Zahira responds yawning with a smile of contentment.

Romana gives Zahira a bewildered look. "I don't know about that, you didn't seem fine when it happened."

"Really mama, I am fine."

Romana looks at Zahira with a suspicious eye.

"Well, get up, wash, and dress. We have to go to the market and we are already late."

As Romana leaves the tent, she turns back to Zahira and says, "And your little girl companions are waiting outside to see you. We still are going to talk about this missy."

Zahira quickly dresses and soon notices that the pain in her side is no longer there. She then runs outside to see her friends Tejima and Salasa.

"What happened, Zahira," Tejima ask with concern in her voice, but Salasa know better. The look of disgust makes it abundantly clear. Tejima continues,

"We ran. I thought you were with us. If we had known that Hamas had gotten hold to you, we surely would have stopped. You should have screamed out."

Unable to listen to any more of Tejima's lying, Salasa butts in saying, "You are speaking lies Tejima. I told you that we were leaving Zahira behind and you kept running."

"What are you talking about Salasa," Tejima vehemently reply.

"You know what I'm talking about. I tried to turn and come back for you, Zahira, but Tejima grabbed hold of me and pulled me along with her. She said there was nothing we could do to help you and that it didn't make sense for us all to be attacked by them."

"That's a lie, Salasa," Tejima screams. "If I had known the boys had grabbed Zahira I would have helped her. I would have fought them. You are just jealous of me, Salasa. You hate the fact that I am popular!"

"It's all about you Tejima, you don't know how to be anyone's friend." Salasa screams.

Tejima and Salasa starts to argue back and forth getting louder and louder. Soon people begin to take notice.

Zahira puts herself in between the two bickering girls trying to calm the situation. "Please, please, it is okay I am fine. There was nothing the two of you could have done. The boys would have gotten you as well . . . I will be okay. Now please, we are friends . . . you are the only friends I have, so stop."

Tejima and Salasa look at each other with cold stares, but to appeal to Zahira Salasa finally extends her hand to Tejima.

"I'm sorry for what I said. I was just upset by what happened to Zahira and feeling guilty that we didn't help her."

However, Tejima, being stubborn, is not quick to accept the apology, but Zahira places her hand on Tejima's shoulder and gives her and endearing look.

"Come on, Tejima. Salasa said she was sorry. Now it's your turn."

Tejima looks at Salasa with her face slowly softening.

"I'm sorry, Salasa."

The two hug one another and Zahira joins in.

"Zahira, it's time to go to market," Romana calls out. "Tell your companions you will see them later."

Zahira wave to her friends goodbye and she and Romana heads in the direction of the market square.

The market is always the liveliest spot of the community. As usual children are running around chasing one another, bumping into patrons. The adults shake their fists at the children who rudely continue with their antics. Customers argue with the merchants over unfair prices. In the middle of the market is the entertainment, men playing their musical instruments and reciting poetry, while the women dance.

As Romana and Zahira approach the heart of the market, there are carts filled with the different fruits and vegetables of the land, melons, leeks, berries, to mention only a few. Grain can also be purchased at the market, slaughtered goat meat along with ripen dates and many spices.

The aroma that issues forth from the pots prepared by cooks filled with rich spices make Zahira's stomach rumble with hunger. Romana turns and catch ear to Zahira's growling stomach.

"Perhaps next time you will awaken a little earlier, my sweet."

Romana search through her pouch and hands Zahira a coin.

"Take this and purchase something to eat for yourself."

"Thank you, mama." Zahira takes the coin and run to one of the carts and purchase a piece of bread.

As she follow behind Romana nibbling on her bread she looks to her right and notices a familiar person, its Elnak's son Siraj. He is walking with the older men, listening to their winsome words and asking many questions. They walk right by her and eventually out of sight.

Both Siraj and Zahira are of the same age. Siraj stays close to his father, learning the many ways of the clan and mimicking the assertive nature of his father. Even during his youth, Siraj carries himself like a prince, ignoring many of the childhood games, clinging only to those that are a member of his personally formed circle of scholastic associates.

Zahira turns back towards Romana and notices that she has progressed further ahead, as she race to catch up to Romana to her horror she runs right into Hamas. A startled look of dread appears on her face.

"Watch where you are going rodent," Hamas snarls.

Zahira immediately run to Romana and quickly takes her hand.

She is both hurt and angry, gritting her teeth tears start to flow from her eyes. Romana notices her tears and ask,

"Are you ready to tell me what happened yesterday?"

Zahira shakes her head no, clinging to Romana's hand tightly.

"Okay, when you are ready . . . but we are going to have to talk about this dear."

Zahira lowers her head and softly reply, "I did have a strange dream mama; at least, it seemed like a dream."

"What was it," Romana ask.

"Well . . . it is a long story . . . hmmm. It was some grass lady sitting in a really big chair. She had two pet lions. It was something mama. They were big, and she spoke with me. She told me that there is only one deity and all the others humans worship are not real. She also told me that they are aliens and have been here for a long time. She told me that Adul will die and his son will—"

"Now, now, Zahira," Romana interrupts, "I am not too fond of him either but we don't want to wish death for anyone."

"I know mama. I didn't say this, but the lady in the forest did. She said he will die."

"Now why would she say a thing like that Zahira? What kind of lady is this?" Romana ask while propping her hands on her hips.

Getting more anxious and impatient Zahira exclaim, "She is the lady of the forest. She knows about me having special abilities—"

"Shhh," Romana quickly covers Zahira's mouth with her hand. She then grabs Zahira sternly by the arms and whispers, "Remember, you are to say nothing to anyone about your gifts. We have had this conversation before Zahira . . . that is our secret. Do you hear me?"

Holding her head down, Zahira calmly answers, "Yes mama."

Romana embrace her tightly and says, "It may seem as though all is lost and that there is no hope, but the day will come when you, my dear, will rise above others, proud and strong."

Wanting to tell Romana more of her experience, she refrains and vow within herself to never speak about it to anyone again.

As Hamas and his companions continue through the square in search for Siraj, whom they finally catch sight of conversing with the older men of the clan, Hamas' eyes become filled with rage. He is no admirer of Siraj for he longs for the favor that Siraj hold with the older men, even though it is Siraj's by right his disdain is fueled by jealousy.

Siraj is next in line to be leader of the clan, to succeed his father as Chief. Hamas' reasons for desiring such a position is purely of a selfish nature. He is not interested in the welfare of the clan his interest is only in his own welfare. At the young age of thirteen, he craves power, lust for the accompaniment of women and dreams of being Chief over the tribe.

Hamas and his friends catch up to Siraj and confront him,

"So, if it isn't the great Siraaaaj." Jeers Hamas, "to what do we owe the dishonor of your presence,"

One of Siraj's companions step forward to attack, but Siraj stops him.

"There is no need to react. They are only specks of dirt on the bottom of my sandals. They are nothing. Their attire speaks of their minute existence. They are not even worthy of our acknowledgement."

Siraj attempted to go around Hamas, but Hamas stepped in front of him blocking his exit.

"You *will* acknowledge me."

Siraj's companions lunge at Hamas and his companions and a fight ensues amongst the children. But the fight does not last long, for the older men of the clan soon come aware of the scuffle and intervene.

"What is the meaning of this?"

The boys immediately stop looking disheveled and unkempt.

Pointing at Hamas and his companions, the eldest of the older men command, "You boys go to your homes . . . your worth here is valueless, how dare you fight with Siraj, he is indeed a child of the scrolls one to be a leader soon . . . you must be more respectful of him. Your fathers will hear of this."

Hamas and his companions reluctantly turn and leave, each going to their own tents.

The older man then turns to Siraj with disappointment in his eyes and says,

"Siraj, what is this? Why have you stooped to such a level? You are to be the future clan leader. You must not fill your mind with such childish antics. You must focus on your training and the position you hold. Your father would be ashamed to hear of such behavior."

Siraj put his head down, ashamed that he allowed Hamas' taunts to provoke him into fighting.

"I am sorry . . . my actions were not becoming of a future leader."

"As long as we learn from our mistakes and do not repeat them," replies the man, "then all will be well. Now go to your home."

Siraj quickly leave for home as directed.

Meanwhile, Hamas enters his father's tent swole with anger, his father notice his sons bewildered look.

"What is wrong with you," he grunts.

"Siraj is what is wrong. I hate him, father."

"He is next in line to be clan leader. Perhaps it is not good to make enemies with him."

"I do not care. He thinks he is better than me. He said I was not worthy of his acknowledgement."

"Do not let his pompous ways affect you so. The day will come when you will be a man of great prestige. Trust in my words, son."

His father's words ring deep within him.

CHAPTER 5

An Untimely Death

Later that day Hamas and his companions meet once again. They lay in the grass, by the river conversing about the day's events.

"I hate Siraj," Hamas exclaimes, staring into the sky. "I wish he was dead."

"Yeah," the others chime in, agreeing with him like obedient little puppies.

"Maybe we could drown him in the river," Hamas adds.

"Yeah," the others reply without any hesitation.

Then one of the companions chuckle saying, "It should not be hard to do. I'm sure with him always having his head in a scroll he never learned how to swim anyway."

They all let out hearty laughs. Hamas then sits up and glances around at his friends with a sinister gaze.

"I don't know when and I don't know how, but I will kill Siraj." He states grinding his teeth and clinching his fist.

"Ha-ha-ha," laughs an intruding voice behind them. When they turn around to see who it is, there stand Siraj and one of his friends with their arms folded.

"In your dreams," Siraj states boldy. He and a friend of his comes back to confront Hamas and his friends despite the warnings by the older man.

"Let's finish this now." Hamas yell's rising to the challenge. Without warning Hamas charges into Siraj and both the boys fall to the ground wrestling. Their friends crowd around cheering the fight on. The two viciously strike at one another, landing blows to the face and body.

Mustering what strength he can Siraj delivers a blow to Hamas chest causing Hamas to fall to the ground clasping at his chest for air. Siraj dust the dirt from off his clothing and offhandedly walks back towards home, with his friend with him.

For a brief moment Hamas lay on the ground, dazed from Siraj's blow, but as soon as he recovers he jumps to his feet in pursuit of Siraj. He picks up a big stone, runs up behind Siraj and hits him in the head. Siraj falls to the ground motionless. Blood pours from his head profusely. Hamas and his friends stand motionless staring down at Siraj with surprised looks on their faces. Hamas kicks at Siraj's body, but he does not flinch. Siraj companion who was with him looks in disbelief as well. He kicks at him again, but again there is no response.

"You killed him, Hamas," one of the boys cries out.

"Don't be an idiot! He is not dead," Hamas reply nervously. "Get up and fight, you worthless piece of trash," Hamas screams to Siraj. But Siraj does not move.

"What have you done, you have killed him!" shouts Siraj companion.

"He is dead," another boy cries. "You killed him! You killed him! Look at the blood!"

Hamas' body starts to tremble violently.

"What are you going to do, Hamas? If they find out they will certainly kill you."

"You mean, 'What are we going to do?' You are just as much involved as me."

"What, how can you say that," cries Siraj companion. "You are the one that hit him with the rock. You killed him."

Hamas finds a brief moment of courage and sticks out his chest in a proud stance, "Yes, I did kill him, as I said I would, but you are accomplices in this whole thing. Therefore, you are just as guilty.

That is what the elders will say if this matter is found out. So this is what WE are going to do. We will take his body far away from the village and bury him. We will bury him so that they will never find him."

The boys look at one another, fear seizing each and every one of them. Fear even grabs at Hamas, who tries desperately to appear at ease with the situation.

"Well, what are we waiting for? Grab his body and let's go." Hamas shouts.

The boys slowly walk over to Siraj's body. They each grab a limb grudgingly and carry him down the path behind Hamas.

"He's heavy," one of the boys carrying Siraj grunts. "You could at least help us carry him since you killed him.

"Look," Hamas replies in a demanding tone, "I have to search out the best spot to bury him, he can never be found. Everyone knows we were bitter. If they were to find his dead body I would be the one they look for, perhaps."

No one says another word after that.

After walking for some time, one of the boys cry, "Please, can we rest for a bit? I am so tired." The other boys chime in agreement.

"Okay, okay! I didn't know I was dealing with a bunch of whiney girls. You can rest for just a little while."

The boys lower Siraj's body to the ground.

"Oh, just drop him," Hamas snickers, "He won't complain." The boys look at Hamas irately not one of them finds humor in this.

"You guys are no fun." Hamas grunts.

"Hamas, you killed someone. What is funny about that? Aren't you scared? Do you not feel sad," one of his companions asks.

"No, I do not feel any remorse! He had it coming. He walked around thinking he was better than everyone else. Now he is dead . . . no glory in that." Hamas laughs, grabbing hold of his sides.

"I don't know Hamas this just is not right," another boy retorts.

"Enough! Pick him up and let's go."

The boys stand and pick up Siraj's body up. They then continue their journey to find a place to bury him.

After walking some distance Hamas shouts, "Stop! This is the perfect spot. We will bury him here." The boys gently place the body on the ground.

"What are we supposed to dig with, Hamas," one of the boys asks.

"Your hands, what else, do I have to think of everything?"

"Well, it's not like we're experts at killing and burying people Hamas," another boy exclaimes.

"Just start digging so we can get out of here." Hamas bellows.

One of the boys shakes his head with disbelief at Hamas reaction. Nevertheless, they dig the hole.

"How deep should we dig it?" one of the boys asks.

"I don't know . . . just keep digging. I will tell you when to stop," Hamas reply.

After a while one of the boys sit up and protest, "I am not going to dig any more until you get down here and help us, Hamas. This is your doing . . . you are not going to stand there just watching us." The other boys clamor in agreement.

"Alright, alright, I'll help dig, move over." Hamas gets down on the ground with the rest of the boys and starts to dig.

They dig for some time using their hands and small tree branches until finally reaching a depth of about five feet.

"This is good," said Hamas. "This will do fine. Drag him over here." Two of the boys pick Siraj's body up and brings him to the grave site.

"Drop him," Hamas says. The boys slowly lower Siraj into the hole. They then start to push the dirt back into the hole over Siraj's body. When they had finished, Hamas takes his foot and press the dirt down. The others watch with saddened faces.

"Mission accomplished. He is gone forever. The animals of the field and insect in the ground will get rid of any remains," Hamas declares.

"Let's go, I have had enough of this day time to go home now." one of the boy's lament.

"Me too," says another.

"That's fine with me," Hamas reply.

On the way back, Hamas tries to engage the boys in some light conversation. But understandably, none of them are in the mood to talk. Hamas eventually gives up.

When they get within a few yards of the village, Hamas turns to his companions and sternly warns, "Okay, we can't tell anyone about what happened. This is between us and only us. Does everyone understand?" They grudgingly shake their heads in agreement.

"Don't shake your head at me!" rumbles Hamas, "Open your mouth and say that you understand!"

"We understand," they all say in unison.

"Okay."

They continue their way to the village. Upon reaching the village the group disperses heading to their separate homes with heavy minds.

When Hamas enters his dwelling his father Adul turns to him and ask, "Where have you been all day. You missed the dinner Romana prepared."

"I'm sorry father. I was out with my friends and lost track of the time."

Adul looks at Hamas as if trying to read his thoughts. "Well, I hope you enjoyed yourself because tomorrow you will be helping Romana with chores all day. She also tells me that you have still been picking with that girl Zahira."

"I don't know what she is talking about father." mutters Hamas.

Adul replies, "Nevertheless, you are to help Romana with the chores, I need this done quickly because I have plans for that yard in the back."

"Yes, father," Hamas lazily reply. However, usually when Adul tell Hamas that there are chores to be done he meets it with resistance, but this time is different. His compliance and sullen face rises Adul's concerns.

"What have you been up to, boy?"

"Nothing father." Hamas quickly answers.

Again, Adul looks at Hamas with suspicion.

"Okay. I want you up at dawn so we can get an early start."

"Yes father."

"Now go and have Romana fix you something to eat, and then go to bed."

"Yes, father, but I'm not hungry. I ate some berries on the way home."

"Very well . . . good night."

"Good night father."

Meanwhile, that evening, Chief Elnak sits on the floor of his tent reading scrolls while dining on rabbit legs and fruit. One of his maid servants walks in and asks,

"Will there be anything else, my lord?"

"Has my son returned home?" He asks.

"No, my lord . . . no one has seen him since he left earlier today."

A look of concern quickly comes over Elnak's face. "That is not like him. He has never been away from home this late. I am deeply concerned. Call my trusted servants and have them come to me."

The maid servant quickly runs to call for the male servants who in turn make haste to Elnak.

"Yes, my lord?" One of the servants asks.

"Go and search out my son. He is late in returning home we have much studying to do."

"Yes, my lord. We shall do so immediately." The servants quickly leave Elnak's presence in search for Siraj.

Two hours pass and Elnak paces the floor of his large decorated tent worried about the whereabouts of his son. He senses that something bad has happened, for Siraj is never away from home for long periods of time unless with his father. His stomach begins to ache at disquieting thoughts. Siraj is his pride and joy, the beginning of his reproductive powers.

Finally one of his trusted servants comes to him.

"Have you found my son," Elnak frantically ask.

"No my lord, he is nowhere to be found. We have searched all of the tribe and its fringes and still we are unable to find him. We have even involved other servants in the search."

Elnak rips his garments and places his face into his hands. His heart starts to ache and the pains in his stomach worsen. He walks over to the servant and begins frantically shaking him.

"Where is my son?! Where is my son," he cries.

"I am sorry, my lord. We do not know of his whereabouts . . . but we are still searching diligently."

"Search the neighboring villages. Find my son!" Elnak shouts with extreme frustration.

The search for Siraj continues for days. Everyone in the village is talking about it. During that time Hamas keeps busy with his chores, which make his father even more suspicious. Romana sees it as peculiar as well, for his attitude towards her also improves. As for the rest of Hamas companions, they remain terrified that their crime will be discovered. Their loyalty toward Hamas begins to wane.

Adul eventually confronts Hamas about his sudden interest in caring for his duties.

"Hamas, come to me son. There is something I want to talk to you about."

"But father, I am not done with my chores." Stresses Hamas.

"You can get back to that later. Come to me."

Hamas complies under duress but goes to his father.

"Yes father."

"How come I do not see you with your friends anymore? Have you had a disagreement with them?"

"I have grown weary of their childish antics, father." Hamas moans, "I am a man and need to behave as such."

"I see. So your sudden interest in doing your chores would have nothing to do with Siraj's disappearance. I know that you and he were at odds with one another. You would tell me if you had gotten into some difficulty, wouldn't you?

Hamas gets very defensive. "Father, I told you, I am a man. I have to do the work of a man. And as for Siraj, I do not know where he is! I had nothing to do with his disappearance! Don't you believe me, father?!"

"Yes, son . . . if you say you do not know anything about his disappearance, then I believe you."

Adul gives his son a hug and sends him back to his chores.

After fourty days of intense searching, Elnak gives up hope of finding his son. He is convinced that his son is dead. He retreats into his sleep chambers and there he remains for thirty days grieving. A funeral is performed in Siraj's honor and the tribe then gathers around Elnak's home and mourns the loss of Siraj.

Finally, Elnak resurfaces from his chambers unkempt. He summons the maid servant to bring water to him so that he could bathe and a change of clothes.

Suddenly he is approached by one of his servants who frantically races to him with two of his generals.

"My lord, while you were mourning, we received word that the tribe of Ashaza has mobilized against us and are approaching. They may be here in a matter of days.

Elnak looks at his generals and declares courageously, "We have beaten them before, and we will beat them again. They will not have this land or anyone else."

Elnak is infuriated and the loss of his son furthers his crazed fury.

"Rally our men and we shall meet them head on!" He shouts raising his sword to the sky.

The men then prepare for battle against the tribe of Ashaza. Elnak is dressed in his finest armor. He calls for his beautiful black stallion Melchin and decorates him for the war as well.

"Are you well my lord, do you think you should march out with us?" ask one of his generals, due to Elnaks loss.

"Of course I am," he barks back, "am I to mourn forever . . . the gods have brought me this fight so that I might regain who and what I am about."

However, unbeknownst to his generals and military Elnak still grieves terribly over the death of his son Siraj. Deep down inside he knows that he will not be returning from this battle.

Elnak's men number two hundred, fifty on horseback. They march out the next morning towards the borders of their land where they meet the tribe of Ashaza on the battle field.

Before the fight Elnak and the opposing chief sends out their best generals to fight in a dual. Elnaks and the tribal chielf of Ashaza send out three men each. The fight is short but vicious with Elnak only losing one of his generals, where the opposition loses all three.

After that the men encourage their forces with war rhetoric and then the bloody battle ensues.

CHAPTER 6

Casualties of War

The battle between the tribes is long and grueling with many lives lost and spread out upon the field like a blood stained blanket. The crows and vultures fill the sky as they soar over the feast that awaits them. The Beshari rises victorious in the battle with the remaining thirty men of Ashaza taken as slaves.

Although the Beshari are victorious, there is not much to celebrate. Chief Elnak is killed in the battle and his body is discovered by one of the soldiers beneath a pile of Ashaza soldiers. Another found dead is Adul, the father of Hamas, who also joined the men in the fight. He was drafted into the battle by Elnak, even though only being a temporary resident amongst the Beshari, as part of his payment for Romana.

They carry Elnak's body back to the tribe territory. They put him on his divan and summons the maid servants to his chambers to clean his body. The maid servants weep bitterly while cleaning his body. After cleaning him up they put on his finest armor for it is customary to bury a Beshari Chief in this attire. Drummers announce Elnak's death with the whole tribe gathering at his home, wailing and beating their breast with the women letting down their hair.

He is then taken to the burial field of the Beshari leaders on a decorated prepared cot. The hole in the earth awaits his placement. After the priests say a prayer to their gods in his behalf he is then lowered into the hole and covered over. The mourners continue their frantic cries and beating of their chest.

Adul's funeral, on the other hand, is not as elaborate. He is buried along with the other soldiers that fought by his side. They are carried on the fringes of the Ajulag forest. Hamas, Romana, and Zahira along with a host of other mourners follow close behind.

As Zahira watch them lower the bodies into the graves she cannot not help, but admit to herself that she feels no remorse over Aduls death. She think back to the times he would allow Hamas to terrorize her without any discipline for his behavior. She also recollects how her mother Romana was nothing more than an object he could have his way with. There were many a time that despite her mother's attempts to appear cheerful, she could see the pain in her eyes, and there was nothing that she could do about it. But now that he is gone his tyranny is over. But would someone else continue where he left off? Who would gain ownership of them now?

Zahira then turns and gaze upon Hamas who himself keeps his head lowered with tears racing from his cheeks. It is the first time she actually felt some sympathy for him.

Thirty days pass since the funeral and the demeanor of the people gradually builds back up from their loss. Tafari is now Chief over the tribe and his oversight is welcomed by all. He is a good man and shows concern for all those of the tribe, both poor and rich, unlike many of Beshari's past leaders. He also brings with him a new belief, a crude form of monotheism which he learned from his travels and studies abroad. At first the people are taken back from the new teachings but the logic soon take root and the true understanding of the nature of the universe and all life that surrounds them become manifest. This new belief in their deity as being only one and the sole creator of all life resonates with Zahira, for she remembers this statement mentioned by the strange creature she met in the Ajulag forest many months ago.

One day, like many other days, Romana and Zahira are carrying out their chores when Romana is visited by Chief Tafari. Romana quickly kneels before him as was customary to do for the women of her tribe.

"My lord." She remarks over his presence with her head lowered in submission.

"Rise, Romana . . . there will be no more of that. I am only a man, and there will be no kneeling before me or any other man. Save that for the one true source of life, it is he you should not kneel but fall upon your face to. The very one I am starting my education syllabus here on. And never call me lord."

"Yes Chief." Romana exclaims with a smile.

"Better." Tafari replies, "You are spoken well of amongst the people. I have come to take you into my dwelling, you and your child."

Romana is overwhelmed by his invitation and attempting to hold back her enthusiasm she replies,

"My lord . . . I'm sorry, I mean my Chief . . . I would be most honored to have you as my owner."

When the news reaches Zahira she leaps with joy. Finally after years of serving under tyranny she and her mother would now have peace in the home of the Chief Tafari.

CHAPTER 7

The Migration

One sunny day, Chief Tafari calls the great council of elders together concerning the plight of young Zahira, for now her true nature is a concern of both his and Romana's, for times are changing. The Beshari leads a traditional lifestyle with little to no contact with the outside world. Their dislike of outsiders developed as a precaution to the foreigners who had at times endangered their survival, but now a power unlike any of their enemies have focused on them and the threat increases.

"Elders, it is with urgency that we must meet. The Dark creature Rathamun has taken control not only of Azmaria but many of the surrounding lands as well, even as far as Kush and the southern bantu lands. His kingdom is now growing and word is that he is moving towards our direction. If our people are to survive, it is necessary to move further away from this evil kingdom."

Tinochika, a subordinate of Tafari responds, "Tefari if I might speak . . . the problem that would make us a threat can be removed with ease. We hold in our possession the young child Zahira, the very one you kept secret all these years from many of us even and now we learn of her true nature. Do we really need to relocate our whole tribe from this rich land that has provided for us generation after generation, or do we merely get rid of the problem by handing over to Rathamun what he wants . . . Zahira. Now that we are aware of her nature, even though the hidden mystery for so many years, we must do the right thing in preserving ourselves alive . . ."

"Have you gone mad," interrupts Tafari. "It was in our care that the child was entrusted. It was not the time to disclose her origin to anyone, not even Chief Elnak. These words were explicitly told to Romana and I by the girl's father before his death. I did what I had to do to protect the interest of not only her but this tribe as well."

Another elder addresses the counsel saying, "That was the past. A solution must be found now, for it is the child whom he seeks. As long as the child is with us we are in danger. How could you possibly fathom, for even an iota of a moment, that we could escape the wrath of a god? We are surely housing death for ourselves."

"He is no god," shouts Tafari, "have any of you learned anything from the studies we have been engaged in. He is from another dwelling from amongst our vast universe. He is nothing more than another species of life that has retreated here for who knows what—"

"There is only one solution," Tinochika interjects. "We are a small people. We are seen as nothing more than pests by surrounding nations. Are you prepared to go down in history as an insignificant, demolished group of people because of our foolish notion to defy this prominent power? Well, I am not ready for such a destiny. I would be more than willing to sacrifice the girl for the sake of our people, god or not. She is the difference between life and death for us."

"How dare you speak such treachery Tinochika," Tafari grumbles. "Your words are those of a foolish man. We must not commit this act of treachery. We must take further counsel to find another solution. It is written in the scrolls of the Ged'l, that one leader will come forth, regain the cities of Sagala and pronounce Azmaria once again the land of hope. She is our hope, our key to survival. She must be protected!"

Tinochika quickly rise and shouts, "And you put this girl as our hope?"

An argument erupts amongst the elders and the idea of Zahira being preserved is increasingly an unpopular decision amongst the bulk of the elders. If she remains in their company it can possibly mean death of the Beshari.

Rathamun's lust to gain power leads him on a sadistic hunting campaign, which exterminated the ancient Azmarians, the only vestiges that stood in his way. However, one Azmarian remain, Zahira, and she possess the retreating power that allows her to escape his grasp and survive her people.

Realizing his efforts to spare the young child's life is futile Tafari later that day secretly summons Romana to his tent and convenes with her over the matter.

"Chief Tafari, you requested my presence?" Romana ask standing at the entrance of his tent.

"Yes, my child. Please, come in."

As Romana enters she is offered a seat on a large plush pillow next to Tafari, he looks at Romana with a serious look in his eyes, a look of concern and anguish.

"Reveal what I am about to speak to no one." He whispers, "The council of elders is demanding Zahira's life. My efforts to spare her life have been in vain. If she is to continue living she must leave here at once."

"Why do they wish to take my child's life? What harm has she done? She has done nothing, but brought joy to my life and hope to our people."

"It is not what she has done my dear, it is who she is. You know this as well, a secret both you and I have held quiet up until now . . . is she not the child of the late great Azmarian general Zada? You know as well as I that the child possesses the gift of the Whitestar. It is because of this that the kingdoms of this death monster seek her out."

A look of pain comes across Romana's face as she wrestles with the idea of sending Zahira away, this day she knew would come, but the idea of them parting tears at her heart. In a sad tone she humbly replies, "Then I must prepare her for departure. I promised her father I would protect her, and if it means I must let go of her to do so, then it is done."

Tafari continues, "Kimoni, general over our warriors and his best men will go with the child to ensure her safe departure." The Beshari are fierce warriors, with the men arranging their curly hair in a distinct bushy Afro, wearing long white cotton cloaks, carrying curved swords and oval shields. They keep their long hair covered in a turban around their heads and face. Kimoni himself is our best warrior and general, surviving the fight against the Ashaza.

She will go to the eastern land of Azal where she will be taught and cared for by the Muhas. I had already sent word to them before taking counsel with the elders for I sensed their betrayal. The Muhas are fully aware of her purpose even more so then you or I and are eagerly awaiting her presence. She will learn to better utilize her hidden gifts."

Tafari now reaches behind him and picks out of his bag a brown leather wrap, rolled up tight and tied together. He opens the wrapping and unrolls five long sheets of parchment with strange writing on it and says,

"These were given to me by Zada, Zahira's father before his end. On them are explicit instructions for Zahira when she is older. The words are written in the Azmarian tongue. We will bury these in a chest in the ground under your home. I don't want to give them to her now or to Kimoni quite yet, she is much too young, but I and a trusted entourage will deliver them to the Muhas at a future time. It is essential that they receive this before her leaving their company. Keep them hidden, keep them safe."

A troubled look remains on Romana's face.

Tafari takes her hand and gently caresses it in his.

"Fear not, my child. Your precious one will be well taken care of. She will be safe in the hands of the Muhas."

Unbeknownst to the conversation taking place between the two, young Zahira and Salasa are playing outside in the tall grass just outside of Romana's tent.

As the day wear on, Romana eventually returns to her tent and calls Zahira inside. Her voice is unsteady, but she manages to keep her composure.

"Zahira, come near to me, child."

"Yes mama." answers Zahira who cheerfully runs over to Romana and plops down onto the floor right beside her.

"Zahira, my love, a situation has arisen. Come near to me so that I may hold you close to my heart."

"What is wrong mama? Are you sick?" Zahira states with her lips pouted.

"No, I am not ill, but all is not well. You know well of your true ancestry, the one thing I told you to hold secret."

At this point Zahira is more in tuned to Romana's words, she whispers in agreement,

"Yes mama . . . what is wrong."

Romana continues, "I have to be blunt with you dear . . . I can no longer honey coat this . . . what was held back from you is that your existence is not welcomed by everyone."

Zahira pulls away from her mother, unsure of what to say.

"I do not understand mama."

"Oh how I want to hold you close and shield you from the ways of this world. It is just like you came from my own womb . . . my only child. You have meant everything to me and there is nothing I wouldn't do for you; and it is because I love you so that I must let you go."

Tears start to flow from Zahira's eyes as she grasp onto Romana's waist and hold tightly. Romana fights to hold back her tears, but instead she gives way to a torrent.

"Mama, I do not want to leave. I want to stay here with you. I will be more social and will talk more."

"My love, that's not the problem . . . you have to leave for I fear your years on this land will not be long. The dark kingdoms of the south fear your existence they know you are alive, the last of your kind. You are from noble people, so hold your head erect and take pride in your heritage, nothing more we can do for you here, you need training and good protection, you will go to a school that will help guide you. I want you to remain proud and strong no matter what happens throughout your life. Be the light to the world and the hope of mankind against this evil that approaches . . . that is why you are here."

Zahira falls to her knees, crying uncontrollably.

"Zahira, you must be strong, my love. This is what has to be done, sweetheart. Be courageous and always know that I will continue with you no matter where you are. Just search inside your heart."

Wiping the tears from her eyes Zahira ask, "When will I have to go?"

"As soon as possible, I thought I would have more time to prepare you better, but things are moving faster than expected. This is all by order of Chief Tafari . . . you know he is a righteous man and has your interest at heart. You will leave at nightfall when everyone is asleep."

Zahira wipes the tears from her eyes and stand before her mother attempting to display the strength expected of her.

"I will do exactly as you wish mama. I will be strong for you." Zahira laments.

"Your life will not be an easy one." Romana continues, "It is said that you will face many perils; and tests will come before you. But know that all things are measured from that which is not seen, and if you choose the right path your life will be fixed well. Chief Tafari has taught us so much regarding the truth of our existence and the realities of our universe, our governing by one essential power being that overlooks all life. Oh my beautiful child, I shall never love anyone the way that I love you."

At that moment Romana turns and reaches into a sack and pulls out a beautiful solid gray scarf woven from a strange cloth like material unknown to the Beshari,

"This scarf was given to me by your father and it was woven by the finest tailors of your people. Keep this with you and all ways keep yourself covered with it, even over your head. For this is a way of safety for you dear Zahira. Modesty is what you are to display wherever you go, for the world of men is indeed immoral and depraved.

This will serve as a safeguard for you and a remembrance of me. Now go and rest, for your travels will be long."

They share a tight and long embrace. Zahira then drags over to her cot and eventually falls fast asleep.

Later that evening an idea occurs to Tafari. Although Zahira is an exceptional child possessing the power of the extinct Azmarian peoples, she is a child none the less and she possessed the fears of a child her age.

"Perhaps the accompaniment of a close companion would make the transition a little easier to bear," he thinks to himself. Knowing that Zahira is close friends with Salasa, Tafari quickly summons Romana with Salasa's parents and hold a secret meeting in his tent with them.

Tafari informs Salasa's parents of the dire situation and after giving it careful thought they to agree to send Salasa with Zahira in order that her life might be spared, due to the approaching doom. They know that despite their constant moves, they will eventually have to face the mighty power of Rathamun. The forces of Rathamun, by far, possess more power than one can imagine. By sending her with Zahira they know she would be spared the horrific torture the tribe will surely experience once confronted by the minions of Rathamun.

After meeting with Tafari, Salasa's parents sit her down, explaining the plans for her to join Zahira's journey. But not wanting to upset her, they lead her to believe that the journey is temporary and that she will return soon.

Salasa loves Zahira and enjoys every moment they spend together. The idea of taking a trip with Zahira away from the roving eyes of their parents appeals to her.

As night fall, assisted by servants, Zahira begin to prepare for the lenghty journey that lay ahead.

Salasa enters the tent rubbing her eyes she asks, "Everyone has gone to sleep. Why are you still up, Zahira?"

"What about you, Salasa," Zahira asks.

"I can't sleep. Is that why you are up," Salasa ask as she sits on the cot next to Zahira.

Zahira turns to Salasa and whispers, "I have a secret, but you can't tell anyone."

"Oh, I love secrets, tell me what it is. I promise I won't tell, tell me, tell me." Salasa gleefully whispers coming closer.

Zahira pauses for a moment, looking into Salasa's eyes she exclaims, "I have to go far, far away from here. Some bad man that killed my father wants to kill me too. If I stay he will find me and kill me."

"That's terrible. Why would he want to do that," Salasa inquires with a disturbed look on her face.

Zahira continues, "I don't know. But my mama and Chief Tafari told me about where I really come from and I think I should not say anymore about it. I am going to some place called Azal and they will tell me more and watch over me."

"I am coming with you," Salasa gleefully exclaims.

"You are coming with me," Zahira ask with excitement in her voice.

"Yes . . . my parents told me . . . it will be fun. We share a bond that death itself could not break Zahira."

Zahira smirks at her statement and ask, "Those are fancy words Salasa . . . who have you been ease dropping on?"

Scratching her head slightly embarrassed Salasa looks to the ceiling and says, "I heard one of the men say it to the lady Jeneia. When he said it, he looked sleepy, like she was playing with his mind or something. But she did smile and kiss him. It must be a good saying."

Zahira stands and Salasa follows, she then gives Salasa a hardy embrace and states, "Well, let's make it our saying from this point forward."

Early the next morning, after preparing their personal belongings, Kimoni and the four warriors assigned to accompany Zahira on her journey meet with the girls outside the camp.

Romana embraces Zahira one last time unable to speak being choked by her tears. She pulls away and smiles. Zahira is too filled with sorrow and tears, but they manage to separate from each other.

"This is all going so fast mama." Laments Zahira. However, Romana only nods and give her last words, "may the one God go with you my love.

After saying their final goodbyes to their loved ones they all saddle their camels and take a small entourage far north to the coast of Menatet where they will await the ferryman to take them across the Waters of Al Qalzam.

As for the Beshari, they ready themselves to travel and leave the area. They migrate with their flocks and herds over large wilderness between their summer and winter grazing lands.

After a couple of days they finally arrive at Menatet. Zahira and the others load their belongings onto the boat and prepare for their journey across the waters to the other side.

The boat measures twenty feet in length and is ten feet wide. It has black sails that blend into the night sky when looking up at them, measuring thirty feet high. The ferry man whose name remains unknown wear a long ash gray colored cloak. He has a long black beard and mangy, matted hair with large bone earrings. His crew mimics his poor appearance as well.

After paying him, they board the boat and start on their way.

It is during their travel across the waters that Zahira meditates heavily on the abrupt departure that took her away from her mother.

"Will I ever see my mama again," she wonders over and over. She sits by herself at the end of the boat staring into the night sky.

Kimoni goes over to Zahira, feeling her pain and attempts to console her.

He is a man in his mid-thirties, virile and handsome.

Kimoni experienced the loss of his parents at a young age as well, but Zahira has much more to battle, someone wants her dead. The feelings of a twelve year old are feelings that not even Kimoni can imagine. Nevertheless, Kimoni approaches Zahira hoping to offer her some comfort.

"Zahira, I notice you have not eaten since we left Menatet. That is not wise, child. You are sure to become ill."

Keeping her back to him and looking into the sky she reply in a dry tone, "I do not want to eat, Kimoni. I know I promised mama I would be strong, but I want to be with her. I may not see her anymore. I try to stop thinking sad things, but I can't. I wish I was dead."

Kimoni places his arm firmly around her shoulders and exclaim, "You speak foolish words, child. Speak no more of death for I assure you your years on the land will indeed be plentiful. I understand your sorrow, but what was done had to be. Now I will not speak a lie to you, whether you will see your mother again is not known, but I do know that the love the two of you share for each other will be forever. You posses a strength no other young person possesses. Believe what I am saying to you."

Zahira turns and faces him with tears flowing from her eyes. She then embraces Kimoni tightly, so tight that he chuckles softly.

He rubs her back and states, "Careful child, not only do you possess strong emotion, but physical strength as well."

Zahira then ask, "Kimoni, is it really true that all the spices of the world are in Azal . . . those nice spices mama buy from the caravans?"

Kimoni rears back in laughter. "Well . . . I am thinking you are referring to the popular frankincense and myrrh of the Sabaeans . . . hmmm, I don't believe the school in Azal has them, but near the coast where the trading is the land abounds with it."

"Will you take us to see it Kimoni . . . will you?" Zahira asks enthusiastically.

"Well now . . . that depends on you Zahira, how how good of a girl you can be . . . and that shouldn't be a problem at all for you."

CHAPTER 8

A New Home

After a long days travel they finally reach their destination on the other side of the sea and enter the land. Azal is truly a land of great awe. It is a small area right outside the land of Sana'a. The training camps of Azal are located on a towering hill surrounded by other hills of its kind, overlooking the landscape. The most remarkable feature of this ecoregion is the luxuriant vegetation and dense woodland supported by the coastal fogs, in direct contrast to the adjacent desert interior.

As Zahira, Salasa, and their guardians approach the camps, five elderly men, who in appearance appear to be from the growing Sabaean tribes, come out to meet them accompanied by four guards. The old men have white beards that fall below their chest and they wear cloaks the color of charcoal gray. They are the Muhas, teachers of the school and masters of what is called the power of the White Dust.

There stands one man ahead of the others who wear a tan colored cloak girded with a wide thick leather belt. He is the leader, eldest and founder of the school. His name is Ahura. It is said he has lived for over eight hundred years, due to the power of the White Dust.

Kneeling down on one knee and softly placing his hand upon the frightened Zahira's shoulder, Ahura speaks to her in the Sabaean tongue, a dialect that she knew well through her training.

"Do not be afraid, my dear, for here is where you will be protected and loved. You are special. That alone should give you comfort that all will be well for you. This place was designed only for young boys possessing the power of the White Dust; good boys that will use their new found abilities for the good of our planet. However, you Zahira, you are the first and only female that has ever entered this school and will become the greatest of all here."

Zahira looks around in amazement at the beautiful school in the distance. The camps consisted of tight-knit tents and clay homes all joined together in a receding spiral with an arena to the south of the camp. Continuing south of the school are the Escarpment Mountains, consisting of three ranges that together form a long breathtaking chain.

There is a large library elaborately carved and tunneled through a mountain that possesses a wealth of literature for the students to learn language, art, the sciences, and history. The main palace where the Muhas reside is a beautifully decorated edifice. Its structure too is made into the belly of a mighty mountain.

In the arena the students are trained in the use of their powers, physical abilities, and disciplines, gifts from the so-called White Dust of the star.

Zahira, Salasa, and their guardians, whose names are Tegene, Taye, Tahro, and Zere slowly, follow the attendant directed by Ahura to their quarters down a narrow roadway turning into what looked to be a small community. In actuality, it is the homes and work rooms of both students and workers. However, Kimoni stays behind talking with Ahura over the proceedings and future events.

"Whoa . . . what a place," Tegene exclaims. "I never knew anything like this could ever exist."

"Well, I guess you don't get around much," Taye states. "Have you forgotten about the halls and palaces of Kush? And what of Azmaria, well at least the ruins, many say . . ."

"Ok, ok, I get the point," Laughs Tegene, "but this is marvelous nevertheless. I didn't know the people from these parts could accomplish such feats."

Finally, they reach their living quarters.

The attendant remarks, "This is where you will reside during your stay here. Many amenities are afforded to you as well, and there will be servants assisting you."

The houses are meticulously crafted stone homes with Sabaean writings engraved above the entrances. Each one face the other divided by brick roads. They are sectioned throughout the school making separate streets.

The streets are lined with torches that are lit at night.

"Now this is definitely a place that I can appreciate," Zere chuckles, "we could never have imagined this with our tribe, at least to this degree."

All but Zahira and Salasa enter their rooms to relax from the long journey.

However, before entering his room, Tegene ask the attendant, "What about the girls? I will wait with them until . . ."

"Say no more my friend." One of the attendants interrupts. "A maidservant has been assigned to care for the two girls."

Running towards the group is Zeira, a beautiful young woman assigned to live with Zahira and Salasa. She is covered in a long white garment from head to toe and fair complexioned.

"Greetings, I trust your travels were pleasant." Speak Zeira.

Zeira then turns to Zahira and Salasa.

"And look at what fine young women we have here." She states smiling from cheek to cheek.

Salasa rudely run pass Zeira and into the house they will be living in, Zahira slowly follows behind.

Tegene quickly addressed Zeira saying, "Please understand the reason behind their actions. It's going to take . . ."

"Don't worry, I have been informed about their situation," Zeira replies, "It is remarkable how much you and the other warriors care so much for the young girls. I will do so as well. You have nothing to worry about."

Zeira steps into the house behind the girls into the front room. She closes the door behind and then turns to the girls to properly introduce herself. She smiles and kneels to their level.

"As-Shlama" Zeira greet in the Sabaean tongue, a greeting of peace, "my name is Zeira, and I will be tending to you during your stay. Might I ask what your names are?"

Wiping a tear from her eye, Zahira stand and boldly announces, "I am Zahira!"

But Salasa is more aloof and bitter, missing her family. She does not respond but stands behind Zahira with her hands hiding her face.

"That is a pretty name." says Zeira, "Would you believe it is a name from these very parts? It means 'the shining one', and how fitting. The two of you have nothing to worry about, for the greatest of care will be given to you. Whatever you need you may ask of me and I will be your fulfiller. Just think of me as a mother..."

Salasa quickly interrupts yelling, "You're not my mother... I have a mother... I want my mama!"

She then burst into tears, jumping onto the cot with her face buried in the pillow.

Empathizing with her grief, Zeira softly laments, "You are right. I could never take the place of your mother. But I would at least like to be your friend. Don't answer at this moment. Relax. Now why don't we get you two out of those dirty rags? You have had a long trip and its time for the two of you to get some rest. Perhaps we can sit up tonight and you can tell me wonderful stories of your beautiful land."

After saying that Zeira tenderly kisses Zahira on the forehead then walks over to Salasa and gently rubs her back.

When Zeira leaves the room to get their clothing, Zahira creaps over to Salasa and whispers,

"Come on now. Stop crying please. I thought you were excited about this trip. Everything will be ok..."

"No," Salasa screeches, "don't say that. Don't bother me. Go away! Go away!"

Zahira reluctantly leaves Salasa's side and retreats to her own cot. After sitting for some time in deep thought, rocking back and forth, she soon starts to cry as well.

Sometime later, there is a knock at the door. Zahira rises and opens the door. There standing at the door is Kimoni. He cheerfully opens his arms and Zahira races into them.

"Just coming to check on you girls, where is Zeira?" Kimoni ask.

"The lady is preparing our clothes for bed and we are about to tell stories of our homeland" Zahira cheerfully answers.

"Now that sounds great," Kimoni laughs with excitement.

He notices Salasa curled up on her side lying on the cot. He walks over to her and sits besides her, tenderly placing his hand on her forehead.

"Salasa, I want you to come to me for whatever you need. I am here for you."

Turning her head to face him, he beholds soak drenched eyes swollen from the many tears she cried.

In a jittery voice she laments, "Kimoni . . . when . . . can I go home? Please . . . take me home to mama."

Kimoni leans over and kisses her forehead tenderly. At that moment Zeira steps back into the room.

"Sorry, should I leave?"

"No, no." answers Kimoni, "Sit, because I want you to hear this as well. Salasa . . . Zahira . . . I love the both of you dearly and that goes without question. I would gladly walk to the sun and back for a piece of its light just to see smiles on your faces. But as you know, we cannot go back. Salasa, your mother and father sent you here because of their enormous love for you. They would not have had it any other way. I know that what I am saying is not much consolation, but in time, you will learn to understand why things happened the way they did. Zeira is here to help you. So please, do not scorn her efforts. She is willing to do whatever she must to accommodate you."

"I understand," Zahira answers softly.

However, Salasa continues crying, placing her face back into her pillow.

Finally, Kimoni leaves after kissing the girls goodnight. Salasa does not change, but instead eventually falls fast asleep on the cot. But Zahira changes into clean clothes and eagerly sits in Zeira's lap to tell about the wonders of her home in Be'ja.

Zeira is amazed and pleased that Zahira, as young as she is and heartbroken over her abrupt departure from Romana promptly embraces her so eargerly.

During their stay in Azal, Zahira and Salasa are given the best of care. Growing up within the confines of Azal's many mountains, they spend most of their time in the palace halls, running around columns and playing old childhood games from Be'ja.

Zahira becomes an advent student of the ancient books passed down by the Muhas that speak of their world. She takes her classes seriously and humbles many of the young boys with her knowledge. Many become jealous, whereas others admire her knowledge and her beauty.

As far as Salasa is concerned, although she acquires a bit more ease with her surroundings, she still remain somewhat aloof. She stays under Zahira, constantly demanding her attention, even when Zahira is engaged in her studies.

Although Salasa become an expert in hiding her pain, the sudden departure from her parents is still a troubling concern of hers.

Nevertheless, the two girls grow to be shining lights within the large school. Yet, there are many tests yet to come.

CHAPTER 9

The Rebirth of Tribulation

Three years pass since Zahira's first day on arriving in the land of Azal. She is now fifteen years old and Salasa is fourteen.

The girls come a long way and gain much knowledge since their earlier days at the school.

Zahira's progress impresses the Muhas so that they soon wish to involve her in specialized training. Unbeknownst to Zahira, the Muhas desire to use her for special missions, enhance her skills and perception abilities, and bring forth the suppressed energies of her special powers.

With her growth her latent powers grow more evident. Zahira's knowledge of her true ancestors' fate continues to fuel the desire for revenge. But she knew that there is an appropriate time for everything, and now was not the time to act. What she need she does not have and that is maturity, skill, and knowledge.

Some classes are taught with other students present, but the majority of Zahira's classes are on a one on one basis with Ahura.

Zahira is a beautiful sight and her physique is in peek condition.

Salasa too is beautiful, with brown skin and braided ebony black hair. The two are always together and very supportive of one another.

Zahira is constantly positive, thinking things through before acting, a very rational thinker. She is an honest girl in all her dealings, soft-spoken, but will act when the situation call for it.

Even though Zahira is the logical one, she sometimes allow Salasa's nagging to break her will, falling into things she would otherwise think not right.

Salasa hardly speaks to anyone other than Zahira and those men that escorted them from their tribe. She uses Zahira as her mouth piece, speaking only when lashing out at the young boys.

One bright morning, when classes are not in session, the two girls leave for the school yard to sit and reminisce about old times. Zahira laid a blanket on the grass and the two sit on it, snacking on fruit, laughing and talking under a shaded tree from the warm sun. After some time of their merriment they are visited by five young boys standing over them with their arms folded.

"As-Shlama," Zahira says initiating conversation. She recognizes them from one of her classes.

"You're sitting in our spot," one of the boys bark. His name is Ahd.

"Excuse me?" Zahira asks a bit confused.

"I said, 'you are sitting in our spot!'," he repeats but in an insistent tone while pointing at Zahira.

"I didn't know that sitting areas were apportioned by Ahura in his yard," Zahira sarcastically retorts.

"Well, I guess you wouldn't know," Ahd laughs, "now would you, being that you're a girl and all. There is certain information you are not privileged to."

"Then if it is privileged information, how could I know . . . dummy." Zahira exclaims.

Upset, the boy viciously states, "Well, the point is now you know, 'so get up!'"

At this point others in the yard overhear the commotion and heads over to get a better look. The situation is now getting uncomfortable for the girls, seeing that they are the only girls in the whole courtyard.

Not wanting to draw any more attention to themselves Zahira rise and calls Salasa to come with her. However, Salasa is indignant and feels that they do not need to leave on account of the bullies.

"Why are you getting up? Are you crazy? Who are they to demand who sits where?" Salasa fusses.

"Salasa, they can have the sitting area, I don't care. The sun shines just as brightly somewhere else."

Salasa pouts and loudly declares, "No! That's not the point. You can't just give in to them like that. They will do it again and again until they think they are in control."

"Salasa, lets go!" Urgently demands Zahira. "There is no need to go looking for trouble. If it makes them feel manly then so be it, as long as they are not . . ."

"Hitting you," Salasa abruptly interrupts. "That will be the next step they take if you let them get away with this!"

Nevertheless, Zahira grabs Salasa's arm and pulls her away to another location in the yard away from the boys.

After sitting, the two continue their conversation when Zahira is later struck in the back with a date. When she and Salasa quickly turn to see who threw it, they notice it is from the direction of where the young boys Ahd and his friends are sitting.

The boys giggle while quickly looking in the other direction, pretending it is not them.

Ahd laughingly states, "Sorry . . . I was about to pop it in my mouth when it slipped through my fingers. No harm done, right?"

Nodding ok, Zahira grabs Salasa's hand once again but this time leaves the yard, with Salasa aggressively trying to resist.

Upon leaving the courtyard the two girls bump into another boy walking towards the courtyard from one of his classes. He is fifteen years old, tall, and handsome. He is of a very dark complexion and bald-headed with slanted eyes.

"I'm sorry . . . As-Shlama, I am Abassi. Might I ask your names?"

Looking at him suspiciously, Zahira slowly returns the greeting, "Alykom Shlama . . . this is Salasa . . . and I am Zahira. We are on our way home . . . excuse us."

But not wanting her to leave so soon, Abassi continues saying, "Everyone knows your name. You don't recognize me because of the size of our class, but I see you every day."

He then turns and addresses Salasa.

"And you are Salasa. That's a pretty name."

Zahira giggles while Salasa continues her agitated expression.

"I hear you are quite skilled with a sword. Is that true," Abassi ask Zahira.

"I am ok—"

"Ok," Salasa interrupts. "She's the best. There is none like her."

"Oh," Abassi smiles rubbing his chin. "Then I guess you wouldn't mind attending the sparring competition in two days."

"Sparring competition," Zahira replies inquisitively.

"You mean to tell me you haven't heard about it?" ask Abassi.

"No."

"Well, a few of the guys have formed a club of sorts, where we get together and test our use of the sword. Do you want to come?"

Salasa abruptly answers for Zahira saying, "Zahira could beat you and your gang in anything—"

"Enough Salasa," Zahira bashfully interjects.

"Well, so I guess you will be there then." Abassi continues.

"Ok, I will be there." Zahira boldly agrees.

"Good . . . then it is official."

Abassi smiles and softly pats her on the shoulder. He then leaves on into the courtyard.

While the girls head down the brick path to their room, Zahira ask, "Do you think I should have accepted?"

Salasa whole-heartedly answers, "I would normally say no . . . but in light of these idiot boys, of course I do. These boys think they rule the world."

"In a sense, they will soon enough." Zahira replies.

Salasa suddenly stops in her tracks shocked at Zahira's response.

"No. Have you lost your mind Zahira? They think they rule the world, but they do not. How could you think that? You are the said future savior of our lands and you believe man rules it?"

Gently grabbing hold to Salasa's arm and pulling her forward she reply, "Come now Salasa, the kingdoms were not built by women, but men."

"That might be true," Salasa counters while putting her hands upon her hips and rolling her eyes, "but without their mothers to inspire them, they would not have accomplished what they have."

"Look, don't get me wrong Salasa; I am not saying that men are greater. I'm just saying . . . never mind. I will explain another day. Let's go.

Later that night while Zahira is lying across her cot engaged in her studies, Salasa approaches her with a sad expression on her face.

"Zahira, you study day and night. I feel as though those scrolls and books are your best friend."

"That's not true Salasa. We share a bond that not even death itself could break, remember that, it was your saying. There is just so much for me to learn and it seems like I have little time to do so. But I will make time for you. Come and let's talk. What is on your mind?"

Salasa comes closer and heaves a heavy sigh. She then plops down on the edge of Zahira's cot.

"When you are immersed in your studies, I have a lot of time to think. I constantly think about our families in Naldamak and long to see them once again. Do you not share these feelings?"

"Yes, I think about them and I want to see them too. But we cannot return. There is too much at stake."

"We were children when we left," Responds Salasa now tearing, "our appearance has changed since then. No one would recognize us. It is not even necessary to exchange words with them. We can observe from a distance. I just need to know that my family is well. Do you not wish to know how your mother is doing?"

"Of course I want to know if mama is well." Zahira confirms while rubbing Salasa's hair, which she starts to braid, "I think about her night and day. She frequently appears in my dreams. But you know that is not what they would want us to do."

"All I ask, Zahira, is that you consider what I have said." Salasa reply, "This is not a decision you need to make now. Consider what I have said once you have rested."

Unbeknownst to the women, Tegene overhear their conversation while walking by outside their window. He then leaves quickly to tell Kimoni. On hearing this Kimoni is disturbed for he knows the consequences of their return to Naldamak. He commands Tegene not to reveal their conversation to anyone else.

Kimoni immediately leaves for Zahira and Salasa's home. Upon entering, he greets Zeira and requests a word with Zahira.

"The girls are sleep Kimoni," says Zeira, "but I will wake Zahira for you."

Zeira goes and wakes Zahira up and brings her to the larger living room. On seeing Kimoni Zahira smiles lazily due to her sleepy state and walk over to hug him. Kimoni whispers,

"Zahira, I must have a word with you."

"Of course, is there something wrong?" she asks.

He continues, "It has come to my attention that you and Salasa desire to return to Naldamak. I must warn you that such an action could result in calamity for you and your families. Now, I am not a harsh man and I have been very good and fair with you girls. I understand your desire to see your families, but you must remember why you were sent here."

Zahira rubs her fingers through the back of her white hair, wondering how he knew about their conversation.

She reply, "Kimoni, you must be mistaken. Yes, I do miss mama, but I have not forgotten why I was sent here. It is not my desire to return to Naldamak. Who told you this?"

Folding his arms and walking in his usual distinct fashion he boldly declares, "Where the information came from is not important. What is important is that you understand that to return to Naldamak or to stay in Azal is not a choice you have. You will remain here with the Muhas."

After that he tenderly kisses her forehead and leaves the house. The conversation with Kimoni disturbs Zahira and causes her distress. She is torn between those she deeply cares for.

CHAPTER 10

A Girl's Challenge

Two days pass and Zahira is ecstatic about the sparring competition. Though she is quite humble, she is very competitive and welcomes a good challenge.

It is a beautiful morning and the girls both put on their scarves, as customary, and leave their quarters heading to the site where Abassi told them to meet him. It is behind the palace at least a mile away, near a collection of tall dense trees, out of the view of others.

As they wait for Abassi to show up, Salasa nervously rejects, "I don't know about this,"

Irritated Zahira reply, "What are you talking about? You were the one that pushed me to do it."

"Yes . . . I know. But why does everything have to be so secretive? Will any of the Muhas be there to govern the sport? Have you not forgotten what these boys can be like? Remember back home in Beshari—"

Shaking her head in disbelief, Zahira begrudgingly answers, "I don't know Salasa. Let's just wait and see."

Soon in the distance they can see Abassi running towards them down the long pathway. When he arrives, panting heavily, he apologizes, "Sorry I'm late. How long were you waiting?"

Zahira answers, "Only a few—"

"Too long," Salasa restlessly interrupts.

Abassi smiles and says, "I'm sorry. I got up a little late this morning. Oh well, let's not waste anymore time. Follow me."

The trio heads deep into the woods, toward the tall hills.

Salasa's uneasiness intensifies as she notices Abassi constantly looking over his shoulder in all directions making sure they are not being followed.

"Just where are we going!" Salasa grunts.

"Oh . . . the boys meet at the black hill." Abassi answers, "It's not too far. It's inside the cave just—"

"Did you say, 'Inside the cave?'" Salasa ask interrupting.

"There's nothing to fear. I will not let anything happen to you or Zahira."

Abassi grins and smile at Zahira who is shaking her head in aggravation over Salasa's constant nagging.

When they finally reach the cave and start to crawl through the small opening, Salasa's fears overtake her and she objects, "This is ridiculous! Where are you taking us? No, no, no! I am not going in there. Zahira let's go home."

"Salasa, what are you talking about," Zahira urges. "We have came this far. Let's go and see what's going on."

"No! I am not going in there with a bunch of boys. You're crazy!"

Zahira motions with her finger for Abassi to give her some time to talk with Salasa in private. She gently grabs hold of Salasa's hand and pulls her to the side.

"Salasa, do you think I would let anything happen to you?"

"Zahira, you might be this 'chosen one', but that doesn't mean you are . . . unbeatable! You are still human."

Zahira sighs and reply, "I know, but a different kind of human, at least that's what I've been told all my life. Regardless, this Abassi seems pretty decent. A good ambiance is flowing from him."

"You're crazy," Salasa shouts. "You don't really know that. You just like him, that's all. You have a crush on him!"

"No I don't," Zahira fires back attempting to hush Salasa.

"Yes you do. I can see it in your eyes and the way you keep smiling when he looks at you. You act like you don't know anything."

Zahira closes her eyes momentarily to gain her composure back, after calming down she softly counters Salasa saying, "Come on Salasa . . . I don't think I do. But just this time, come in with me. You know I'm not going in if you don't."

"I know." Salasa pouts folding her arms.

"So please, let's go just this one time." Zahira pleads, "You know how you feel about all these boys thinking they are better than girls. Now we can prove them wrong."

Zahira giggles, tapping Salasa's shoulder,

"I will make them eat their words . . . along with the dirt that imma shove down their mouth. You know I will."

Salasa thinks for a moment while Zahira looks endearingly at her with sorrowful eyes.

"Ok, just this time." Salasa sighs, "But don't ask me to do this anymore!"

"Thank you so, so much. I owe you one."

"Yes, you do," Salasa sarcastically reply as she turns her back to Zahira.

The two girls walk over toward Abassi who patiently is waiting sitting on a nearby rock with his head down with a silly smile on his face.

When he see them coming he immediately jump to his feet gleefully exclaiming, "So, are we going?"

"Yes," Zahira halfheartedly answers.

"Ok, follow me and stay close."

They start to crawl through the small opening toward the faint light that burn deep inside ahead of them.

When they reach the clearing the cave is wide and open, with its ceiling measuring at least fifty feet high.

There are at least ten young boys between the ages of fourteen and seventeen standing in a circle around a large circular floor measuring forty feet wide with a flat surface covered over by stretched camel hides sewn together. There are ten six foot torches lined around the floor giving light to the dark cave.

"Hey worms," Abassi jokingly yells as he enter joining the boys. All the boys gleefully greet him and asked why he is late.

Shortly after Abassi enter, Zahira and Salasa follow. The boys immediately get silent on seeing the girls.

One of the boys step forward, his name is Melku, and he is the eldest and organizer of the event.

"What are they doing here? Is this some kind of joke, Abassi?"

"No Melku. I thought we could add some flavor to the competition."

"Flavor," Melku bawls. "The only thing they can do for me is serve me my supper!"

The boys laugh hysterically over his jeering.

"Is it not true … that in your land of Kush … women rule," Abassi asks Melku. "I believe they are called Kandake's."

The response angers Melku, for there is truth to Abassi's statement.

Ignoring his remark Melku continues, "They can't compete with us. Send them outside to get us some dates and milk."

Again the boys laugh out loud and start to point at the girls, jeering and taunting them.

Abassi approach Zahira with a downtrodden expression and says, "I'm sorry for bringing you here. I didn't think they would be this ignorant about it. Let's go."

Angry, Salasa starts to stump towards the exit of the cave, mumbling under her breath, but Zahira stops and look into Abassi's eyes reassuring him,

"Are you really going to leave because they don't want Salasa and me here?"

Melku calls out to Abassi saying, "What are you doing? Tend to your girlfriends later! We have man'ly things to do here and when done, me and the boys will visit the village of Sakah, where the real women are."

The boys in the cave are overtaken by constant laughter.

Abassi turns back and gives Zahira an endearing smile. "Let's get out of here."

A chill runs down Zahira's spine, and she cant hold back from blushing over the fact that Abassi would leave his friends for them.

"What are you doing? Let's go," Salasa yells again impatiently waiting for Zahira near the exit of the cave, hot with rage.

"Go ahead Salasa. I have a competition to engage in," Zahira confidently states while looking into Abassi's eyes.

"Are you sure about this?" Abassi ask with concern in his voice.

"Of course I am. Why not," Zahira says as she parades past Abassi toward the group of boys.

Approaching Melku and looking him straight in the eyes she announces, "I will take any one of you boys in this dirty cave and beat you back to your mamas."

Salasa reluctantly returns, disappointed at Zahira's decision to stay.

"You have no place here. Get out, this is a disgrace!" Melku bawls with his chest stuck out proudly.

"Are you afraid of losing to a girl?" Mocks Zahira.

"No way," yells one of the boys.

"Then what are we waiting around for?" Zahira screams. "Let's do this!"

"Ok, ok, if you are so anxious to be humbled, then fine." Melku fires back.

The boys all stand back and start to throw lots as to who will be chosen to fight Zahira. The lots fall on Shaku, he is chosen to compete against her.

Shaku is a boy of small stature, frail in appearance, but very fast and skillful.

Melku then announces to Zahira, "No offense to you Shaku . . . but this is all you get. He is tough, but one of the lesser ones here; and I don't think you will last a rocks fall with him."

Abassi approach Zahira again uncertain of her decision.

"Are you sure about this? You know we can leave. Who cares what they think."

"I am so sure." Zahira answers with great anticipation as she clinches her fists with her eyes fixed on Shaku.

"Hey Abassi," Melku yells, "By the way . . . if she loses, you lose our respect."

"You're getting soft," another boy barks.

Ignoring their taunts, Abassi heads over to the sidelines and take a seat on the ground to watch the event. Zahira and Shaku step onto the floor arena. The rules are announced by Walo, who is judging the event.

"There will be no eye poking or groin hitting. There are five rounds. You will receive three points a round. The first to fall will lose a point for that round. The first to fall out of the circle will lose the round. The one with the most points will be the winner—"

"We're using Shatha fighting style . . . right?" Zahira interrupts. Shatha is the fighting style taught to the students by the Muhas's. It is a martial art form that teaches restraint under mercy and discipline before rage.

The boys burst into laughter over her question.

Finally Melku states, "We don't use that old way of fighting in here."

"But that is the style the Muhas teach at the school," Zahira exclaims. "It promotes discipline and—"

"It promotes nothing," Melku abruptly interrupts. "You talk like you are a Muhas. You're only fourteen—"

"Fifteen!" screams Salasa heatedly from the corner.

"I don't care how old she is. She is going to lose anyway . . . besides any fighting style counts!" answers Melku.

"Let's do this!" screams Shaku in anticipation.

"Then get started," Melku reply.

Walo waves his hand and quickly moves off the circle leaving Zahira and Shaku standing face to face.

The two quickly grab hold of their mock weapons, wood shaped into the traditional swords of the era. They are small swords which gave use to rapid movements and used for training purposes.

They circle the arena, focused intently on each other.

Shaku takes the first attack and moves in toward Zahira with his weapon held back to make a strike. Zahira quickly evades with Shaku almost falling out of the arena, straining to keep his balance.

"You are not as fast as we thought." Abassi yells out to Shaku mockingly.

Shaku shakes his head in disappointment and again takes his combat stance. He charges at her again, but this time he moves more cautiously. Swinging at her, his sword eventually connects with Zahira's, sending a loud echo throughout the cave. He then aggressively starts to strike down on her sword with the intent to overpower her. However, she manages to successfully ward of his attacks. With his last blow she swiftly evades and rises behind him, striking him on the back so hard that he lose his balance and falls to the floor.

"Point," Walo yells.

The boys begin to 'boo' at Shaku as he stands up from the humiliating fall.

"Shut up," Shaku screams, still slightly dazed from the blow while trying to hide the pain felt.

Again, Zahira and Shaku take their combat stance facing each other. The boys shout, cheering Shaku on, "Break her, break her, break her!"

Salasa sits at the exit of the cave watching uneasily, biting her nails due to her unsettling nerves.

Repeatedly, Shaku races toward Zahira using different techniques to try and break her defense. But again, she evades his attacks striking him on different parts of his body. It is not until the last round that Shaku manages to get two points, but not enough to bring him close to winning.

"I hate you," he blurts out at Zahira. Then a strange thing happens. Shaku's eyes begin to glow and a faint aura seems to appear around him.

Salasa immediately stands up dumbfounded and hysterical yelling, "Zahira, get out of there!" But Zahira pays no attention; for she too starts to generate a powerful glow in her eyes.

They stand before each other, their bodies aglow when Abassi jumps onto the floor of the circle between them and announces, "No, you cannot use your gifts! This is getting too heated."

"Who cares," Melku chimes in. "We all have it, but none of us can really focus it . . . it is all a big show. Besides, it gives a little more light in this dark cave."

Abassi repeats but this time more sternly, "No powers are to be used! We are too young to exercise our properly. Melku, you know what the Muhas say about this."

"You are like a baby Abassi. You are getting way to soft for my taste." Melku retorts.

Zahira then simmers down with her glow fading. She then turns to leave the ring. Suddenly, Shaku, in a fit of rage, charges at Zahira with her back turned. Zahira immediately turn to face him and delivers Shaku a hit with her blunt sword into his abdomen.

He once again falls to the floor in agony. While he is crouching over holding his abdomen, she thumps him in the head with the handle of her wooden sword. Shaku's aura quickly dissipates as he lay on the ground in excruciating pain.

A long hush comes over all the boys in the cave.

She then turns and head toward Salasa who is grinning ear to ear. She says to Salasa, "Come on. Let's go."

The two girls leave the cave and the boys are left in disbelief.

"Take me on, you dog," Melku screams with a challenge to Zahira. "You are nothing but a bastard."

Zahira ignores him and continues exiting the cave. By this time it has grown dark outside.

Almost home Abassi chases after the two girls yelling, "Zahira . . . wait!"

Zahira stops and turns around waiting for him to catch up, but Salasa grabs the sleeve of Zahira's garment and tugs saying, "Come on. Forget about him. He's one of them."

"Wait," Zahira whispers, "let's see what he has to say."

When Abassi catches up with them he exclaims, "That was outstanding! I had heard of how good you were, but that was tremendous."

"Thank you," Zahira reply blushing, all the while Salasa impatiently pace back and forth.

"I would much like to see you again. Maybe we could be friends?" Abassi states cautiously.

But answering for Zahira, Salasa quickly interjects, "That position has already been taken . . . and besides that is not allowed."

"Perhaps there is no harm Salasa, we are at the same school and I could use help in some of my studies." Zahira calmly remarks.

Salasa turns her head and heaves a sigh of disdain.

"Well, I know you and Salasa need to get back home," Abassi states, "but I hope to see you again Zahira, maybe in class."

"That's a possibility." She agrees.

They then go their separate ways.

On their way back to the house it is a quiet walk. Soon Salasa breaks the awkward silence asking,

"Why are you doing this?"

"Doing what," Zahira answers with a bothered tone.

"Why are you getting so close to him and wanting to be accepted by them . . . why?"

"It's not that I want to be accepted . . . well maybe. I just want peace. Look, we are going to be here for a long time. Why do you want to remain separate? Maybe we should be nicer to them."

Salasa throws her hands in the air and exclaims, "What do you mean Zahira, we are suppose to remain separate from them . . . do you not pay attention to any of our ways. I don't trust them Zahira. They are trouble."

"Well, we can't just stay like this while we're here." Zahira exclaims.

"Like what?" Ask Salasa.

Zahira shrugs her shoulders and states, "You know . . . outcasts, alone. We have to make more friends."

They soon reach their living quarters. On entering Salasa warns, "You better be careful, Zahira. You trust too easily. Soon it's going to hurt more than you. Mark my words. It will hurt people you are close to as well. The boys should stay with the boys and the girls the girls. It's a thing that makes us safe."

CHAPTER 11

The Trusting Heart

During Zahira's stay in Azal, she remains the most favored of all the students among the instructors. Many of the students resent her for this.

In her science classes, Zahira will often sit behind Abassi, secretly infatuated and dazed over his presence.

Whenever the Muhas back is turned in class Abassi will turn and whisper endearments to Zahira. She blushes and smiles while playing with her right earlobe, a habit she is known for.

There are even nights when Abassi will secretly make surprise visits to Zahira's bedroom window to talk with her. These visits frighten and disturb Salasa and she often threatens to wake Zeira if he does not leave. However, Zahira is always able to convince her otherwise.

One night, exactly twenty days after the cave competition, Abassi makes his normal visit to Zahira's window. Upon getting her and Salasa's attention, he whispers through the window, "What are you girls doing?"

"Trying to get some sleep, no thanks to you," Salasa rudely answers.

Zahira whispers back, "What are you doing here? I told you Zeira is just in the other room."

"I know, I know. I just wanted to see you."

Zahira gets out of her bed and whispers, "I just saw you in class today."

"Yeah . . . but now I'm here to see you again," Abassi says with an endearing smile. "That was much too long ago."

"Too long ago," Zahira giggles.

Abassi now implores, "I need to ask a big favor of you just this one time, please."

Still agitated over his presence Salasa mumbles, "What do you want? Go home. You are a pest."

"What is it . . . wait Salasa, please," Zahira pleads, gently pulling on Salasa's gown.

Abassi leans back from the window and looks around both corners of the house to see if anyone is coming. He then creeps back and whispers to Zahira, "I want you to come with me somewhere."

"Oh no!" protests Salasa, "Zahira is not going anywhere with you. Get out of here," Salasa starts to push on his shoulders at the window for him to leave.

"What are you up to?" Zahira ask now suspicious of his motives. "I do have morals now."

"Come on Zahira." Huffs and puffs Abassi, "That was not on my mind, trust me, I have far more respect for you than that. I really do have something nice, innocent and clean for you to see. I have been at this school for way too long and have learned too much to just throw my reputation away like that."

Zahira rubs her earlobe contemplating his request, all the while being subject to Salasa's constant bickering.

Finally she implores Salasa saying, "Please do not say a word. I will be back soon. If I'm not back by a reasonable time please tell Kimoni . . . well, maybe not him. Tell Tegene, ok Salasa?"

Salasa fretfully reply, "I don't know about this. You better—"

"Please, trust me." Zahira implores staring into her eyes sorrowfully. Salasa reluctantly mumbles her approval and Zahira quickly climbs out of the window to join Abassi.

"You better be right back, I mean very soon!" Salasa whispers forcefully. Zahira nods in agreement and she then commissions Abassi to wait for her by a date tree near the courtyard. She puts on her garments and scarf and leaves out the window as quietly as possible.

"I mean it!" Salasa grunts her last warning. On meeting Abassi by the date tree Zahira ask enthusiastically, "Where are we going, and why so late?"

"You will see." He responds with a sly smile.

The two race through the night heading south out of the school. They finally reach a long range of hills and mountains. One of the mountains has a long steep trail going up its side,

"Now let's test what youre really made of," Abassi smirks.

The two race up the trail with Abassi leading the way. The trail seems to get steeper and steeper the higher they get, but Zahira is more than able to keep up.

"Wow . . . you are pretty good. But we still have a long way to go," Abassi laughs as he keep the lead.

"Will we return before dawn, right," Zahira ask.

"Possibly, but we really have to keep moving."

At last, they finally reach the top of the small mountain expended, the two falls to their knees gasping for air.

Zahira sits on the ground still catching her breath when Abassi calls out to her saying, "What are you doing, you are missing the view."

When Zahira stands and turn his way, she beholds the most beautiful breathtaking landscape she has ever seen.

She is in awe over the high mountain ranges that drop into the Al Qalzam seas many miles away. Resonating sounds of the sea's tide crashing into the mountains base and birds hover over the sea in the night's sky looking for a quick meal to snatch from the waters. There are steep lush hills plunging down to the deep still bays below. Also inland from the sea are clear, deep, still waters surrounded by beautiful bushes, with deer that appear like silhouettes drinking from the stream.

The sky is black and ominous with stars spread about like snowflakes against a black carpet. The moon is crescent and shows clearly in the sky.

"The glory of the one Creator and sustainer of life is indeed witnessed from atop of this mountain," Abassi says, looking up and raising his hands to the sky. "You can vaguely see across the sea of Al Qalzam straight into Kush. Turn south and witness the hills and oasis of Sana'a. Turn north and east and view the mountains and wondrous terrains as far as Sumeria. The world is beautiful. When I sit on this mountain, I think back to my people in Punt across these waters."

"Where is Punt?" Zahira ask, taking her seat on a nearby stone.

"Where is Punt," Abassi reply with a sound of surprise. "I see you have not gotten around much."

"Well . . . no. I have lived my entire youth with the Beshari, a very small tribe from Be' Ja in Naldamak."

"So you are a Kushite?" Abassi enthusiastically ask.

"Well, not really." Zahira answers a bit unsure, "I believe we are related in many ways. My Chief Tafari of my tribe said something about my people being a branch of Kush or something like that."

"Of course you are," Abassi laughs, "aren't we all, that is, all those from the whole of that continent? Back home in Punt I was taught that Kush is the mother of all our worlds. So if you are not a Kushite, then what are you?"

"Human," Zahira answers with a cynical laugh.

"You know what I mean." heaves Abassi.

"I'm not sure about all of that Abassi, all I know is what I have been taught that we are all creations by the one source of creation, he knows best. I can't say it started from Kush and you also know that is not what the Muhas have taught us here. We have been taught though elements of this planet were used to design mankind our start was really from another dimension. The place of the unseen, but I am sure in time we will learn the truth of that as well. However, on a fleshly note, back to your curiosity, my true heritage is Azmarian."

Abassi answers, "That's true Zahira, I do tend to cling to the ways taught from the schools of Ikengia from my homeland Punt. The Muhas have taught us the truth in so many aspects; they have not deviated like much of the other schools, that's for sure, but back to your heritage . . . Azmarian, hmmm."

"Yes, Azmarian," Zahira repeats, "have you heard of them?"

"I thought they all died out. I should have known you were an Azmarian . . . stupid me!" He replies hitting his forehead with the palm of his hand, as if a light had gone off inside. "Your white hair is your birth mark. In Punt we studied a lot about your people and their purpose. We are actually just south of your land."

"That's interesting . . . but regarding Azmaria, it's no longer my land."

"Why do you say that?" he asks.

"I was raised in the country of Kush. I knew nothing about Azmaria, only what was told to me by my mother."

"But it is still who you are." He confirms.

"I wasn't born there," Zahira reply now growing agitated.

Abassi comes closer to her. Softly grabbing hold of her hand he says, "Look Zahira, you do not have to be born there to identify with it. That is your birth mark and you will represent it no matter where you go."

Zahira's moral instinct causes her to quickly remove her hand from his. After regaining her composure she firmly reply, "But they are all dead—"

Abassi politely interrupts,"They are dead, but you are their champion due to your being alive, you are now their representative. Your existence is their victory. But you know, the wonderful thing about all of this goes far beyond race, color, culture and the like, we have something else that bonds us that far exceeds all of that stuff. It is the mark we carry, the mark of the star, this power that only certain ones are gifted with. We are a brotherhood, chosen from times memorial to be who we are today.

The Muhas have taught us that our allegiance should be to those marked by the Whitestar and dust, not the evil that comes from the

Blackstar or its dust. The Whitestar is pure thus our heart should not harbor any love for the Blackstar users, even if they are of our kin. That is the beauty of our new forming race, a race not of color or ethnicity, but one united based on the gift given to us. Sometimes I have to remind myself of this often as well.

Zahira smiles and comments, "True, and well said. This is our unifying mark . . . our heritage of the star."

Abassi responds, "Not all of us cling to this belief. Many of our brothers with this power in the vast lands of the world set themselves apart so that they can gain greater glory. That's all foolishness. That is why Rathamun is able to take over so much of our world in such a quick time. He saw the division of our lands, the lack of unity and used it against us. It is your people, the Azmarians that set the example for us all to learn from. They are the forerunners, the ones that were initially given these powers that separated them from other humans, and they proved themselves righteous users of it as well. You are the last representative of that great race . . . that is so amazing to me."

"Very thought provoking," Zahira states laughing, "where did all this knowledge come from?"

Abassi smiles and responds, "Some of it has been shared with me from my father back in Punt, but most of it is only what we have been taught by the Muhas. All of this you know as well Zahira."

"True," she replies, "but always good to hear it again. That's why living here I am increasingly feeling at home, even though I have to contend with the idiot boys here and their quest for superiority."

Abassi laughs. Zahira then ask,

"The Muhas briefly mentioned about what will happen once we are done here, what is your take on it?"

Abassi answers, "Once we leave the school, each of us will go back to our country and serve as the protector for the land under that king. We will take with us the knowledge of creation and our world we've learned here and share it with our people. Hopefully, this will ultimately bring the lands together again, one people, like it was with the Azmarians who fought for their freedom from tyranny and brought peace back to their lands. I think it will be a grand occasion."

"You are very knowledgable in your belief Abassi, and strong on it." Sighs Zahira, "these things I do know, but I like to hear others opinions . . . thoughts on the matter."

After that, the two sit the entire night on top of the mountain laughing and talking, enjoying the company of one another.

Zahira finds her emotions stirring for Abassi. However, she thinks seriously about the repercussions of foul behavior with him or any other. She grapples with her feelings for him so where she at times appear harsh and mean to him. She knows her place and struggles to keep it.

Soon they fall fast asleep, with Abassi's head eventually falling onto Zahira's lap.

CHAPTER 12

Love and Ignorance

Finally dawn ascends. Zahira quickly awakes to find Abassi snuggled up on her lap.

"Wake up! Wake up," Zahira shouts shoving Abassi off her lap with his head hitting the ground.

Startled Abassi ask, "What's . . . wrong?"

"It's morning!" Zahira retorts, "We have been here all night. We are in big trouble!"

"In trouble?" ask Abassi still waking up from the deep sleep, "What are you talking about?"

"Get up," she shouts again, this time shoving his shoulder with her foot.

Impatient Zahira grabs hold of the back of his shirt and forces him up, racing back towards the trail back down the mountain.

"Wait, wait!" Abassi screeches, "My shirt is choking me."

"Do you not care that we are going to get in trouble," Zahira screams.

"We haven't done anything to be worried about . . . or did we?" Abassi laughs.

"No you fool, nothing happened, and nothing ever will." Zahira yells.

"Then what are you so nervous about?" He asks.

Ignoring him, Zahira continues her way down the trail of the mountain, with Abassi struggling behind her still trying to pull together.

When they finally reach the bottom, Zahira races back toward the school.

Abassi is hard pressed in keeping up with her. He is still quite tired from the abrupt awakening.

"Wait up," he screams, but Zahira pays him no mind. She is focused solely on getting back for in her mind what she did was unwholesome and would be looked down upon harshly by not only the Muhas but Kimoni and the others as well.

When they finally reach the school grounds, activities appear to be in process with the student moving about hurriedly to their classes.

"Ok, we can split here . . . ," Abassi explains, but when he turns toward Zahira she is already off like a flash into the crowd of students, attempting to blend in so as not to be noticed coming from off grounds. She soon finds the ideal moment then departs from the crowd home.

She quietly sneaks into her window and ease into the room. She notices that Salasa's cot is empty. Not even having time to bathe, she scurry and change her clothes to head out to her class. When done she leaves open her door to the larger room where the exit is and there waiting is Zeira, standing with her arms folded and a look of anxiety on her face.

"Now where have you been young lady?" Zeira ask.

"I, I . . ." Zahira stutters, attempting to explain, but Zeira interrupts her saying.

"Salasa jumped up this morning and ran into my room screaming that you were still gone. I tried to convince her that she and I alone could go and find you but as stubborn and fool-hearted as she is, she ran and reported your disappearance to Kimoni and his men. They are out looking for you at this very moment."

No sooner after her saying that there is a loud frantic knock at the door.

"That is probably one of them now." Zeira sighs.

As Zeira walk toward the door to answer it, Zahira nervously hide in the corner anticipating it to be Kimoni and her fears are correct. There standing in the entrance way is Kimoni, along with Tegene, and Ahura. Salasa also is with them.

Kimoni rushes in saying, "We started our search in the woodland . . ." but before he can finish he eventually notices Zahira quietly standing in the corner.

"Zahira . . . come here," Kimoni shouts hysterically.

Zahira slowly comes forward.

"Are you mad? What were you thinking? Where have you been?" shouts Kimoni greatly agitated.

Before Zahira can respond, Salasa interrupts yelling and pointing at Zahira.

"I told her she better watch it. She's sneaky and stubborn—"

Kimoni intervene saying, "Quiet Salasa."

But Salasa continue with her bickering. "It's easy for her to do what others want, especially boys—"

"That is enough," Kimoni exclaimes.

"She thinks she knows it all—"

"I said that is enough, Salasa!" states Kimoni in a firmer tone.

Yet Salasa is not one so easily silenced, again she remarks, "And . . . and that boy Abassi who she likes—"

"I said be silent!" Kimoni screams. "Go to your room!"

Begrudgingly Salasa leaves, mumbling as she walks away. Kimoni realizes that he is allowing himself to get to emotional and might lose Zahira's attention by allowing this confusion to escalate. So he finds his poise and calms down. He turns back to Zahira and asks,

"Now . . . where have you been?"

"Kimoni, I took a walk.—" she answers, but is interrupted by Kimonis frustration,

"A walk, an overnight walk? Where could you have possibly walked that it took this long for you to return? Have you lost your sense of reason? There are dangers out there beyond these grounds. You were instructed to stay in this school and to venture nowhere else. There are those who want you dead Zahira, do you not know this? You are to listen to me and—"

Zahira at once run into Zeira's room with her eyes filled with tears.

Kimoni attempts to follow her, but Zeira humbly and quietly suggests that he leave her for the moment and she would speak with her. Kimoni sighs and reluctantly leaves the house with Tegene following behind.

However, the head Muhas Ahura remains, who stand to the side silent during the commotion. He looks toward Zeira and asks in his normal calming voice,

"How are things here with you and the girls?"

"All is well Muqarahein." Muqarahein being a nick name given only to Ahura, she continues, "Salasa has warmed up considerably since her first day here, but she still does not talk much. However, Zahira is just as sweet as she can be. I have never had problems with her my."

Ahura paces the floor of the room back and forth with his head down and hands behind his back in deep thought. "Zahira is changing." He replies.

"I realize that, that is what I try to tell Kimoni . . . she is going to like boys and—"

Ahura rears his head back and laughs hardily. He then interjects saying,

"That's not the type of change I am referring to Zeira, though that will happen as well, but as you and I both know there are laws of etiquette here between males and females, and we keep them separated, but not segregated."

"Yes Muqarahein." Zeira humbly reply. He continues,

"What I mean is that the energies within her from the power of the whitestar are growing, and special care is needed with her. We have to be very careful especially in these times we are living in. She will soon have to understand her meaning here and the importance of all this and that which awaits her."

"I know, Muqarahein." Speaks Zeira, "But being that the girls are the only female students here, they are going through so much. Perhaps the other few women in the entire compound are the only female faces they see, but all of us are grown and we work here to serve the school. We cannot relate on the girls level with their education and the like, Salasa is still a bit of a challenge, she is very obstinate in so many ways. We do all we can, but there is only so much we can do. I have noticed though that Zahira loves challenges. She is very competitive, even more so than some of the boys here."

"It is in her blood, dear Zeira." Ahura explains as he takes a seat on one of the large pillows in the corner of the room.

"I realize that," Zeira remarks, "but I think that she is also trying to prove something."

"Explain." Ahura ask rubbing his beard with intent.

"I think because she and Salasa are the only girls, Zahira is determined to prove that they can do just as much as the boys."

"I could only imagine how alienated she must feel," Aura sighs.

"Yes, Muqarahein; she speaks of it constantly."

"I will have a word with her," Ahura says. He then rises from sitting and heads into the room with Zahira.

He knocks lightly on the pane of the entrance way. "Zahira, can I please come in?" he asks kindly.

Attempting to catch her breath and wipe her tears away, Zahira softly answers, "Yes."

Ahura enters past the heavy leather curtain which provides privacy for each room.

"Come over to me please." He asks.

Zahira rises from her cot and slowly moves toward Ahura, vigorously wiping the tears from her eyes.

Ahura sits down on a stool and pulls another stool beside him for Zahira to sit. After sitting he says,

"There is much for you to learn and much time is needed. Do not despair over Kimoni's chastisement. Always speak truth, for this shall be the greatest of your achievements. Many will praise you for it."

"That is not why I'm sad." She laments.

"Then why, my dear?"

"I am confused Muqarahein," Zahira says while wiping tears from her eyes, "I have done a lot of thinking . . . I do not know what will happen to me. So much is expected of me.

Ahura smiles and responds,

"Expectation in you is due to your potential and your calling. You possess greatness, the power to achieve . . . possibly limitless abilities. You have been gifted with power potentially greater then even mine. You are special and being special makes you strange or odd to many and a light to others. Kimoni and his warrior companions know this as well, thus they are aggressively protective over you; and you cannot fault them for that. In time, they will learn to release their hold; I assure you."

Zahira then asks, "Why do you never speak of this . . . Rathamun?"

A bit surprised by her question, Ahura hesitantly answers, "That name, 'Rathamun' is unimportant and an unnecessary burden for you now. You must learn about yourself first, about your path and your purpose. In time his shadow will be an obstacle that you must learn to overcome; and the only way you may achieve this is by conquering your fears of his shadow and focusing on your path alone. Do not race down your path as if you were sprinting to cover long distances. You will tire and eventually give out. Do not walk down your path as if time is afforded you, you will soon despair and fall into doubt for the journey might seem too long. But you are to pace yourself as you journey down your path, allowing the healthy flow of your abilities to push you there, not too fast or too slow, training and learning your way towards maturity. And once you arrive, though you might be tired, you will not have expended your resources. You will be able to rise again and complete your quest for enlightenment.

This is all a test for you Zahira and how you take this test is all up to you. The straight path is never easy, difficulties and trials will always come your way . . . especially if your purpose is a righteous path . . . but do know your trials will be remembered in the end and your perseverance will be your victory and your reward."

Zahira is captivated by Ahura's words of wisdom and his caring nature.

Ahura now asks Zahira, "Now my dear, just where did you go last night?"

Zahira takes in a heavy sigh and reveals where she was, "I and Abassi left to a mountain he knew of. There we sat and talked, and that is all that happened, I promise."

"I believe you," Ahura smiles. "I do appreciate you telling me though."

"Abassi is a wonderful student." Zahira states regaining her confidence, "He is very wise. He constantly speaks of unifying the people across Al Qalzam Sea."

Ahura throws his head back in laughter and responds, "Abassi has many dreams and good ones too. He has much heart and we love him for it. His people are much like him. The kingdom of Punt is truly a place of glorious hearts. In time my dear, in time peace shall reign over not just Punt and our lands, but the planet as a whole. Soon we will come together as one, from the farthest south to the cold mountains of Nordia. All mankind will be free of this evil my dear . . . soon. However, as far as you and him leaving out at night like that together, I think you know that is not befitting a chaste young woman and man, am I correct?"

"Yes, I know" Zahira states holding her head down in shame.

"So please understand our concern," he continues, "it's not merely the fact of mistrust, but it's also not our way, and goes against our teachings here. Just think about it Zahira, if nothing was wrong with it, why did the two of you have to sneak to do it? The laws are in place as a protection my dear."

Zahira nods her head in agreement. Getting away from the subject spoken she sees an opportunity to ask a question that has been her coneconcern for quite some time.

"Am I really the true chosen one to bring an end to this . . . is it really me?"

Ahura slowly rise to take his leave, but he smiles and says,

"Just focus on why you are here. You are here to receive education. Leave the Blackstar to us grown folk. Now rest my dear. Do not worry about your classes today you are excused."

Before he leaves Zahira quickly rises and says,

"A long time ago when I was twelve I had a dream . . . well, it may have been real, but I have never said anything else about it, to anyone."

Ahura turns and sit back down, "Continue." He implores inquisitively.

"I was in the forest in my home town and I was visited by a forest lady. She was accompanied by two large lions, one white as snow, and the other black as the night. She said a few things that have already came to pass. But I still wonder about who she was . . . was it real?"

Rubbing his bearded chin, Ahura states, "Possibly it is the power within you manifesting through dreams, speaking with you and assuring you of your path and what's to come. Keep it to yourself, and hold it sacred. It might be the energies of the Whitestar, which can manifest itself in many ways."

He then rise once again and leaves the room.

Zeira later enters the room and sits down next to Zahira. She then asks, "Are you ok?"

"Yes, I'm fine." Zahira responds rolling her eyes.

"Is there anything you would like to discuss?" Zeira asks.

"No . . . not really," Zahira casually reply.

Zeira gently rubs Zahira's head and starts to leave the room when Zahira halts her departure by asking, "What do you know about boys?"

"Boys," Zeira laugh. She quickly turns around and takes a seat next to Zahira and continues,

"I can tell you a lot about boys and boy can they be a pain."

The two start to laugh and talk for hours.

Zeira expresses her feelings regarding Abassi, and gives Zahira constructive counsel on how to deal with her emotions regarding this issue. Not only does Zahira gain insight and discernment, but she also learns a new riddle that day, the affections of what boys *attempt* to bring, and the importance of chastity of a woman.

CHAPTER 13

A Tempting Offer

Zahira is determined to be the light that she saw in Kimoni, Zeira, Ahura, Abassi and Salasa's eyes. She is determined to do the best she can.

In the interim, Abassi is very hurt about luring Zahira from her home without permission and swore not to do so again. He is reprimanded for what he did by his teachers and chooses now to behave appropriately.

However, love can be likened to a disease, for once it gets ahold of you, the cure is hard pressing to find. Thus, Abassi and Zahira grow to love each other dearly, with Abassi speaking in confidence plans of marriage to her. This, of course, makes Salasa very jealous and she often scorns Abassi when in the company of both in the courtyard.

Zahira often tries to show Salasa that she still is her closest friend, but Salasa merely shrugs her attempts off, enjoying Zahira's persistence.

On one day, Zahira has visitors at her home. This time it is shockingly Melku and four of his companions, one of which includes Shaku, the one she defeated in the competition some time ago.

"As-Shlama, Zahira." states Melku, standing at the door after Zahira's answering it.

"Hello, Melku. To what do I owe this privileged visit?" She replies still surprised.

"Well, we came to talk with you about something that you might be interested in." he whispers.

Salasa walks past the door and see the boys talking to Zahira. She shakes her head and leaves to her room, mumbling to herself in disgust.

"I see your friend is still pretty sore at us." Melku laughs.

"She has reason to be Melku. You and your boys are constantly gossiping behind our backs and putting us down."

"Those days are over Zahira, you know we haven't done that in a long time, since the competition." Melku answers boastfully.

"Oh, really," Zahira remarks unconvinced placing her hands on her hips.

"Yes! We are here to make amends." He implores, "We want to be friends. We are all living here so why should we keep acting like babies. We have to accept you sooner or later, probably sooner than later . . . like now—"

Zahira interrupts him saying, "Melku, we do not need your affections or even your friendship."

"Interesting, but you can't fault me for wanting peace." Melku reasons with her.

"Fine, apology accepted!" Zahira hastily reply and quickly attempts to close the door when Melku places his foot in the way, preventing it to shut.

"What are you doing?" Zahira retorts.

"I am not finished. Please, hear me out." Melku pleads with a sorrowful expression on his face.

Annoyed Zahira reluctantly surrenders. "Hurry, I have much studying to do."

Melku responds. "So, we hear; you are always in those scrolls, researching and studying . . . maybe a lot about your extinct race. Anyway, me and my companions here have something we think you just might be interested in."

"What could that possibly be Melku?" Zahira ask sarcastically.

Melku continues. "Yes, let me finish; have you ever heard of 'the Gate of Agron'?"

Bewildered, Zahira replies, "Nooo . . . I don't think I have."

Eagerly, Melku whispers, "Well, let me educate you sista. First . . . is Zeira home?"

At this point Zahira is irritated and wish to end the conversation. "No, and that is why you have to go now." She demands.

But Melku doesnt give up, for what he has to tell her is extremely important. "Wait Zahira, please, just hear me out. I mean you no harm. Can we come in?" He pleads.

"Are you crazy!" she grunts. But he persistently begs,

"Please, please, trust me, what I have to tell you is purely on an academic level . . . I have no interest in you what so ever."

"Oh yeah, you couldn't possibly," Zahira laughs sarcastically, "You got those older women you claim to visit in some other village, right,"

Melku grows impatient. Lowering his head and gritting his teeth he responds,

"Please, I am on the serious level here. I am not stupid to try or do anything right here at all. Just let me explain to you what we found. You are Azmarian right . . . I know of scrolls that speaks volumes of their life."

Zahira's eyes open wide for this is indeed a shocking discovery if true, she then thinks long and hard finally answering, "Salasa is here. You know she will not have that!"

"Well, meet us in the temple yard." He states, "Believe me. It will be worth every bit of your time."

The boys leave and Zahira closes the door. She sits on a long cot in the front room contemplating whether or not she should meet Melku's request. Her curiosity eats at her, for what possibly academic could they have of any interest to her.

Salasa enters the room demanding, "Now, what did they want?"

"Nothing, they just wanted to discuss a few things about some classes here." Zahira responds quickly with a vacant expression, she then states, "I'll be back, Salasa. I'm going to the temple yard."

"Oh no you are not!" rejects Salasa, "I'm tired of you and your sneaking around. I know what you are up to Zahira."

Zahira stops, faces Salasa and calmly ask, "What am I up to Salasa? I'm just going to the temple yard, out in the open for everyone to see."

But Salasa sensing much more retorts, "There is something else going on and I'm going to tell Zeira."

Zahira is now getting incensed with Salasa's bickering. She surprises Salasa when her eyes take on a white glow of crackling energy and she raises her voice saying, "I do not care who you tell! I am going to the temple yard . . . alone!"

She immediately leaves the house slamming the wooden door behind her. Salasa is shaken over this display from Zahira, for she has never witnessed this side of her closest friend.

Zahira races in the night to the yard and find the boys leaning against the tree talking and whispering amongst each other.

Melku catches sight of Zahira and calls out, "Zahira, over here!"

She races over to them, constantly looking around to see if she is being followed.

Upon reaching them, she irritably asks while clinching her fist, "Now what is this all about?"

"Calm down," assertively speaks Melku. "There's no need for you to take an attack posture with me."

"I'm not taking an attack posture, I am just fed up with you and your—"

"Just listen," interrupts Melku. "You get drunk in your studies and a lot of it is about your long lost people, the Azmarians . . . trust me, this doesn't go unnoticed. The Muhas have only so much information to gratify your curiosities. However, we know of where you can find annals of information about not only how your people lived but details of the language, their religious practices and yes even your papa. Yes, even scrolls about their living and their dying . . . all written by the Azmarians themselves."

"Don't toy with me," interrupts Zahira.

"We don't have to toy with you about this. That would be a waste of our time," shouts Shaku, leaning against the tree.

"Keep it up Shaku, and I will have to humiliate you again like last time." Zahira warns.

Shaku enraged has to be detained by his friends as he attempts to rush Zahira.

"Enough," shouts Melku in an elevated whisper tone. "We didn't come here for this. I see you have gained a little more spunk Zahira, and that is exactly what will be needed for the little challenge I am putting before you. Deep in the mountains there is a place called 'the Gate of Agron'. There in the black dingy lair is great treasure and ancient scrolls of people from the past, lost and guarded."

"Guarded," asks Zahira.

"Yes, guarded by a creature called Agron the guardian. He is a dragon monster that sprouted from the soil from the farthest eastern lands. He has the head of a hideous reptile of sorts, but the body of a man. His appearance is very fearsome, many have journeyed there to steal these treasures but never returned."

"Then why have Ahura and the other Muhas never made mention of him or this place you speak of?" ask Zahira.

"Why would they," sarcastically laughs Melku. "If they did so, all of the students would be itching to go. Do you not hear what I am telling you . . . unimaginable wealth, gold, silver, books of knowledge that stretches to the ends of the earth. We learned of this place long ago by our many adventures me and my companions have taken, to the unawares of our teachers."

"So I presume you've been. Why now, and why me?" Zahira ask.

"We have been many times Zahira, but to actually go in and try our might against him is foolish! But now we feel assured in what we can do, we have grown and learned the use of our abilities. I want the treasure, just as my partners do, and I figured you would have an interest in those scrolls and ancient Azmarian texts, the more of us there the better our chances. Look at you, you are to be greater than us all, this news has spread throughout the school like gangrene. How fitting it is to take you with us on this adventure."

Rubbing her earlobe and looking downward in deep thought she asks hesitantly, "Is Abassi going?"

"Abassi," Melku states with disdain, "do you need to check with your boyfriend to make decisions for yourself?" sneers Melku, "If that is so then we asked the wrong person. Let's get out of here."

With that, Melku and his companions begin to leave back towards their homes leaving Zahira behind with her usual baffled expression when she quickly calls out saying,

"I don't need his permission, and he is not my boyfriend idiot!"

"Well good." Replies Melku as he turns and walks back over towards her, "Then are you in?"

"In what," asks Zahira with her famous vacant expression when in deep thought.

"Don't play dumb. You know what we're asking? Are you going to come with us to the Gate of Agron and get the loot, yes or no? We don't have to be friends if that is not what you want. All you have to do is get what is yours from the cave and go about your merry way. We can do this with or without you."

Rubbing her earlobe Zahira unenthusiastically replies, "Ok, I will go . . . when?"

"In exactly two days, meet us back here behind the temple walls facing south. We will be here when the last torch light is lit."

Without saying another word Zahira jogs back toward home.

While wrestling with the question of whether or not her decisions was a wise one, she bumps into Abassi.

"Zahira, I just left your home and Salasa told me you were out in the temple yard with Melku and some of his cronies."

"She has her facts messed up." she balks.

Abassi chuckles and says, "Well, you know Salasa. She figures things out all by herself."

Zahira nods her head and hurries back to her house, hoping that Abassi would leave her alone. Noticing the bemused look about her face, Abassi follows and gently grabs hold of Zahira's hand. She jerks her hand away looking at him like he was crazy. He then asks,

"Is everything alright? Those guys haven't start bothering you again have they? You look like you are upset about something. I can take care of those guys."

"No Abassi, I'm fine." She quickly retorts, "They just wanted to apologize about the mess that went on in the past, that's all, everything is ok."

"Melku apologizing," Abassi laughs to himself. However he asks more persistently, "Are you sure?"

"I said I'm fine, Abassi." This time she says it as if he is bothering her. He continues saying,

"Well you know I can—"

"Please leave me alone!" she interrupts, "I'm ok. Why does everyone constantly worry about me? Nothing is wrong with me. I'm fine!"

She breaks away from Abassi and storms towards, leaving him confused and saddened.

CHAPTER 14

The Gate of Agron

Two days have passed and Zahira remains very silent, causing Zeira and Salasa much concern for her.

Salasa thinks she is to blame, due to her constant nagging and tries to get Zahira to confide in her; but Zahira ignores her advances.

On the second night, when all are asleep and the last torch is put out, Zahira quietly rises from her bed and places rugs under her blanket to give the illusion oh her presence there sleeping.

She creeps over and gently kisses Salasa on hee forehead. She then sneaks out of the window and runs to the temple, stealthly evading the guards.

She comes across a lit banquet house and there sitting inside is Kimoni, Tegene, Taye, Tahro and Zere, laughing and having a good time talking about the old days and bragging about exploits to one another.

Like a snake, she eases past the window unseen and heads towards the temple.

Melku, Shaku, and three other boys are there waiting for her arrival.

"Ok," whispers Melku, "everyone is here. I was able to sneak these camels and bags out for us. We have a long ride ahead. There are six of us, but I was only able to get four camels, very risky. Zahira you will have to share with someone."

"Fine," Zahira nervously responds.

"Ok, let's go!" Melku whispers.

They mount their camels and head far south into the vast wilderness towards the the Gate of Agron.

Zahira shares a camel with one of the boys named Hassan.

Hassan gives Zahira the option to steer the camel. Zahira gladly abides.

The group gallops a great distance into the night's cool air.

Hassan soon begins to make subtle advances towards Zahira, squeezing her hips and blowing softly into her ear, while sniggling under his breath.

Zahira gets enraged at the thought of Hassan taking advantage of his position behind her. She soon is revisited with disturbing memories of the past, of the boys of her village, Hamas and his arrogant foolhardy friends.

Suddenly, Zahira strikes Hassan in the mouth with her elbow, knocking him off the camel and onto the ground. Hassan jumps up yelling and screaming in excruciating pain. He places his hand up to his mouth noticing blood on his hands and realizes that he is missing two of his top front teeth. He jumps around screaming, holding his mouth and mumbling,

"She knocked my teeth out! She knocked my teeth out!"

Everyone stops and heads back to the crying Hassan.

Zahira remains quiet not sure if Hassans companions would seek to fight her due to her hitting him in his defense.

Shockingly, Melku responds unsympathetically, "Knowing you Hassan, you probably were being a little grabby. Stop your whining and get on with Shaku. We have already lost time as it is."

Hassan gets on one of the camels with one of the others still holding his mouth fighting to hold back the tears.

Melku passes Zahira up, gives her a sly smile and says, "Keep up will yah!"

He then gives his camel a couple of kicks and races back to the front of the traveling group.

After over a full day of traveling, they finally reach the mountain area where the Gate of Agron is located. They dismount their camels and tie them to large olive trees. Melku discusses in detail their plan for gaining the treasure and the scrolls. They then follow Melku toward the dark path that leads to the vicinity.

An eerie thick mist fills the landscape. The hilly terrain has shoots of sporadic weeds and tall brush in clumps across the slopes. Trees are sparse in this land and shelter can only be found by the occasional crevices stumbled upon up the sloping hills. The damp smell of an aggressive water fall pours through the low lands.

When they finally reach the opening of the cave Melku turns and whispers to the group, "Everyone, be as quiet as a rodent. We don't want to unnecessarily wake our host, now do we?"

After that, they quietly enter the cave in a single file line. The long tunnel has very little light with its walls barely a two arm span in width. Every ten feet walked is a turn up or down. The ground is patchy with moist soil and rock.

Soon they can see a dim light ahead and as they come closer the tunnel widens out to a large immense room. Entering the room they are overwhelmed by its magnitude and the ocean of jewels and treasures that blankets the floor. From gold, silver, pearls and rubies, the finest materials to be found and large scrolls and old books decorated with leather covers. All of this lay about in such thick layers that the floor of the cave cannot even be seen.

Zahira's eyes open as wide as an owl's in her amazement over what she is witnessing.

Melku places his finger over his mouth, reminding them to remain silent.

He then motions quietly with his hands for everyone to take their positions at the four corners of the cave.

The moons faint light peers through a hole into the cave from its roof that stands over one hundred feet high. Zahira notices that towards the back of the large cave is a black spot where no light can reach. It is a large space that looks eerie and quiet.

Zahira whispers to Melku anxiously asking, "We need to hurry up . . . where the scrolls and books you told me about are?"

Melku places his finger over his mouth again, hushing her and nodding his head in assurance.

Then suddenly a large rumbling noise with grunts and moans begins to echo throughout the cave. It shakes the ground they stand upon, sending them to their knees.

Suddenly from the darkness comes a monstrosity of a beast, leaping forward. He stands upright thirty feet tall with the body of a man, the hind legs of a bull and head of a Crocodile with large menacing ram horns. He also possesses a long bulky tail that drags behind him swaying from side to side and large powerful wings folded behind his back.

Everyone quickly begins to bury themselves under the heaping piles of treasure of gold, jewelry and coins in the cave so as to hide themselves.

The beast appears very ancient. He slowly looks around the cave and in a thunderous voice states, "*I do not see you . . . but I smell your stench!*"

There is a long silence no one says a word.

Then the beast yells more urgently, "*Speak Pilferer!*"

Melku boldly speaks forward, but stays clear of the giants turning head and roving eyes.

"Perhaps, because you are blind in one of your eyes my lord?

The creature aggressively responds, "*Perhaps, but my other senses prove true . . . and will be your demise!*"

It was Agron, the guardian of the cave. Agron has guarded this cave for a half century and it was intrusted to him by an unknown entity because of the wealth of knowledge and power within it.

Hot steam flows from Agrons nostrils, his teeth grind, echoing throughout the lair like a chain pulled across ragged rocks. He growls, "*Make yourself known coward!*"

Melku continues to stay clear of the beast and replies, "Would it matter if I did . . . how would you know who I am, great Agron . . . your vision is dim, is it not?"

"*Bother not my vision anymore . . . reveal who you are . . . though your voice sounds familiar.*"

"Of course my lord, I am the one who seeks refuge." Melku responds.

"*Oh . . . it is you?*" reply Agron, now familiar as to who Melku is.

At hearing this, Zahira begins to grow even more concerned. She thinks to herself,

"Do they know each other . . . why would he not tell me this?"

Agron then ask, "*Did you bring what I asked for? Waste my time no longer . . . 'One who seeks refuge!'*"

"Of course, I would never go back on my word great lord, especially with one such as yourself, oh great Agron," Melku craftily replies.

"*I sense . . . others with you . . . who are they?*"

"Only my companions, the trip was long and we needed each other to serve as look outs. So, my lord, may I receive my payment."

Agron roars making the walls of the cave vibrate and the jewels of its floor dance, he answers enraged, "*You get payment . . . when I've received that which is due to me.*"

"So be it, my lord," Melku anxiously replies. Melku then turns his head towards Zahira's hiding place and states, "Gaze to your right, oh great Agron, just below your statue beneath the hill of gold coins and your present shall you receive."

"Fool," yells Agron. "*Do I look like a slave to you? Bring it to me . . . and hide it no longer?*"

With that all the boys fretfully rise from their hiding spots and head over to the statue where Zahira is hiding.

Zahira cautiously rises and creeps toward the boys, anticipating their next plan. But to her horror they all grab hold of her and drag her before the giant.

"What are you doing," Zahira shouts fighting to free herself from their grips, but to no avail.

Melku exclaims, "Here is what you've requested my lord, the last Azmarian!"

Agron let's out a tremendous roar and stumps the floor of the cave with his hoofed foot lamenting, "*Finally . . . I have captured what Rathamun seeks . . . one of the foretold knights of the crescent, a child of the whitestar. I shall be the power . . . to be reckoned with once I absorb her power. Go fledglings . . . take only what I've allowed, and never return. She will remain with me!*"

The boys throw her to the ground before Agron and hurry taking only of the treasures allowed by Agron in their prior pact.

Zahira immediately rises in disarray over the betrayal. She runs over toward Melku,

"What is this you have done!" she screams hysterically. Suddenly she is caught by large swirling tentacles that entrap her, shooting from Agron's large staff, wrapping her body up in a cocoon.

Melku smiles and shakes his head stating to himself,

"What a waste." He then continues taking his share, quickly filling his bag.

The boys finally finish up and heads swiftly towards the exit of the cave.

Upon leaving Shaku lags behind looking round about for any other choice jewels he could cram into his bag. He is the last to leave the cave, but right before leaving he looks up above the caves exit and notices a shiny red ruby fixed into the stone. On it is many hieroglyphs of celestial entities and written words engraved, but prove to be not one of the items allowed to be taken from the cave. Thinking it will not be missed he swiftly takes his dagger and chisels it out of the rock. He then shoves it in his bag and runs out to catch up with his companions.

Suddenly a loud roar echoes from the cave, the roar of Agron.

"*Thieves!*" He shouts.

The boys turn to see the giant Agron leaping from the top of the high mountain, spreading his powerful wings soaring in the night sky above them.

"What happened," screams Melku to the others in a state of confusion.

"I don't know," they each yell in reply.

Agron lands right in front of them shaking the ground beneath him.

"*How dare you pilfer from me!*" he thunders.

"My lord, we did not steal from you," Melku frantically exclaims. "We took only what you told us to take."

Agron then puts them to the test.

"*Each one of you ... empty your pouches before me, and if there is found a liar—*"

"Then kill us all," Melku boldly interrupts, assured that none of his companions stole anything from him.

"*SO BE IT!*"

At this point Shaku is so terrified his blatter releases. He then slowly walks away from the group slyly, so as not to be seen and hide behind a large tree.

When they all empty their pouches, not one of the boys had anything that was told to them not to take.

Agron then exclaims, "*There was another ... I smelled him!*"

Melku now grows very nervous, not seeing Shaku he now knows that Shaku could have possibly taken the ruby.

He fearfully pleads, "My lord, please excuse us for the treachery of our companion. Take him instead."

"*Silence ... bring him forward!*"

The boys start their search for Shaku until finally they find him cowardly hiding behind the tree. They grab him and drag him before Agron.

Agron then exclaims, "*Empty your pouch!*"

He empties it and the missing ruby falls to the ground.

"*For this treachery ... you all will die!*"

Melku and his companions realize there is nothing they can do to change Agrons mind, so they start frantically running through the forest only to be pursued and cut down by Agron's relentless streams of fire he release from his staff, disintegrating and scattering their atoms.

Melku is the last to be caught. He trips over a rock and twists his ankle.

Agron approaches slowly with each thundering step shaking the earth. Melku looks around and sees remnants of his disintegrated companions lying around, daggers, swords and satchels. He looks up tearfully at Agron and pleads for his life.

However, Agron pay's no heed to his pleas for mercy, but delivers a horrifying death different then his friends.

He raises his heavy hoofed foot above Melku and stumps him into the ground, crushing his body flat.

After that Agron turns and leap back into the air. His wings spread wide and he soars up back to the top of the mountain. But just before he enters, he hears the voice of another call out from behind him.

"It is not over yet, you foul beast!"

He sniffs the air and catches scent of another boy. When he turns to face his enemy there standing courageously is Abassi. Salasa had informed him of Zahira's disappearance. He then followed their tracks left by their camels and finds his way to the gate of Agron.

He is clad in a special bronze colored armor of the Muhas he stole from the inner most chambers without their notice. The armor is called 'Al Madyn Kunya', or the cosmic metal. The style of the armor is of the far eastern fashion complete with a helmet and full body protection. The armor is also made from Kadmadyn and works as a catalyst to those that carry the gift of the white dust power. He also carries a short glowing sword in his right hand, another weapon taken from the Muhas.

"Another that wish to Die!" snarls Agron.

"Release her or suffer!" Abassi boldly screams.

Agron lets out a hearty laugh.

"*Do you know who you stand before . . . boy?*"

"I know who you are. You are Agron the malevolent." Shouts Abassi.

"*Then you know . . . it would be unwise . . . to upset me?*"

"I care not for your anger. I only want my friend back!" answers Abassi.

"*Then come and get her . . . boy. But know this, you defy Agron . . . and such defiance . . . warrants death!*"

"I do not fear death!" Abassi hesitantly replied.

"*But you will fear me boy! I am the slayer of millions. My legs are the pedestals of the earth . . . my arms are the pillars of the heavens. My armor is a thousand moons deep . . . my power rivals even the fire of the sun, my rage . . . . insatiable. Come to me ant . . . dine at the table death has prepared for you?*"

Abassi says nothing further. He leaps into the air toward the giant, propelled by the power of the armor, only to be knocked back to the ground by one swift swing from Agrons mighty hand.

Abassi hits the ground with a terrible crash, breaking the earth, but with the protection of the cosmic armor Al Madyn Kunya he quickly regains footing. However, he knows even with the armor his lack of experience does not stand a chance against the giant, so he takes the fight higher up the mountain as he thinks of a plan.

Agron leaves his staff down below as he climbs up the mountain side swinging and busting rock, trying to grab hold to Abassi. All the while Abassi narrowly dodges all of his attacks.

After a long grueling climb, they finally reach a spacious leveled part high in the mountain. Abassi runs to a corner and waits for Agron's approach.

Agron climbs up and faces Abassi, "*Poor fledgling . . . such an early death for you.*" Agron mocks.

Abassi boldly comes forward and exclaims, "If I am to die today you will indeed join me in the afterlife . . . but your reward shall be the pains and misery found in the abyss of torture. But as for me, I will indeed bask in the confines of glory!"

At that moment Abassi's whole body starts to illuminate like a star, lighting the entire area where they stand. His eyes crackle with light and his countenance grows savage.

Then suddenly he leaps into the air with his sword held back soaring with lightning speed

Toward's Agron. He hits right into Agrons face, striking with his sword. The impact is so devastating that Agron, even with all his strength and leverage is not prepared for the sudden attack.

Agron falters back disoriented from the blow where he loses footing and falls backwards off the edge of the mountain landing. They both fall over the edge of the mountain, plunging toward the valley of mountain rocks over three hundred feet below.

On hitting the ground a cataclysmic crash resonate throughout the area, sending shockwaves throughout the vicinity. Then suddenly it all abruptly stops, with the silence of the woods reiging once again.

In the meantime, Salasa informed Kimoni, Tegene, and Tahro of Zahira's absence and they begin their search. They track the trail made by Abassi and finally arrive at the cave. The land carries an eerie silence. They notice the daggers, swords and satchels of the boys scattered about and their camels running lose.

Kimoni commissions his companions to search for the boys. He soon finds the entrance of the cave and hastily runs inside searching for Zahira.

When he comes to the large opening of the room, there lay Zahira on the ground appearing unconscious, loosely wrapped in rapidly decaying tentacles.

Kimoni rushes to her and lifts her up off the ground cutting away the remaing tentacles from off her with his dagger. She slowly opens her eyes and immediately starts jerking violently and pulling saying,

"Where are they," her eyes white and filled with tears.

She swings in the air at Kimoni, not recognizing who he is for she is partly blind.

He grabs hold to her tight, holding her close to him saying, "It is I Kimoni . . . they're dead. Agron killed them all, we found their remains laying about!"

When she finally recognizes Kimoni she starts to cry unceasingly.

Kimoni takes her into his arms and without any further words carry her out of the cave.

Tegene exclaims, "We found his body, but Agron is nowhere to be found."

"Thank you," Kimoni replies. "Now let's go home before he returns."

Zahira overheres Tegene and inquires of the body he spoke of, "Whose body . . . whose body?"

"Please dear, enough damage has been done tonight. You don't—"

But Zahira is persistent and interrupts Kimoni by clumsily jumping out of his arms and running towards where they body was they carried on a cot. There, lying under a blanket is Abassi dead, his armor badly singed from the explosion.

"No . . . no . . . no!" Zahira tearfully screams in disbelief. "Why was he here . . . why did he come here?"

She falls on top of Abassi's body and wails, the tears flowing uncontrollably from her eyes.

It took some time for the men to pry her from his body.

"Kimoni, we have to get out of here," exclaims Tegene. "the creature he fought his body is no where to be found."

Kimoni agrees.

They finally leave Zahira lying across Abassi's cot and carry them both back to the school in Azal.

CHAPTER 15

Origins

Zahira is now eighteen years of age. She has grappled with the reality of Abassi's death for three long agonizing years. Now, she is finally learning to cope. Kimoni and the other warriors has been a great support for her during this difficult time.

Kimoni has been like a father to Zahira and Salasa, always concerned over their well being.

After Abassi's death, Zahira engorges herself into her studies and never allows for any more distractions, even neglecting to spend time with Salasa.

She is soon noted to be the highest achiever in the school and many awards are given to her for her great achievements. All the students eventually come to love and respect her. Zahira illuminates as a shining example to all.

At eighteen, she has matured in phenomenal ways. She is placed in a class with greater gifted students like herself, even more than the students she shared classes with in the past. In this class, she learns the definition of her latent powers as they mature. The Muhas that educate her is the renowned Beltazar from the land of Elam of the far east. He is noted for his scholarly discipline of the cosmic arts and his superb teaching ability of these latent gifts.

On one eventful morning, Zahira rises from bed and rushes to get ready for her new class. She enters the classroom and like the other students acknowledges the teacher as Muhas.

Fifty students have taken their seats on the decorated expensive rugged floor and the class commences.

"Greetings my students," Welcomes Beltazar, "May you have peace and prosperity and might you become illuminators in a darkened world . . . by the will of the divine creator." Beltazar pauses momentarily and looks around at each student silently, pacing the floor in front of them with his hands clasped behind his back, he continues.

"In an age of uncertainty and evil, the light of hope has simmered slowly from the mind of man. Man has fallen into despair and has given in to the evils of the shadow from the south. You, my students, are the renewed lights in this dark world. You are the guardians that will give man the will to carry on. Later generations will deviate from understanding and will worship your memory and offspring as gods and raise you on high as the source of their being. However, this is not what you, nor is it the way of the Muhas, nor is it what has been taught unto you. But regardless of what man is told the ignorant will not heed such counsel. The proper knowledge of the one true source of creation spreads over the lands, and the false gods of the peoples will melt away like the snow melts away from the nordian pathways once the glory of the sun beacons its rays.

The nature of your being causes confusion in some of you, but others have gained proper insight due to knowledge and understanding given at early ages."

"Then what are we Muhas?" asks one of the boys. The Muhas answers saying,

"It is time you know the full story of who and why you are. You are the offspring of those that were infected by celestial energies from the heavens, better yet, aliens. These cosmic creatures gave your ancestors many extraordinary powers and perceptions. They are astral beings from another world, trapped here on our earth and only able to survive here by possession alone. Their possession of your ancestors left genetic trails in their blood patterns, thus passing these gifts unto you many years later."

"How did they get here and how did they come to our world Muhas?" Ask another student. The Muhas answers,

"That we do not know, for this is still a mystery. Me and my brothers here, including the Muqarahein himself are also of this power, but still some things are vague. We do know that these astral beings are also referred to the Azin, along with many other names."

"Can you tell us more about the powers we were gifted with?" another boy asks. The Muhas answers,

"We will discuss the variety of powers afforded by many of you that we have come to learn about here in the school. We will discuss how it will serve your kinsmen as you protect their cities and provinces when you return to your land as their guardians . . . in time.

Now many might have concerns over the powers possessed by the children of the Black Dust or even the all-powerful Blackstar, for these creatures dwell in darkness. To answer your concerns . . . with this there is much that remains aloof, for these are the evil astral energies that exist here as well. We have found that there are some Black Dust users that have displayed use over powers similar to yours, but they are as varied as the stones beneath the sea. But regardless to what power those evil forces hold, you must be prepared to stand against them, and rein victoriously . . . your reason being here."

The Muhas Beltazar continues his lecture for the next ten hours. Many secrets the students learn and many woes they are taught about their ever changing world. But the details of the coming star and Rathamun by name are still held back from the students.

Zahira is absorbed in her lessons. Twice every month she and the other students would engage in intense training using the fighting style of the Muhas for the advanced students, 'Shandola', and learning to control their powers. Still the actual emission of their powers remains hidden, for still they grow within them.

A year has pass and the nineteen-year-old Zahira is indeed a shining light to the school. Ahura looks upon her with much approval and appreciation. She has matured into a beautiful warrior with astounding perception.

One day, like other days, when Zahira is leaving Beltazar's class she is stopped by Ahura in the outer temple.

"Greetings and peace Zahira,"

"Greetings and peace to you as well Muqarahein."

"Many good things are being said about you. You are ascending to greatness. Is all well in your special studies and training?"

"Yes, Muqarahein, I have nothing but admiration for Muhas Beltazar and the lessons he teach."

"Good." Ahura smiles, "Then you will be pleased to know that we have chosen you for an expedition, one that will truly test your training."

Excited Zahira asks, "Will I be going alone, Muqarahein?"

"That question will be answered tomorrow." Answers Ahura. "Come to my chambers by first light tomorrow and we will discuss it further."

"Yes Muqarahein." Zahira answers enthusiastically.

On her way back home she thinks deeply over what is in store for her. On arriving home, she is greeted by Salasa at the door.

"How was class, Zahira?"

"Fine, as usual. Every time I go to Beltazar's class, I learn something new. He is like a library of information."

"Well, I guess they would be," laughs Salasa. "They claim to have lived hundreds of years. Sometimes I wonder . . . are they making that up just so they can keep the edge over their students."

"Come on Salasa, you can't be serious." Sigh's Zahira.

Salasa laughs and replies, "You know I'm kidding. Just look at them, they look like they've lived for thousands of years." They both have a good laugh and enter's the house. Zahira goes to her room and change her clothes in preparation for her workout at the gymnasium.

Salasa walks in and shakes her head saying, "You are either training or studying. Do you ever tire?"

"You know what is expected of me, Salasa. I don't want to fail any of those expectations. For goodness sake, the whole world is resting hope in me . . . me, a woman with not even the slightest idea of what I'm doing. You of all people should understand why I am doing what I do, my hearts position."

"Oh, you know what you're doing, even more so than a lot of these other students here." Salasa replies, "You are just over-taxing yourself, but there is something else that has been weighing heavily on my mind, Zahira."

"What is that?" Zahira asks.

"Do you ever think about home?" laments Salasa.

"Now Salasa, we have gone over this a million times—"

"I know, I know," Salasa interrupts, "I just can't help but to wonder, you know. I think often of my mama and papa. Many times my eyes swell with tears and I tell you nothing. The time we've been here seems to have hardened you Zahira."

Zahira turns and look consolingly into Salasa's eyes saying,

"No Salasa, I know there is nothing we can do about it, so I don't constantly beat myself over it. Kimoni and the others brought us here under explicit orders, from not only Chief Tafari, but our parents as well. Don't you think they knew what was best for us?"

"Possibly . . . but we were only children then. Now we are adults and can choose for ourselves. Besides, I was fooled to believe that this was a temporary thing."

"So what are you asking," asks Zahira.

"Nothing, nothing, never mind. You just go and train . . . that is what seems to be most important to you." States Salasa in a cynical tone.

Zahira continues, "Salasa, please, all I'm saying is—"

Salasa interrupts saying, "Look, you go and exercise. Don't worry about me. Now go!"

After that Salasa leaves for their bedroom. Zahira is hurt, for she does reminesce many times about returning to visit the Beshari, but she quickly dismisses the notion, for she knows the horrors such a visit could possibly bring. She then leaves for the gymnasium and stays until nightfall.

CHAPTER 16

The First Mission

The next morning Zahira rises bright and early and leaves for Ahura's chambers. When she arrives she notices four other students waiting at the door as well. After the greetings are given, they all stand their quietly barely even glancing at one another.

When the doors finally open, they all enter and sit on the floor on large plush pillows before Ahura's table, which is elevated on a higher step and behind it is a beautiful purple rug that he would sit on facing those he addressed.

Finally Ahura enters and sits on his rug before them. They all greet him saying, "Greetings and peace to you Muqarahein!"

He returns the greetings and says,

"Today will be different then other days. We will not be learning the fine cosmic arts of your abilities, or the meaning of the forces of the earth today. However, you will be readied for something even more challenging.

Each one of you was hand selected out of over two hundred students in this school. You are the elite. You were chosen for a special task, a task that could claim your very lives if performed negligently. We have taught you the importance of unity, and now this will be tested.

To the west across the waters of Al Qalzam is Kemet, what many have termed 'valley of the gods'. There in that kingdom dwells an evil ruler that has falsely positioned himself as a god, he refers to himself

126

as Ammun Ra, father of the gods. He rules the land with an iron hand and has turned the people corrupt. As you might have figured out, he is a progeny of the Black Dust. He has captured one of our Muhas, a Muhas by the name of Azhad.

Azhad went to Ammun to convey instructions about the coming of the Blackstar and how to ward off attack by his armies. We were fooled to believe that Ammun was of the White Dust through reports given by our scouts. He was at one time of the White Dust, but was tainted by the evil of the Blackstar minions, this is how we know that even those of the White dust can change allegiances for the Blackstars influence is not to be underestimated. So our Muhas left unaware of this change, thus being captured and imprisoned.

Because of being away from Azal for such an extended amount of time Azhads power begun to fade, thus giving Ammun a greater leverage. Ammun tortured him through inconceivable measures trying to get the location of Azal's secrets, but like all the trained Muhas of our temple, he spoke nothing.

Ammun will not kill him, for he wishes to learn of a way to absorb his power the way the Blackstar does. If he gains this knowledge of absorption he will use this gift to wrought control over our land and all within it . . . his greed is severe. Azhad has remained a prisoner in the caverns of Ammun for the past forty years."

"Excuse me Muqarahein," politely interrupts Zahira. "Why have we never heard of this? Only now it is brought to our attention. Why have not the Muhas attempted to retrieve him?"

"The time was not right, my child, but now the time has come. Though we possess great power, this power is limited only to our land and slowly diminishes the further away we are from it. Azal is our talisman. We would possibly have been useless in retrieving Azhad once entering Kemet. Thus from our students we have chosen the six of you to go and retrieve our brother."

The students begin to look at each other puzzled. Noticing their concerns, Ahura states, "Have no fear. You were appointed for this task based on what we do know about you. You may now rise and introduce yourselves to your fellow classmates. Let's first start with you, Durjaya."

The slender young well-formed man stands and prepares his introduction. He is fair complexion with dark eyes and possesses long straight ebony hair, which he wears in a tight long pony tail that falls to his lower back.

"Greetings, I am Durjaya from the eastern lands of Indra. I have come here as a representative of my land to bring peace to all the threatened lands, which will ultimately stretch into my land. I am under the service of the Muqarahein."

Another student rises. He is dark brown in complexion and wears tight braids upon his head. He too possesses a well defined lithe but more muscular build.

"Greetings, I am Keon from the land of Punt, from the province of Ikengia 'School of thought'. I was sent to Azal after Ikengia was taken over by minions of the Blackstar. Here I have continued my studies in the practice of the cosmic arts. I shall avenge my land. I am under the service of the Muqarahein."

The next student to take his stand is of a tan complexion and also wears a pony tail in the back of his head, but his reaches only to his shoulders and it is the only patch of hair on his bald head.

"Greetings, I am Anen from the land of Kemet in the province of Ammu. I am pleased to go on this expedition even more so, for it is my land that is under scrutiny in this quest. I will release her from the grip of the Black dust. I am under the service of the Muqarahein."

The fourth student is fair skinned and wears his hair shoulder length. He possesses prominent features and is of a hardy structure.

"Greetings, I am Shavir from the land of Sumeria from the city Lagash. I am pleased to join you in this battle. I come with sword and honor and my goal is to eventually see an end to the Blackstar. I am under the service of Muqarahein."

And finally Zahira stands to introduce herself.

"Greetings, I am Zahira from a lost land in a dark world . . . my only purpose here is to see light shine once again in the shadow of my world. I am under the service of the Muqarahein and mankind."

After her introduction, all the young men turn and look at her peculiarly.

Ahura smiles and continues, "Good, the task before you will truly test your loyalty, courage and obedience, your allegiance to truth and your strength of faith will be tested and honed. You will be given explicit instructions for your journey, only if you adhere to these instructions and all that you have been taught here at this school will you be successful. If you are heedless to your training and avert the lessons given to you, your failure on this mission can mean your lives.

Each one of you is a brother and sister to the other. Uphold this unity, and work together, focused on your mission."

Ahura continues all that morning and up into the evening providing pertinent information for the long perilous journey before them.

Zahira is amazed over the things that Ahura speaks regarding the many possible dangers that could arise on their mission.

After the meeting the students rise and bid their farewells until five days later when they will rejoin to embark on their journey.

Just before Zahira leaves Ahuras chambers he pulls her to the side alone and asks,

"Is all well my dear?"

"Yes Muqarahein." She answers with an uneasy look on her face. "I think I will be fine." She smiles. Ahura sternly warns her saying,

"Know this Zahira, the Blackstar still searches for you. You and the others are to stay on the path I apportioned for you. Do not deviate in any way. It could mean your life. Many of his minions and scouts are on the hunt for you and will prove relentless in their search.

However, do not fret, for if you follow the counsel that was given you, you will return safely. Resist taunts and challenges and do not allow noone, I mean no one dupe you into doing something unwholesome.

There are many more questions you might have, but do not bother about asking them now. Go home and relax your mind, for there is much that awaits you. We will talk further later."

When Zahira turns to leave, Ahura lastly states, "Zahira, it is in you that I foresee the success of this mission."

Zahira smiles and finally leaves Ahuras chambers, carrying with her mounds of burdensome thoughts.

CHAPTER 17

The Commencing

On the fifth day, the students meet once again in the chambers of Ahura. They are all dressed in the same uniforms given by the Muhas, long sleve shirts, and plated skirts over their baggy pants. They also wear a very light upper armor made for the deserts relentless heat with wind scarves to protect from the sandy winds of Kemet. The boys wear small turban headdresses while Zahira wears her Azmarian scarf given to her by Romana.

Each one of them is provided with a camel, food satchel, water pouch, and other supplies for their lengthy journey to Kemet. Resilient Sabaean swords are also provided for each of them. Durjaya also carries along his long traditional staff sent from his land long ago when only a child.

It is morning and all of the students appear ready for the mission. There is zeal and anticipation in their eyes as they stand before Ahura, awaiting his final address.

"Again, you have learned much here and are counted to be some of our finest students. Be courageous and strong. But do not despair or feel down trodden when fear takes hold of you. It is a natural emotion and many a kingdom has crumbled for lack of its proper use. It will keep you alive and will strengthen you. It will help keep your senses alert and your wits strong, but . . . it can mislead you if you do not control it, it can make the weak hearted compromise otherwise honorable principles learned. You must master it, or it will master you.

Remember all the things that you were taught here and continue in the light. When the sun darkens and the stars dim, know that your obedience, zeal, faith and honor is always monitored and recorded in your book of deeds, it shall also be a light to your way. You will see wondrous things in Kemet, but do not be fooled, always remember that the greatest power that exist is that one singular power that exudes from the one true deity that defines and controls all things. He is the provider, he is the sustainer and unto him are all the most beautiful names. Despite mankind's debauchery and ignorance in worship to stones, wood and altered beings, there are no other gods accept he.

Now go my students and meet evil with that which is righteous. Bring evil to the abyss of destruction. Stray not from one another that you might not loose hope, support each other. When there are disagreements, comply with one another in truth and evidence.

On your way, do give ear to those that yearn for help, for such charity will be remembered of you in the hereafter that we the Muhas have come to understand exist. Do not despise those in need, thinking that it will delay your mission. For if you despise them, you have already failed in what you were sent to do.

When you battle that which is evil, do not battle with blinding hate or with the intent of gratifying yourself, but battle with honor and loyalty to those that yearn for release, and for the sake of the greater power that exist and defines all things.

Do not give in to wine or fatty foods, or any substance that might intoxicate you for these things are forbidden not only here in Azal but also amongst those trained accordingly from our school that leaves our borders.

Let not your loin's lust for illicit sexual relationships. This too you were trained in and will be a test also of your devotion and loyalty to your training. Stay on your path and prove yourselves resilient and honorable, as shining examples in a dark world."

These and many more were the wise words of the Muqarahein, Ahura, who spoke with love and admiration for the students embarking on a journey that could possibly claim their lives. However, he has faith that due to their training and upright ways in the school they would succeed in their rescue mission.

After those words they mount their camels and head northwest toward the Al Qalzam coast.

Upon arriving, they board with their camels a larger vessel supplied by the ferryman, Urshanabi, then sail across the waters toward Ge.

From Azal to Ge across the waters is a whole day's travel. They arrive late that night. Much cannot be seen in the vicinity due to the cover of night. It is an open land, very grassy with few trees. The ground is very hilly and antelope thrives in the distance.

They pitch camp and sit around a quaint fire, getting better acquainted with one another and talking about many things that were of concern to them regarding their mission.

Anen stretches his arms out with a yawn and declares, "I cannot wait until I can get my hands around the throat of that Ammun Ra. How dare he come into my land and dethrone Mentut, a respectable Pharaoh, I might add."

Keon turns to Anen and states, "I can understand how you feel Anen, but do not let your emotions get the best of you. We all want him dead, regardless of what land he has chosen to play dictator over, but remember why we are here . . . to save the Muha."

Durjaya then comments, "My land is far, Far East from here, and even though my people have not felt the grip of this Blackstar, they will soon enough as it moves further east in its conquest. Anen, I am with you in your zeal. The zeal that you have will make you a better warrior against this Ammun Ra."

Shavir then asks, "Do any of you know anything about this Ammun Ra, what we are up against?"

Keon responds, "No more then you and the information given to us before we left. You should've asked the Muqarahein when he asked if we had any questions. Why didn't you?"

"I didn't want to sound stupid." States Shavir, "They make you feel so simple-minded sometimes."

"That's not the way they are Shavir," replies Keon.

"I know . . . but they carry this aura as if they are untouchable . . . I don't know, never mind me. I'm just blabbing from the mouth."

Looking at them all Keon then says, "The Muqarahein and the Muhas's are all interested in our welfare to the highest degree. They do not abuse their authority over us as if they were tyrants. They are kind, gentle and welcome whatever questions we may have. Do not start to doubt their wisdom."

"Who said we doubt their wisdom?" blatantly asks Shavir.

"All I said was let none of us begin to fall into doubt." Answers Keon.

For a brief moment there is silence. It is broken with Keon turning to Zahira who sit silently by the fire in deep thought, he ask her, "You are a quiet one. Is all well with you girl?"

"I'm just a little tired, that's all," She softly replies, "and this girl has a name."

"My apologies . . . Zahira." Keon quickly corrects himself.

"Speaking of doubting wisdom," interrupts Shavir, "there are a few concerns I do have. Have any of you ever wondered if the Muhas are holding back on us, at times?"

"Holding back," responds Zahira irritably.

"Yes, my feisty one, holding back . . . and maybe even confused on some matters." balks Shavir.

Zahira then states,

"We owe everything to those ancient teachers and scholars; they have guided, protected and molded us into what we are today. They are the last true scholars of our age, we owe them respect."

Shavir then rise to his feet shaking his head in disbelief as he pace the ground back and forth. He then remarks,

"There is truth to what you say Zahira, I don't doubt all of it, but it goes much deeper then that my friend. The true nature of the Blackstar, his personal identity, this is never revealed to us, as if speaking the name of the Blackstar is taboo or something. I need to get it off my chest . . . . Rathamun, Rathamun, Rathamun, now was that all that hard. Actually it relieved some stress a bit."

"There is no need to be hung up on a name. If they choose not to speak of it by name then I trust their judgement. We just have to be patient." reply Zahira.

"You could say that Zahira, have they not shown you a special interest or attention due to their misguided belief of your saving the world or something like that." snaps Shavir.

"Ok that's enough Shavir," interjects Keon.

"No, not quite my friend, there is more." Shavir abruptly continues, "How about the fact of why there are no female students in Azal's schools but just this one? Not counting the workers."

"Does it matter . . . would you like more women in the school Shavir?" laughs Keon.

"I do not find that funny at all and of course it matters; there is more to it than the reasons given to us. Not once have I heard the reasons why females, outside of you Zahira, do not possess the power of the star. But never fear my friends the secret is out, and I have it."

"What is it?" desperately ask Anen. Shavir smiles cynically and answers,

"It is said that the power of the star, either dark or light chooses the dominant of the species, it chooses the male equation or factor. Some kind of way, the power is only transferred to the male seed, some type of science of the inner body that I cannot quite understand, but was told to me by a reliable source . . . more knowledge the Muhas hide from us."

"Then how do you explain Zahira having the power Shavir?" Ask Keon.

"That, is a mystery my friend, but an answer worth digging for." Shavir responds.

"I too heard of this," spoke Durjaya rubbing his chin.

"So what is your point Shavir?" ask Keon, but this time in an annoyed tone.

"My point is simple; I refuse to walk around blindly being lead by everyone but myself. I am responsible for my own destiny not the Muhas—" argues Shavir.

Keon stands and walks over to Shavir and ask him, "Are you truly that ignorant, or stupid to believe that?"

"First off don't call me stupid," protests Shavir, "and yes I do believe it."

"You know what, I don't have time for this Shavir," states Keon who walks away throwing his hands up frustrated, "let's just get some sleep. Looking around you is the only disgruntled one here amongst us."

After that Keon lays back down and everyone starts to settle down. Keon was made the leader of this mission by Ahura so they all agree and lay down to get some much needed rest for their journey tomorrow.

CHAPTER 18

Bandits of the Dessert

They awake the next morning to birds chirping and the fresh aroma of the dew covered grass. The land is more visible now and the eyes awaken to a vast landscape. The animals are plentiful in the surroundings but keep their distance from the group of travelers.

"Ok, we have a long way yet," speaks Keon as he rises letting out a long yawn, "get your things and we will travel again until night, then set up camp."

"Wow," yawned Shavir, "I could sleep a little more, time flew by."

"Where is Durjaya?" ask Keon. The team starts to call out his name and separate looking for him, but stay in close proximity of each other. Finally Anen spots him sitting atop of a cliff that overlooks a large valley below where a thick mist blankets the canyon.

"Durjaya!" calls Anen. But Durjaya remains silent. The team regroups and catches up with Anen who is still behing Durjaya calling his name. Keon walks on up the clif past the others and lightly places his hand on Durjaya's shoulder.

"My friend, are you alright . . . . Durjaya, are you okay."

Finally Durjaya awakes from his stupor and quickly turns facing Keon.

"Oh I am sorry . . . I was just meditiating . . . in deep thought."

"Are you ok?" Keon ask again.

"Yes, I am just concerned about my family in Indra. I think of them often, their welfare. I guess I am just anxious to return."

Keon extends his arm and assist Durjaya up.

"Well, I feel that way often myself. But just think of it, once we leave Azal, we will be better able to assist them and our countries as a whole. Stay the course, and though they suffer now, they will indeed benefit in the long run from our training. Sometimes you have to except some of the bad to receive the good."

Zahira listens closely to what Keon is saying to Durjaya, for she and Salasa have spoken many times about their family they had to leave behind when little children.

They head back to the camp and collect their camels and continue their track south west toward their next destination. Zahira takes in the beauty of the flat opened landscape. The wind blows lightly and the sun soon makes it to its zenith.

After sometime they make it past the rich flora and come to a more desolate landscape, a rocky area with not much growth with mountain ranges still gracing the far distance but this time along with sand dunes that lay spread about. Vaguely in the expanse of the now sweltering horizon they spot what looks to be a small caravan of travelers on camel back.

"Are we headed in the right direction?" Ask Shavir.

Agitated Keon replies, "Yes, I am going by the map given by the Muhas."

"I don't know Keon," States Shavir, "this doesnt look right to me."

"There is only one way from Ge, south west, that will take us to Ammu." Keon exclaims.

By this time the small caravan draws closer to them, but they do not appear very welcoming. There are at least seven camels, all loaded with large bags that burst with gold and silver jewelry. Water canisters flop against the camel's sides. Riding and leading the camels are large brawny dark men, with unkempt clothing. They wear battle gear like large scimitars and axes worn and stained with blood from past conflicts. Some of them have hair that is long and dreaded, mangled covering their eyes, while others wear loose turbans and draw scarfs.

There are fifteen in all. One of them does not wear a shirt and on his chiseled physique are many battle scars. Tattooes decorate his back with strange symbols. He stands seven feet in height and wears his long mangled hair in a pony tail, his eyes are black with no white present and jewelry decorates his ears and nose.

As Zahira and her companions continue to observe the intimidating caravan they notice a woman atop of one of the camels, her hands are bound and she is covered with a long black cloak. She appears distressed and freightened.

"Look!" quickly points Zahira, "did they kidnap her?"

"I don't know—" reply Keon, but he is swiftly interrupted by Shavir who states, "It's not our concern, just keep walking."

"Are you mad!" states Zahira, "We cannot just let them pass by with her like that. It is our duty—"

"It is our duty to rescue the Muhas," shouts Shavir, "have you forgotten girl? And why am I even debating this with you, you are not our leader here. Keon, she is crazy, they are not our concern."

"That seems to be a bit to late Shavir, they already spotted us," responds Keon, "do you actually think that rabble would past us by without so much of a 'who are you?' And, Zahira does have a point."

"And whats that?" Shavir answers quite agitated.

"She was trying to say before you interrupted her, that it is our duty to help the misfortunate. That is what we are all about being students of Azal, did you not even pay attention in your learning. Or must I conclude that Shavir, prince of Sumeria is a bit . . . scared?"

"Wo," Shavir quickly rebuttals, "I am afraid of nothing or no one. One day even you will have to eat those words Keon. I just don't believe that we should detract from our mission by getting involved with every misfortune soul we meet, that is foolish. We are traveling through hostile lands, can you imagine how much depravity we are liable to pass. That's all I am saying."

Suddenly, during their discussion the caravan finally reaches them. Six of the men leave their camels with the others and boldly approach Keon and his group. Keon and the others also dismount their camels and ready themselves for whatever is to happen.

The men start to aggressively speak in a language that is unidentifiable to Keon and his group.

"I am sorry, don't understand," reply Keon while shrugging his shoulders. The leader, without the shirt, leaps from his camel and walks slowly over to the confrontation.

"Well, I see you speak Sabaean." He grunts.

Surprised Keon answers, "Yes we do. How do you know the Sabaean tongue?"

The man comes closer to Keons looking down at him, envading his space. With a sinister smile he answers, "Let's just say, I get around . . . boy."

He then looks Keon up and down in a belittleing fashion. He slowly walks amongst the others of Keons group looking them up and down and sneering at them. When he approaches Zahira she is unmoved by his intimidating appearance and size. She stares unwaveringly at him. He looks at her and lets out a loud laugh.

"I see you children have brought some entertainment. She looks to be a feisty one; I can see it in her eyes."

He approaches closer to Zahira and stares down at her. Keon and the others come to her side and ready for attack. Smiling, he bends slightly downward and whispers,

"Did you lose something sweet cow? I guess your little boyfriends here havent had time to teach you proper manners when before real men . . . there are some needs I have of you."

Keeping her stare Zahira mockingly returns the smile and reply, "Tell you what, you take me back to Azal and I will be glad to show my respects to some real men. But my mama taught me long ago, never to feed the wild dogs, they just don't know when to stop coming."

"Ha, Ha, Ha," laughs the large imposing man, "feisty indeed, I like you girl." By this time, Keon and the other boys hem their way between the man and Zahira.

"Look we want no trouble here," anxiously pleads Shavir, "We are just heading east to the market in Kemet."

"Quiet Shavir," rebukes Keon. The Man laughs again along with his shabby companions. By this time the cloaked woman sitting on the camel turns and looks at Zahira with tear filled eyes. Her face appears battered and soiled. Zahira's heart melts at the sight of her.

"Keon, we can't leave her with these men." Whispers Zahira.

"Don't worry," He reply, "we will—"

"You will what!" shouts the man interrupting Keon.

Keon turns to the man and boldly declares,

"You will release that woman that you have more then likely kidnapped over to us. And you will be about your way."

The men start to laugh out loud. The leader finally reply saying,

"Tell you what boy, I have a better idea. You will instead give us that sweet cow that is traveling with you, your camels and than we will kindly castrate you boys to releave the pain you will have by not having her with you."

"Why do you want trouble!" shouts Shavir deliriously, "keep the girl, we will continue on our way. There is no need to fight."

"Quiet!" Keon shouts to Shavir once again.

"So be it," states Durjaya, "if it is a fight they want, than I am with you Keon, a fight we will give them."

With that all of them with Keon pull out there Sabaean swords and face the men. Shavir reluctantly does so as well. Anen follow suite after observing Shavir.

"Get'em!" the man yells. Suddenly all the men come rushing at the boys. The swords of Keon and his group begin to glow with their focused power. They then start a victorious battle cutting the men down, severing limbs and slashing deep wounds. The men are excellent sword men, with a couple being even more skilled then Keon and his team, but Keon and his group's powers afforded them the advantage over the men. The ground soon is saturated with the blood of the men. After the massacre, only four men remain including their shirtless leader. Enraged the leader comes forward and pulls from off the side of his camel a large prodigious war hammer. To the surprise of Keon and his team, the hammer starts to emit a bright green glow.

"I knew it, I knew!" shouts Shavir, "the leader is touched by the dust of the star, just like us. But he is of the black dust."

The man swings the large hammer in front of him causing the earth to rip away from his path and form an arch over his head. He then twirls the hammer above his head and causes the formed soil to explode with pieces hitting all in the area. The attack was not meant to damage but to send a message of his power. Soil splatters onto Keon and his companions.

"I am Vardan, I too am gifted children, for I am of the black dust." He growls. "How else do you think I and my fifteen men leveled cities? We had many more women then this little cow that rides with us, we played with them until they were used up. The men and children we buried alive under the earth in a chasm I created alone. The elderly we made eat dirt, seeing that is where they will soon be anyway and as for you . . . hahaha, get ready to meet your gods."

Keon rushes at Vardan and strikes out at him with his charged sword, Vardan blocks with his large hammer and swings at him narrowly missing Keon's head. Durjaya and Zahira leap to Keons aid, but Vardan raises his hammer and throws up a large wall of rock to shield him from their attack. The rock knocks the two back sending them to the ground. Keon raises and strikes again with his glowing sword at Vardan's leg this time. But Vardan reacts quickly by raising the dry foliage from deep below the ground and entangling him and slams him to the ground. Durjaya rises and takes his staff, he swings at the wall of earth busting through it. He then charges at Vardan and manages to strike his back causing Vardan great pain. Vardan then turn his attention to Durjaya and taking his hammer swings downward but is knocked from his feet by Zahira who charges him from behind and sends him to the ground crashing on his face. Anen finally runs over to the fallen Vardan in an attempt to sever his head but Vardan quickly turns and takes notice and points his hammer at him sending a barrage of flying rock that pelts him violently sending him crasing into the ground.

Vardan then raises quckly and swings backwards at Zahira knocking her away from his vicinity. She manages to roll with the blow and is surprisingly caught by Shavir.

"Its my turn," Shavir halfheartedly state.

Keon manages to break free from the vines and confront Vardan once again.

"Time to end this dog," yells Keon.

"You're the one eating dirt so who's the dog boy." shouts Vardan.

The two charge at each other, on meeting savagely clashing their weapons together. Debris of the earth follows Vardan as he progresses. As they engage in combat rock and soil swirls around the two like a small tornado making it difficult for the others to come to Keon's aid. Zahira and the others cannot see a thing through the dense soil, foliage and smoke.

During the commotion, Anen and Shavir head over to the four remaining men and after a struggling battle kills them all.

Finally after some time the debris caused by Vardan slowly subsides. When the smoke finally clears one figure can be vaguely seen standing victorious, it is a battered Keon, huffing and puffing while standing over the dead Vardan. Keons blade is stained with Vardans blood. The faint aura that encased Keon slowly fades as he regains his composure.

Zahira quickly runs over to him.

"Keon, are you ok?"

"Yes . . . I am fine, a bit exhausted, my side feels hurts, but I will be fine." He smiles and pats her on the shoulder, "Go and get that woman, see what her story is all about."

Zahira runs over to the cloaked woman on the camel and starts diligently untying her. Once she is untied she tearfully reaches out to Zahira and embraces her neck. Zahira returns the hug and gives consoling words.

"She hugs Zahira, and you were the one that killed that Vardan man." Sneers Shavir to Keon.

"Don't worry about Zahira, for she has done more then her part today," Keon replies, "as for you . . . well this will be discussed in detail with the Muqarahein once we return."

"I am not worried about that," rebuttles Shavir, "but what of all this stolen gold and silver, I know we will surely take it for ourselves."

Keon approaches the woman and ask,

"Where are you from?"

She is unable to speak their language. She speaks a broken dialect not familiar to them. She motions for them to come and follow her, motioning for them to take the gold and silver.

"No, no, we can't," Keon replys motioning with his hands, "You take it back to your people."

The woman pulls Zahira's arm for her to come with her but reluctantly Zahira motions that she is unable to return with her.

"I am sorry, I can't go with you. We can take you as far as Ammu, come with us." Zahira answers motioning with her hand to follow her.

The woman catches what Zahira is saying, agrees with a nod of her head and follows along with them to Ammu.

They search and find shelter near caves and set up camp for the approaching evening.

CHAPTER 19

Sensual Delights

The next day, the group rises, load their beasts and continue their journey. After some hours of traveling they approach a large hill they traverse over. When finally making it to the top they can finally see a meager sparse forest below. Below at the bottom of the hill is a small clay building, standing alone beneath large olive trees, it is covered in thick moss. It appears abandoned, but as they slowly descend down the hill towards it they can hear faint sounds of laughter and talking inside.

"Come on, let's see what's going on in there," whispers Shavir. "they sound pretty friendly."

However, Keon senses warn him against going in there, he responsd, "Are you mad."

"It is an oasis, a place where we can get some rest, looks to be an inn of some sort for travelers," answers Shavir. "Besides, it is on our way, we have to pass anyway. You are pretty banged up Keon, you could use it as well."

"No we don't Shavir," quickly answers Keon, "I am fine and we can go around farther east to—"

"You are out of your mind," belligerently interrupts Shavir. "I am tired of camping outdoors and eating garbage."

"And this is what you call paradise? A place covered in moss and—"

Before Keon can finish his statement, three women run out of the door of the buildings entrance. They come out laughing and staggering as if they are drunk. They soon catch sight of the group.

"Hey there, hey there," the women call out, "are you travelers, do you need a place to stay for the night?"

Neither Zahira nor the others say a word but turn towards the path at the bottom of the hill and starts walking away, though Shavir is reluctant to leave. Again the women call out,

"Wait . . . wait, why do you leave, you have a lot to carry, hmmm, a lot of gold as well. You must be tired, looks like you met up with some unsavory folk."

The women immediately run over to the travelers. To the surprise of Zahira and her companions, the women are clothing so scantily that only their genitalia are covered with silver plates, the remaining parts of their body is naked, with the exception of bone necklaces, wrist and thigh bands. Their hair is long and flowing, decorated in beads and flowers of varying colors. Their skin smooth and white, lips rose red and their shapes are without match in beauty as well. The young men look upon the forms of the women longlingly, tempted by their well sculpted forms and aromatic allure.

"Why are you leaving so hastily?" ask one of the women to Shavir as she plays in her hair with her fingers. Zahira interjects saying,

"We are just passing through and headed—"

"Kemet," interrupts the woman. Zahira and her companions remain silent, the woman then continues,

"Well you have to be headed that way, for is that not the direction you are traveling, farther west. All your camels are heavily stacked, as if for a long trip—"

"What is it to you," Zahira asks with a tone of mistrust.

"Nothing . . . I presume, just asking." The woman snickers, "If that is the case, then perhaps you need food and wine. This building behind me is the home of Antaneen, lord of this estate, it's an oasis; many travelers stop here for entertainment and rest. You too are welcomed."

"We have already rested, thanks for your offer, but we will do fine." Zahira abruptly reply.

Looking at Zahira with disgust, Shavir quickly speaks up saying,

"Speak for yourself, I am going in; I could use fine wine and a meal that would please my palate."

"Shavir," Durjaya says, "we only have money for our travels; this was not anticipated . . . and you know we do not drink wine."

"Are you crazy," Shavir laughs, "all this gold we took from those barbarians, we have more then enough . . . and a little wine won't hurt, besides what the Muhas don't know won't hurt them."

"That gold is not ours!" Durjaya grunts.

At once one of the women speak up in response to Durjayas remark saying,

"There is no need for money; your stay here is free, if only one night you need."

"Free," ask Anen, "how do you make a living, giving free room and board to strangers?"

"Antaneen is a rich lord, and governs this land with his inheritance," she boisterously responds, "making this place free to young warriors like you. It is his way of showing his appreciation for those that fight for the greater glory of the Whitestar. My lord Antaneen knows those that are touched by the Whitestar dust and only to them does he provide such comfort."

"We did not tell you we fight for the Whitestar, nor did we tell you who we are, how do you know this about us girl?" Suspiciously ask Keon.

"He has given I and the others inside this ability," she laughs, "for he, himself, is of the Whitestar dust."

There is a brief silence. Zahira finally break the silence and ask while pointing at the small moss covered building,

"If your lord is so wealthy and such a wonderous man, why does he choose to entertain the righteous in such poor conditions?"

"Our lord is indeed a humble man, it is his way in showing humility and piety. But inside you would find a heavenly abode designed to tantalize your delight."

Without saying another word, Zahira brusquely turn away and heads down the path westward. Keon, Durjaya and Anen slowly turn and follow, but as for Shavir he stubbornly proceeds toward the building.

Zahira turns and notices Shavir is not with them. She then shouts at Shavir saying,

"Shavir, what are you doing?"

"I am about to enjoy some entertainment, food and good sleep." He balks back, "You are only a girl, you wouldn't understand mine nor none of our needs as men. Anen, are you coming?"

Anen stops and looks at Shavir in confusion. The two are very close friends and have been since their entrance into Azal as young boys. Anen wants to remain with his friend, but his desire to return to his homeland and free it from the menace burns inside. Shavir shouts out saying,

"Do not worry about Kemet; we will join with the others tomorrow. We will even possibly beat them there—"

"That is not the point Shavir," interrupts Keon, "we were told to stick together and not forsake the other. These are the very words of the Muqarahein himself. These are the codes we have lived by since our coming to Azal."

"Don't lecture me . . . you stupid maggot," yells Shavir, "You would blindly follow these men and their wayward words to your very grave. Yes they are wise, but even they cannot read or tame the heart; they cannot invent what you have already become. I am in power of my own life, no other. Anen, come!"

Zahira approaches Anen and compassionately whispers,

"Shavir has already made up his mind; he has forsaken the wise instructions given by the Muqarahein. You need not do this as well. Come with us and even though we take the harsh path, your glory will be given to you. Do not let—"

Shavir now grows hot with anger and interrupts Zahira calling out to Anen once again,

"Are you going to let this woman dictate to you your lot in life? Who is she to play the prince over us? In my land women are second place citizens and we, the men, are the lawgivers. Only when I came to Azal did I see such an abomination of values, by claims being made of Zahira as the hope for the lands, how ridiculous!"

Enraged Zahira shouts saying,

"The last boy that sought to demean me ended up dead, and the one before that and the one before that one. You know, come to think of it, all those idiots that sought to destroy who and what I am all my life died. So you think your machoism and bravado will be any different in this scenario, then you have thought wrong. You will also suffer the same fate as those before you. Your heedlessness and aversion of the laws given to us, the training provided to us for our protection will be your undoing . . . do you have any love for righteousness, are you that foolish to allow your desires to take place over righteous principles and standards."

Shavir grinds his teeth with rage and runs over to Zahira in an effort to confront her.

"Oh yeah, well—" He yells, but is intercepted by Keon.

"I see your problem Shavir," Keon states, "You are afraid of Zahira's strength, you are afraid that her glory will overshadow yours . . . you coward."

"There is no fear found in me Keon . . . perhaps in you, but not in me." Shavir blurts.

With that Shavir turns and head towards the building leaving the group. Anen turn and reluctantly follows Shavir. Keon desperately calls out to Anen saying,

"Remember my friend you don't have to do this. Dont allow your friendships and lust blind you and ultimately forget your oath!"

Anen answers saying,

"I have not forgotten Keon . . . however; there is truth to what Shavir was saying. What is wrong with enjoying the good things in life from time to time, especially when it is not afforded you daily. I will meet you by first light. Meet me by the river on the other side I . . . we will be there, I promise."

With that, Anen catches up with Shavir and the two enters the building with the women.

Angry, Keon take his fist and strike the side of a tree.

"The fools," murmurs Keon in a fit of rage, "How could they be so empty headed."

"Do not worry about them Keon. Even though they strayed, we will stay on track," Zahira reassuringly responds. Keon sighs and reply,

"By first light, when they return, I will show Shavir his place in this group."

Zahira approach Keon and catches his eyes in hers, she then softly state,

"There will be no tomorrow for them, save your passion for the mission that lay ahead of us. We need our leader on key Keon."

Disturbed over Zahira's response, Keon stands there for a moment and take one last look at the building. Finally he joins Zahira and Durjaya who have already progressed some distance down the path.

Meanwhile, Shavir and Anen enter the room and sit on the floor on large plush pillows and are awed by what they observe inside. The inside speaks far more grandly than its outward appearance. It looks like a palace hall. The floor is covered in leopard skins and the walls are trimmed in gold shavings. Gold infest the room and not one person in the room lacks it. Large idols of human bodies with animal heads adorn the walls and magnificent flowing curtains drape ceiling lining. The room is filled with only women, with the exception of an elusive man sitting on a large throne in the shadows in the far corner.

"Who do you think he is?" Anen whispers to Shavir,

"Probably the lord of this place, but with all these beautiful naked women . . . who care's!"

The two are treated like kings, being fed and massaged. The women start to remove the clothing of the two who show no resistance.

They take the men over to a large pool inside made of marble and starts to bathe them thoroughly. Shavir rests his back against the wall of the marbled pool, soaking in the attention given by the sensual women.

Anen, finally relax and allow the women to pamper him as well. One of the women slowly licks Anen's left cheek and softly places her lips upon his, kissing him gently. This entices Anen so that he grabs hold of her by the waist desperately returning the kiss. Strangely, though, he notices himself weakening as he kisses the woman, as if his very strength is being drawn from him.

Immediately he pulls away from the woman, thumping against the tub and gasping for air. Shavir laughs saying,

"You see what the Muhas have done to you; they took away your will to live, and I mean to enjoy the pleasures of life."

"No Shavir," Anen pants exhaustingly while pushing back from the determined women, "It's not that . . . it felt as if her kiss . . . was drawing my strength from my body . . . I felt as if I was going to faint!"

"Ah Anen," sneers Shavir, "That's only ecstasy friend, you were only about to experience what many call—"

But before Shavir can finish his statement, the elusive man that sat in the dark corner nonchaluantly steps over to the pool. He paces the floor above the pool with an eccentric smile. He is dressed in a long giraffe skinned cloak, only his bald head is uncovered. His complexion is as black as soil or pitch and his eyes are yellow.

"Can I help you Sir," sarcastically ask Shavir, "this is a private party here."

"Yes, you can help me," the man responds in a deep penetrating voice, "seeing that I am Antaneen, the owner of this establishment."

"Oh, my apologies Antaneen," Shavir replies, "you have a wonderful place here, I can imagine how many visitors you get here daily."

"Oh yes my friend," Antaneen responds, "many like yourself that seek pleasure and self satisfaction."

Shavir looks up at the elusive man with suspicion over his last statement. In the meantime, during their conversation, Anen grows concerned over the kiss that almost drained his life force. The women presses in upon him voraciously; but he lightly pushes them away, now attempting to exit the pool.

"So my friend," asks Antaneen, "Why do you come this way?"

Shavir answers saying, "We are headed towards Kemet. Many festivities are going to be held there in the cities, so we are going to join in the festivities."

"Is that so?" sighs Antaneen. Shavir sighs back sarcastically in reply,

"Yes, it is,"

Antaneen continues to pace the floor and stares intently at Shavir as the women crawl all over him. Shavir is now getting nervous over Antaneens mysterious nature, but the women eventually cloud his mind once again.

"Shavir . . . Shavir!" calls out Anen, "Perhaps, we should go now,"

"Already," sniggles one of the women, "the enjoyment has just begun, you still must eat and then sleep for your long trip to Kemet."

Again Anen whispers to Shavir, but this time more persistently,

"Let's go! Something's not right here."

Lavishing in the accompaniment of the women, Shavir casually ignores Anen's concern.

Antaneen then ask of Shavir saying,

"The girl that was traveling with you, who is she?"

"A friend of ours," Shavir replies nonchalantly.

"There is more to her tale . . . is there not?" Antaneen further impose.

"A friend, what more do you need to know?" Shavir answers begrudgingly. Again Antaneen paces the floor looking into the water and smiling. Anen finally leaps from the pool and starts to quickly put his clothes back on.

"Shavir, I am leaving; I hope you are coming,"

Again Antaneen ask, but this time more forcefully,

"Who was that girl that accompanied you?"

Insulted by the elevation of the man's voice, Shavir answers blatantly saying,

"If you knew who you address in this fashion then you would quickly grab hold of that tongue. I am no dog!"

Antaneen hold his head back and releases a loud laugh that shakes the very room, rippling the water in the pool. He then declares,

"No my impetuous friend, you need know who I am; then you would answer of what I ask of you."

"I don't think I appreciate your tone Antaneen. Maybe I should fix that tongue for yours." Shavir shouts.

Antaneen only smiles, ignoring Shavir's threat and continues pacing the floor. With that Shavir grows hot with anger and starts to take his leave from the pool, but one of the women grab hold of his shoulders and exclaim,

"Come now, do not be exasperated with my lord, kiss me, please." The invitation is hardly a turn off, her full figured body and white colored sweet smelling skin only entrances Shavir, where he slides back into the pool of water and delivers her a long passionate kiss.

With that, other women join her and start to kiss and hold onto him. Anen can only watch in horror as Shavirs body starts to shake violently with blood spewing from every orifice.

Anen runs over to Shavir quickly, but before he can reach him two of the women jump in front of his path and tackles him to the ground with two more women.

When the women release Shavir, his limp body slowly sinks into the water. He is drained of all his internal organs, his body lays under the water lifeless as white as snow.

Anen screams to the top of his voice and attempts to force the women back from off him but to no avail, they quickly acquire bestial strength.

Again Antaneen delivers a long stark laugh. He then mutters,

"Why do you fight my friend, you are powerless here. My harlots feed off your latent gifts and then they give them to me. There is nothing you can do, but you can be spared alive. You seem to be an intelligent boy, so answer for me what your companion failed to do, then I might let you leave unharmed. Is the girl that traveled with you the last of the Azmarian peoples, the last of the Whitestar?"

"Why do you need to know this?" Anen asks horrified.

"Well let's just say that I am a herald of the mighty Rathamun, and unto him shall I deliver his prize."

"What?" inquires the perplexed Anen, "Your whore's lied; they spoke of you being of the light."

Laughing Antaneen replies,

"No my friend, you probably misunderstood; perhaps they meant I eat of the light. You see, I and my harlots are leaches; we feed off those that possess the power of the dust. But you have a chance yet to remain alive, tell me the truth of the nature of the girl that traveled with you and exactly where they are headed."

Anen looks around in horror at the room as the sensuous women, twenty in number, slowly walk over to him smiling and laughing hysterically. Antaneen stands in the back ground with his arms folded awaiting an answer. With all of his strength Anen manages to throw the women that still hold on to him off and run towards the entrance. He bows his head and begins to focus, exuding the aura of power around his body. He then looks up and states courageously,

"Today, you have chosen your victim wrongly. Now you shall taste the power of the Whitestar. I am the last child of the Whitestar . . . Rathamun was fooled to think it was a girl."

"No, my impetuous friend," grunts Antaneen, "Today, that power that you once claimed shall no longer be yours. I shall feed off you until your power flows from my nostrils."

Suddenly, the women's eyes glow a blood red and they start to scream wildly at the top of their lungs. They all charge Anen, leaping upon him and taking large bites into his flesh, draining him of his strength and power.

Anen, very weak, can do nothing but buckle under the weight of the savage women. For a brief moment he reflect back on how foolish it was to break away from Zahira and the others. Totally unable to fight anymore, he closes his eyes and fight no longer, finally submitting to the leaching women.

The last thing heard by Anen is the fading voice of Antaneen in the background laughing and stating,

"Know this, foolish one, she will taste death, for I do know who she is, the glory of the Whitestar itself."

With that, Anen collapses onto the floor and with his dying breath utters the name, "Za . . . hira,"

CHAPTER 20

Enter the Sekmet

Many days have passed since leaving the small building of Antaneen. When Zahira, Keon, Durjaya and their new female companion finally reach their destination they enter a vast and populace city. Far off into the landscape immense pyramids stand erect as testimony to the Pharaohs wealth. The woman looks at them and kisses each one of them tenderly on the cheek. She offers once again some of the wealth from the camels but they refuse as before. She then embraces them all and leaves into the city.

"Her village must be on the outskirts of this place some where." State's Keon.

"You did a good thing Keon," Zahira reply. Keon answers saying.

"No, we all did Zahira, we all did."

The noisy streets are littered with vendors selling and trading food, animals and their craft work. Way off into the distance away from the commerce square is the regal palace of Amun Ra. They make it through the crowded streets up the ramp that leads to the large palace, which is decorated with many sculptures of Amun Ra and his royal court officials lining the pathways. The symbol of Ra's power in the form of a golden eye atop of the palace glistens in the sun's rays and stand extremely high for all to see. A long line of stone buildings align the edifice with many inscriptions and drawings of daily life and the king and his exploits. They stealthly enter the back of the palace towards the higher level prison holds. They quickly make short work of the guards positioned there.

After entering they pass through a long corridor and come upon a room possessing a vast marbled floor positioned under large pillars scattered about the large palace opening. About fifty feet on the other side of the floor are doors that lead to the balcony and roofs over the prison designed for high ranking captives and where the Muha is being held.

Suddenly, an eerie figure dressed in a long white flowing cloak that covers its entire body walks out onto the floor positioning itself in front of the doors to the balcony. The figure entrance is regal and graceful, but determined. It saunters in the room upright, with its dainty heals barely touching the floor.

A wind gushes into the room and blows the cloak from off the figure revealing a beautiful woman clad in golden Kemetic war armor, only revealing her head, arms and legs. Her hair is pitch black and worn in a long braid coming down past her bottom. Her slanted hazel eyes are almost like a cats and she possesses a creamy complexion. She Hold in each hand beautifully decorated sickle kemetic swords held low on each side of her thighs. The swords are sleek and light in appearance.

"You come for your teacher?" the peculiar woman asks in a muffled tone.

No one says a word, unsure as to what to make of her.

She continues, "Your teacher anticipated your presence, but little does he comprehend, that your attempts to liberate him shall be futile. You stand before Sekmet, the avenging eye of my father Ra and chosen guardian over all Kemet."

Without a moments thought, Durjaya charges toward the woman with his staff reared in the air to strike. Keon attempts to halt him but it is too late. She slowly raises her swords and clangs them together causing a terrifying billowing force to emit and engulf Durjaya, slamming him into the wall behind the others and demolishing his staff.

Afterwards Keon runs over to Sekmet, throwing his sword at her in an attempt to impale her to the wall. However, Sekmet nonchalantly evades the attack and returns another gust of force, slamming Keon to the floor.

Observing the battle, Zahira prepares to join in when Keon screams from the floor saying,

"No! Go and rescue the Muha . . . we will take care of her!"

Sekmet then laughs in response,

"Take care of me, hahaha . . . this battle shall not persist; I will surely make waste of you and send your corpses to the dark pits of Osiris."

Reluctantly Zahira leaves the battle in order to rescue the Muhas.

Slipping by, Zahira proceeds through the doors and runs through the long corridor that spirals up to the ceiling of the edifice. She positions herself atop of the roof on the outside and looks down its edge where she is able to see the window to the prison. She crawls down the side of the building toward the window with the help of ropes she found laying about the top of the ceiling.

Once reaching the window, she grabs hold of the bars and looks into the darkness of the cell calling out,

"Muhas, Muhas Azhad!"

Crawling from the dark corner of the room in mangled clothing is Azhad, squinting to see who it was calling his name.

"Who's there?" he asks cautiously.

"It is I, Zahira from Azal sent by the Muqarahein to rescue you. I am a student."

"Zahira?" Azhad thinks out loudly, "Now this is a sight I thought I would never see."

He then comes closer and Zahira can now behold even clearer an aged man soiled from lack of sanitary conditions. She then states,

"Excuse me, Muhas, we must hurry. The others that came with me are engaging Ammun Ra's guardian in combat. We have to escape this place quickly."

Examining the bars, Zahira thinks hard on how she will get through.

"Focus Zahira," Azhad states, "Channel your power and grab hold of the stone surrounding the bars."

Confused Zahira replies,

"But Muhas, this is not a feat for someone as small as I, another way must be—"

"No Zahira," Interrupts Azhad, "not through muscle will you complete this task, but by the power of your ancestors shall you master even the elements. Focus your gifts my child, concentrate."

Zahria grabs hold of the bars and slides her hands down to the base of stone that support the bars. She then closes her eyes and concentrates very hard. Soon she begins to emit her aura that covers her entire body. Suddenly the stone begins to crumble as her energies rupture through, finally breaking away the stone surrounding the bars.

She then removes two of the weakened bars from their foundation and slides through into the cell.

"See, I knew you could do it," applauds Azhad, "you accomplished what seemed improbable."

"Thank you, but we must go now Muhas." She urgently responds.

Zahira and Azhad escape through the window back up towards the roof of the prison, ascending up the rope she tied for herself.

They flee down the corridor back towards the others.

To her dismay, Durjaya and Keon fight what seems to be a losing battle with the guardian Sekmet.

She sashays through the men like a bird, flailing her blades around and blocking every attack made by them.

Her speed on foot is amazing as she moves amongst them with ease. At this point they can't so much as strike a fringe of her outer garments.

Zahira pauses momentarily to assist them when Keon screams out, "No! Go . . . get the Muhas out of here. We will hold her at bay!"

Suddenly Keon is struck in the back by a powerful telekinetic force that sends him into the wall, this time rendering him unconscious.

The culprit Sekmet then announces, "You arrogant fool. None may hold me still."

Durjaya charges toward Sekmet and manages to make contact, knocking her from her feet to the floor.

He then screams to Zahira, "Get out of here stubborn girl . . . take the Muhas to safety!"

Then with great force Durjaya is hurled from where he stand by an energy blast from Sekmet that crashes him into the ceiling.

Sekmet then laments, "Do you see boy? You cannot stop me! Now I shall rip you asunder."

Zahira surprises Sekmet by charging into her side with her unaware and knocking her to the floor, causing her to release her grip of Durjaya, who falls to the floor unconscious.

Zahira immediately flips from over Sekmet and faces her.

"Imprudent girl, you are naught compared to the blessings bestowed upon me and shall too share the same fate of your brash companions."

Sekmet plants her feet firmly onto the floor and starts to raise her swords upwards. Tremors are soon sent through the floor causing everything in the room to tremble. She then rears back and releases a transparent force of white energy that races toward Zahira.

Zahira, in turn involuntarily creates a white aura that protects her from the impact, dissipating the attack by Sekmet into thin air.

They then charge at one another and engage in swift melee combat with their swords.

Zahira is amazed over her own display of attacks, for she has never been able to produce such power in the past, but her heightened emotions trigger the latent gene within her, releasing a minor portion of its power.

Soon Zahira and Sekmet begin to glow even more tremendously as if two heavenly suns were on the face of the earth. The floor beneath them begins to tremble and form cracks as energy surge and radiate from their positions. The Muhas urges Zahira on from the background, reminding her of her training.

Sekmet is amazed at Zahira's fury, but not frightened.

Due to the length of the battle, Sekmet grows furiously savage, showering her telekinetic prowess over Zahira, trying to rip away her aura and fling her to the floor. But her attacks meet the strong will of Zahira and fail to do what she desires.

Keon and Durjaya look on in amazement as the two women battle viciously. However, Azhad stands with his eyes closed in deep meditation. He then creates a telepathic link with Zahira, which doesn't give her more power but only increase Zahira's awareness and perception in the battle.

The two continue their struggle with soon the reality of Sekmet's power being greater, due to her maturity and higher skill levels.

Zahira begins to slowly falter under her attacks until eventually being knocked back to the floor.

Sekmet slowly and cautiously approaches the defeated and exhausted Zahira saying, "See my dear . . . though you are a worthy foe, the fact of the matter is that your worth is not good enough to prevail against me."

Because of Sekmets attention being taken by her admirable foe, Keon manages without warning to strike Sekmet from behind on the head with a large piece of broken marble, instantly rendering her unconscious.

Immediately the weakened Durjaya runs to Zahira and lifts her to her feet. However, she is exhausted from the scenario where every step she makes she falters. The four immediately runs from the palace managing to slip past the guards. On leaving, they quickly mount their camels and race eastward out of the region.

Unbeknownst to the four, Ra, the lord of Kemet, watches from his balcony smiling at the fleeing invaders. He then thinks to himself saying,

"The fools, Rathamun has much in store for the impetuous princess of light. The coming war has now begun."

CHAPTER 21

The Arena

Six years have passed since the successful rescue of the Muhas Azhad from Kemet, and Zahira is now twenty-four. The Muhas watch and marvel at how she excels in her training. The rescue of Azhad from Kemet and the battle with Sekmet has opened her powers even more, maturing them at astounding levels. She is like no other student they have ever trained. Her abilities now far exceed most of the young men there.

She becomes adept with the Sabaean sword and begins to learn how to focus her hidden cosmic energies through the weapons she wields.

She amazes them with her frequent success in daring missions assigned to her.

Many trials are put before her and long journeys to accomplish them are arranged. But each trial is met with victory.

One evening, the Muhas meet in the counsel chamber to discuss the future of the young woman Zahira.

"Her abilities have grown substantially."

"We must not be so presumptuous," exclaims another Muhas. "She must be tested further in order to call forth her latent powers even more. Let us prepare her to do battle with one who possesses heightened powers as well, our greatest Whitedust user. If she is able to defeat this one, then she will have proven she is ready to move forward."

"Then so shall it be. Have the young woman brought to us so that we may speak with her."

Zahira is brought before the counsel of Muhas. They sit on on the floor in a circle with Zahira sitting in the middle.

She notices a young boy sitting next to Ahura, dressed in the garb of the students from the school, but wearing a band around his head, signifying his training to become a Muhas. From his appearance he looked to be at least eight years of age.

She smiles at the boy, remembering when she first came to the school herself.

At that moment, Ahura, the head Muhas, begins to speak.

"Child, has your time here enhanced your knowledge of your true ancestry and purpose?"

"Yes, Muhas,"

"The new understanding and belief of the one deity essential to all life, the Great Stars and their divisions, the dust they sprinkled, and the people that emerged from it, you have come to know of these truths?"

Zahira answers saying,

"Most of it Muqarahein, you have taught me many more intricate details during my stay here. I am aware of my true ancestry and of those that wish to put me to death. However, there are some things that remain vague to me."

"Then it is time you were better informed." He responds.

Unsure of what Ahura means by this statement, Zahira remains quiet and listens intently to his wisdom.

"The information that came to us is the initial story: A great cosmic star, with enigmatic energy, plummeted to the earth. Upon hitting the earth's surface, the star divided into three separate energies. The Blackstar was hurled to the southern land of Mayota, its capital being Guta'leen. The Whitestar struck the central kingdom of Azmaria, its capital being Sagala and the Koryan landed in the farthest north corner of that vast continent. During the split, residual energies from the star sprinkled parts of the earth and bred other creatures of either cosmic light or darkness, neither being of the pureness of the White and Blackstar. As you may already know, we call this residual the dust of the star, or the star dust, either white or black.

Each began to infect the inhabitants of the land, transforming their very bodies into beings of vast powers that had never been witnessed before. However, the pure Whitestar produced a proud and righteous race of guardians, who built a city and temple in the land of Azmaria to protect the known world from the transformed beings and creatures that would ravage the land, the spawns of the dark portion of the dust. The Blackstar, on the other hand, developed powerful beings of malice and hate. The Blackstar would strive to unite itself with the other stars to become the most powerful evil that the earth had ever seen.

The Blackstar proved stronger then the weakened Whitestar. The earth shook . . . a battle between the two was waged.

However, before this conflict, the keeper of the Whitestar told of a prophecy regarding the cosmic energies of the great weapon. It told of the Koryan in the north later rising and coming forth to unite with the Whitestar and destroying the Blackstar, bringing peace once again to the central kingdom of Azmaria and the world.

The wielder of the Koryan must be that of pure Light or of the pure Blackstar in order for it to be activated. If activated by the Light, peace will prevail. If activated by the Blackstar, the world will be enshrouded in darkness for eternity. Though the Koryan was designed for good, to guide life and be a protector for the righteous, its power if possessed by the Blackstar can be misused, misinterpreted and bring misery to all life.

You, my child, are the only survivor of the guardians of the Light, the last child of the Whitestar. Hope rests in you. When it will transpire is not yet known. What is known is that you are the key to future peace. You are the birth and culmination of all the energies of your deceased people, from the Whitestar."

Zahira interrupts politely asking,

"I am not sure I understand certain things concerning this story. Muqarahein, how can a star come to our earth, from what I have learned from the sciences, such a phenomenon would be catastrophic to our planet, would it not? Are not stars merely balls of gas and energy?"

The Muqarahein smiles and replies,

"Dear Zahira, you have spoken truthfully. Thus the reason I opened this story up as the 'story that came to us'. It was delievered to us centuries ago by our ancestors, who did not have such knowledge concerning the composition of a star at the time, and many to this day still do not. Thus, the phenomenon that happened to our planet, to them the energy that came appeared as stars from the heavens. Actually, they are but astral beings, aliens from another world."

Zahira plays with her earlobe thinking outloud,

"Now it makes sense, the lady of the forest that came to me, when I was a child, spoke of aliens, foreigners of this world."

"Exactly," continues Ahura, "we the Muhas here, have come to understand the events similar but we know the true existence of these creatures. However, that information you will gain at a later time.

Yet there is still more caution to this tale. You must remember from your training here that your full potential is only activated by the use of a catalyst, a material weapon of some sort. Not just any artifact or inanimate object, but one laced only with fragments of the Whitestar. These fragments of metal are called 'Kadmadyn' and can only be forged by blacksmiths that possess the power of the whitedust."

"So the weapons we used here are of that metal, 'Kadmadyn'?" Zahira asks.

"Yes," answers Ahura.

"So why did not the Muhas tell us this," continues Zahira, "they would assign us our weapons when practicing, but they never made mention of this special metal. I along with many of the student thought any weapon can be used to harness our power."

"It was not time, all things are done in a progressive order here, and you know this Zahira. As you grow then your studies grow with you, thus now you are aware of this fact," Smiles Ahura. He continues saying,

"This is the case with all users of this strange power, white or black forces. Many have fashioned their Kadmadyn into fighting sticks, swords, bands, necklaces, crowns, belts and the list goes on. Without their Kadmadyn weapons one cannot bring forth their suppressed powers. They can only show manifestations of it by emitting a rich aura around their form.

"Even the Blackstar itself needs Kadmadyn to activate its power. Depending on the amount of fragments used from the black portion of the star will determine the amount of this power. This minor detail limits all power users in this ever changing world."

At this point, another Muhas begins to speak.

"Your special abilities have not gone unnoticed Zahira. We are very impressed with what you have accomplished thus far. We would like to test your abilities further. One of the tests required is to do combat with one possessing the greatest skills in use of the stardust energies here at this school. We believe you are ready. You will be allowed one week of meditation and training in preparation for your test. Do you agree to the undertaking?"

"If I succeed, what is to come of this?" asks Zahira.

"Know this Zahira, this challenge will open the door for your latent abilities to manifest itself even more. Through strain and tribulation will it come forth, and in combat with another that possess such power. Only this way can we fully gage your progression, maturity at this point. Your presence before us emits a strong flavor of light coursing through your veins. We do not doubt who you are, but we must gage the extent of growth of the Whitestar within you. The choice is yours to make."

Zahira pauses for a moment before responding. She then boldly declare,

"Muqarahein and Muhas's . . . I am ready for the undertaking."

After leaving their presence, extensive training commences for the developing warrior. For a week she dwells within the temple itself, the dwelling of the Muhas, in deep meditation and focus day and night homing in, tapping into her hidden power.

When the week is up, Zahira readies herself and dresses in ceremonial pants and robe. The robe on both sides has long splits and the robe itself is decorated with many writings only known to the Muhas. It covers her neck and arms. Its length comes down to her knees. As usual, she wears her scarf given to her by her mother, this time tightly wrapped around her head. She is brought to the combat circle before the entire assembly of Muhas and students.

As Zahira awaits her opponent, an unusual feeling comes over her.

"Through all my years here, I have not come to hear of such a person. Why?"

Could it possibly be fear? What was she afraid of? Maybe it was fear of the unknown. Would she be able to defeat her opponent? Would his skills far surpass hers? Maybe it was not fear of being defeated as much as it was fear she may in some way bring dishonor to her true identity.

Zahira quickly chases the thoughts of uncertainty out of her mind. She knows that in order to be successful she would have to focus all her concentration on her opponent. She would have to anticipate his every move.

The arena is a large round enclosure able to seat upwards of one hundred spectators. It lacked a ceiling and the walls surrounding the floor appear to be of a strange metallic construction. Above is the first row of seating encircling the entire arena and spiraling all the way around until reaching the last seat twenty feet high. Every seat is filled.

There is no loud cheering as would normally be heard in arenas of the far north and beyond. The purpose here is not to entertain, but to gage the levels of the students.

Zahira knows the moment has come. Soon her combatant enters the arena.

There standing before her is a man standing over six and a half feet in height, a handsome man possessing long straight black flowing hair, a six inch long braided beard, deep brown eyes, an olive complexion with an extremely muscular physique. He speaks very little, but brags much when it comes to displaying his skills and abilities. His name is Shamash, and is from the proud people of north east Sumeria.

It is rumored that his parents were persuaded to join Rathamun in his early quest for power. How he escaped the hand of Rathamun is unknown.

"They must believe in me," she thinks as she stares at the tall, muscular man before her. "Why else would they have encouraged me to accept this challenge?"

As Shamash enters the circle, they face each other. She notices prodigious golden bands with Sumerian writings engraved on it and each fastened on each of his arms, extending from his wrist up to his mid forearms.

They await the signal to begin fighting, neither taking their eyes off the other. They face the Muhas and bow. The horn is blown and the battle between the two commences.

Shamash charges Zahira, glowing like the sun itself. Zahira quickly leaps out of his way with Shamash crashing into the floor of the circle. When Zahira turns to face her opponent, she notices the large crater his body leaves in the ground, glowing faintly.

She thinks to herself, "I cannot beat him using muscle. He clearly far surpasses me in this area."

Immediately, Shamash regains footing, his huge arms glowing radiantly. She notices his fists are glowing unusually brighter than the rest of his body. Once again he charges at her with his fist arched back, ready to deliver a menacing blow. Zahira, being quite agile, flips to safety again.

"Keep still woman," Shamash yells. "Do you fear the power that confronts you?"

"Clearly you don't see a woman before you." Zahira sarcastically reply. Shamash grunts and answers,

"I was told you were something more, thus the reason for this challenge . . . I don't take chances. Many surprises in this merciless world woman, such etiquette is no longer required."

Zahira rises immediately. By now she too begins to glow, her expression changing drastically.

"I thought this to be a test of ability and skill not mindless brawn." Zahira boldly states.

Before Shamash has time to anticipate her attack, Zahira focuses and quickly leaps forward, striking him in the chest with an aura surrounding her two fists clasped together, and surprisingly sending him to the ground. This surprised those in attendance, for none has ever falterd Shamash.

"But if it is brawn you wish for," she taunts, "then I shall deliver it gracefully."

Shamash rises to his feet a bit embarrassed, shaking his head in disbelief. He begins to think to himself, "The star exudes through her very fiber. The Muhas were correct when addressing me. I underestimated her energy usage."

He at once races toward her and the two engage in intense melee combat with their fist. Zahira lacks the raw strength Shamash clearly possesses but she does manage to evade and block every blow he delivers.

They each deliver blows, sending energy crackling with every collision.

Despite his ominous size over Zahira, she manages to temporarily hold off his attacks. However, she soon realizes the affects of his raw strength, when she begins to buckle under his blows.

With a final strike, Shamash knocks Zahira to the ground. He then strikes at her, but Zahira rolls out of harms way.

Zahira then rises and strikes Shamash in his back, causing him to fall to the ground on one knee.

He rears back with his fist but she dodges his attack and strikes him in the face, emitting her aura, sending him backward toward the wall of the circle. Keeping his footing, Shamash leaves a long trench in the odd flooring in front of him.

Filled with rage, Shamash charges at Zahira once again, striking her to the ground. The blow is so devastating that she momentarily passes out.

Shamash walks over to her looking down in pity and thinking to himself, "I was always taught not to lay a hand upon any woman, for what glory is there in doing so. But this female proved too formidable for me to oblige by such counsel. She indeed was a worthy opponent."

Then, without a moments notice, Zahira quickly gains conscious and grabs his ankle between her feet triping him to the ground.

She leaps high into the air, and then with the propelling power of her energy, she comes back down crashing into his chest with her two feet together, embedding him four feet into the earth sending shockwaves throughout the arena. Past thoughts of being mistreated by many males from her past race through her mind. She stands atop of him for a silent moment.

As her temper slightly simmers down and her energy fades, Zahira slowly limps away from the fallen warrior, not even looking back, showing no concern for her defeated victim. He appears unconscious.

After a while of complete silence, Zahira pauses and soon regains her mild spirit. She turns and walks back to aid her combatant.

Upon opening his eyes, he notices her hand stretched out to him but he does not take hold of it. He proudly pushes himself from off the ground clumsily and crouches for a moment with his head bowed to regain his composure. He finally stands erect and faces zahira looking down at her with an unwavering stare. She then slowly places her hand upon his arm and firmly grasps it with a pleasant smile upon her face. This endearing act cools Shamash's rage. They both turn and look up at the Muhas, viewing from their seats. Ahura smiles and nods his head signifying his approval.

CHAPTER 22

Chronicles of Fazeem

After the competition, later that day Zahira is brought back before the Muhas.

"Beyond all doubt you have tickeled the star within you. It has matured to the next stage but still not yet complete. See now that you are not misled. Your destiny weighs heavily upon you and the preparation, which deems necessary, has been set as your proving ground. Hold true young Zahira. Much will come to you in time, a load only you can carry."

It is only a week before Zahira is sent on her first assignment as leader. When in the temple she comes before the Muhas council, Ahura begins to speak,

"In the lands of Arad Alhadad dwells a dark ruler over the army of shadows. In the twilight of his days, he yearned for power above all men. During the year of the stars collide and its divide, man began to change. They were either of the Blackstar, Whitestar or the dust from the chaotic split. We have told you the fate of those affected by the split of the Black and the Whitestar. But those sprinkled by the dust from this vary in their gifts and are scattered around the earth."

At this point, another Muhas, second in command, begins to speak.

"The ruler of Arad Alhadad, proved to be only sprinkled with the dust of the Blackstar. However, he sought to become like those of the pure Blackstar. Journeying to the west in search of Rathamun, the ruler of the Blackstar, he pleaded an alliance with Rathamun, hoping himself to increase in power.

Now Rathamun also quested for power, desiring to unite the stars and become all-powerful. He betrayed the ruler of Arad Alhadad enslaving his army transforming them into his own dark army.

Rejected, he fled back to Arad Alhadad with his life, thus the name of the land, 'The Land of Mourning'. There, in the abandoned Temple Mountain of a once strong but now dead land, he meditated on revenge and conquering the world, becoming all-powerful."

The conversation is now picked up by yet another Muhas.

"Here in the land of Azal, we too came in contact with the dust, but of the Whitestar as well as the Shard, a larger piece of this dust, possessing vast powers. The Shard was given to us and hidden. It was to be joined with the Koryan once it resurfaced, which would help the chosen one bring peace to the entire known world. The shard is the key needed to not only operate Koryan, but to increase its power.

The once strong ruler of Arad Alhadad, who now calls himself Fazeem, out of greed and malice, became twisted and tormented by the power of the Black Dust. Hence, he no longer was a man, but a creature, a being driven by hate and avarice, a being of pure energy.

Hearing of our gift, he desired to have it. He believed that if it were united with the Black Dust it would make its wielder very powerful, possible pure energy of untold compositions. Thus, he stole the Shard in our weakened stage of growth and retreated back to Arad Alhadad. There, he created an army of monsters called the "Beasts of Shadows", and there he fed off the Shard to become a mixture of both light and dark energies from the great cosmic star. It did not increase him in power but instead the conflict of the opposing energies drove him mad."

Ahura now finishes the story,

"The Shard must be reclaimed. You, my child, are the only one who can succeed in bringing the Shard back to its rightful place. As you are aware, we are unable to leave the confines of Azal, our power is confined here. You possess the mark of the Azmarians, the *Children of the Whitestar.* We now await your answer."

"You Muqarahein, you have taught and guided me with your wisdom. I have sworn my allegiance here.

"Zahira responds respectfully. "I will comply with the wishes of the counsil anytime."

Ahura walks over to a long brown chest situated in the corner of the room. He takes out a key and opens it. He pulls out a sword sheathed in a leather holder. "Take this sword 'Nazaar', it was constructed from the metal Kadmadyn from Nabatea, and your catalyst. It will guide you, not only through the perils that will befall you on this mission, but also on missions to follow after you leave this school. Use it wisely and measure your circumstances with scrutiny. For the complications of life might be solved through thoughts of simplicity."

The sword Nazaar or 'gazer' design is crafted much like those of the mysterious orient in the enigmatic east. It has a smooth darkened tsuba and end cap and includes leather and wire wrapped handles.

The blade is made from a single thick rigid piece of Kadmadyn, but its special feature unlike any other sword of its kind constructed is its lacing with small fragments of the shard extending the length of the blade through grip with welded guards and pommels.

The curved blade is 27" long with an overall length of 37", but is as light as a feather.

Zahira marvels over the weapon that glistens with every twist made in her hands. After that, Zahira bids the counsel a good night and leaves for her home.

On her way she indulges in heavy thought and she is dumbfounded as to whom she should take with her on this mission. She remembers Keon and his loyalty and leadership abilities, but he himself is busy on mission training by the Muhas. After much thought she thinks of an unlikely choice, but if he is willing would be a great ally.

Although she had defeated Shamash in the competition, he is still a superb fighter. He had definitely shown he was truly a master of the circle.

She respected him as a true warrior and realizes that not including him on the mission would be sheer ignorance on her part.

The one thing concerning her is that because of his proud nature, he might harbor some resentment and refuse to accompany her. Zahira hopes that would not be the case.

She knows that she needs only the best to go with her.

Later that day Zahira leaves out to Shamash's room, she pauses to collect her thoughts. She then approaches the half cracked open door and asks,

"May I enter Shamash?"

There is a brief silence. He finally responds,

"Enter."

To Zahira's amazement Shamash shows no signs of resentment, he is merely sitting on the floor reading from one of the school books.

"As-Shlama Shamash," Zahira greets. Shamash returns the greeting, "Alykom Shlama."

Zahira gets straight to the point, "I am being sent on a mission for the Muhas. I look for one who is skilled in combat and a loyal companion, also well respected to join me on this perilous mission. You have proven to be one who possesses such admirable attributes. I would be honored if you would assist me on this venture."

Shamash glances at Zahira and then replies, "You come at a time when one's pride has been injured and ask for his aid, woman? Not many would follow such a course. You choose not to gloat over your narrow victory. Instead, you stroke my ego."

"It was indeed a narrow battle," Zahira remarks. "You are much stronger and proficient in the areas of—"

"Wait," interrupts Shamash, "despite the truth in your voice concerning my prowess, I was not yet finished. I admire that . . . I admire you. I would consider it an honor to accompany you woman."

Zahira stares in amazement at Shamash and smiles uncontrollably. She was prepared to go for the long haul with him, trying to convince him to accompany her. She didn't expect such a swift acceptance.

She now feels confident her first mission would be a success. This expedition will be the last of many performed while living with the Muhas. But it will test her in ways she would have never imagined.

CHAPTER 23

The Dead Kingdom

An immense mountain stands high before them, as if touching the clouds. The face of a large temple is cut into the side of the mountain. The wind whistles mysteriously with the stench of death swirling around them.

The surrounding woodlands are dark and dismal with no sign of life in the vicinity.

After a journey of twenty five days on camels back, Zahira and Shamash finally reach the ghostly land of Arad Alhadad. They proceed up to the temple and face the towering door that stands over fifteen feet tall. All of a sudden, they hear a deafening scream and then an abrupt silence.

"To stand here and meditate on our entry is only delaying our mission," exclaims Shamash.

"True my brother," answers Zahira, "but in order to understand the enemy we must understand the elements that surround us. There is a great evil beyond these doors we mustn't be to hasty."

"True," Shamash agrees, "so maybe theres an inconspicuous entrance in the back somewhere, despite the size of this place, it has to make allowances for the disposal of waste," exclaims Shamash.

The two head toward the back of the vast citadel. Behind is a large muddy waterfall that drops from a stream above the mountain spiraling down the hill onto the back of the building into a muddy pool below. The smell is highly putrid; nevertheless they stealthly slide along the wall of the mountain and through the murky waterfalls.

Once making it to the other side of the waterfall inside the mountain they come face to face with a dark small subtle tunnel going through. The floor of it has thick grubby water that reaches their knees. The smell is horrendous, however, they embolden themselves by holding their breath and going beneath as the water raises. They swim further down frantically looking for an opening to resurface. They eventually resurface in a small room. On looking around they notice that the outlet is for waste disposal.

Feeling around the small dark room they finally notice a small hole where more of the dingy water pours into the room. They squeeze through the hole and resurfaces, after removing a small lid, this time into a small, dark and cluttered room.

The two exits the room and come to a long dark hallway with large pillars over fifty feet in height and joining rooms to either of its sides.

Inside the corridors are decaying walls and molding floors, the smell inside remains unbearable.

The skeletal remains of warriors who tried to claim the Shard, but failed, lay scattered across the floor.

As they make their way down the long corridor, the floor squeaks and echoes throughout the structure. They walk as quietly as possible towards a small flickering light at the end of the hallway.

Whispers can be faintly heard echoing through the corridor as they move toward the flickering light.

"This language I have heard before, the calls uttered are chants of Sa'tye, the language of the Shadow beasts. It's a battle cry," exclaims Shamash. Shamash grits his teeth and declares,

"Let them come!" He then runs toward the light and cries, "I welcome the call to battle."

"Oh my goodness," Zahira sighs to herself, "Be still—," desperately calls Zahira to Shamash.

But before she can complete her warning, a blast of energy emits from one of the rooms, sending Shamash hurling through the air into the adjoining room, smashing him into the wall.

Zahira halts in her footsteps.

Again a whispering sound echoes through the corridor, gradually increasing in volume and speed: "SA'TYE SAROUCH, SA'TYE SAROOT, SA'TYE SARAT~!"

The sounds appear to close in on Zahira, as if racing towards her.

She slowly draws her sword from her back sheath. Then there is sudden silence.

Suddenly, from out of the darkness black grim figures begin to pour out as if the walls themselves opened a flood of shadows.

They race toward her with bleak red glowing eyes and sinister calls of the chant.

She manages to channel her energy through the blade of the sword and sends a bolt of pure white energy streaming through the dark cloud of figures.

The blast sends the creatures soaring through the hallways, leaving a path of faint flames that light the corridor before her.

She runs in the room over to Shamash to assess his condition.

As she approaches the room, the chant again calls: "SA'TYE SAROUCH, SA'TYE SAROOT, SA'TYE SARAT~!"

While kneeling and assisting Shamash, she slowly turns her head and looks over her shoulder to a startling image.

A glow of disfigured light approaches from the distance and consumes the darkness five feet of every progression it makes.

"Lift me up. I am able to fight," screams Shamash.

"Your condition will not allow you Shamash. I will have to confront it for now."

Zahira begins to meditate her energies in preparation to fight the unknown figure approaching them.

All of a sudden, out of the chants there is a loud explosive noise, causing the walls in the room to crack.

"Who dare disrupt my dwelling? I am the mountain of Arad Alhadad and the life of those that dwell in darkness. Have you come to steal from me?"

"Thievery?" yells Zahira, "How dare you accuse us of such. We are here to reclaim what you have stolen from the land of Azal. You took it out of greed to enhance the cosmic energies you possess, to become all-powerful and ruler of these lands. But that will not happen. I am a child of the Whitestar, and we shall reclaim what was stolen from the land of Azal! This, we will accomplish today. We will retrieve the Shard, and you will die!"

"How can this be," responds Fazeem, "A child of the Whitestar… Rathamun and his forces decimated the Azmarians. It is irrelevant, for you being the last of your people shall now end as the extinction of your race!"

"Enough!" Zahira yells.

Fazeem progresses toward her, she manages to emit a blast of energy through her sword that shrieks through Fazeem and destroys the wall behind it.

Fazeem laughs sinisterly. He then takes the form of the stature of a man.

"Your levels of cosmic energy are divergent of your foolish boast. Now witness the full recompense which is due for your error!"

Fazeem creates a bubble of energy from his hands and hurls it at Zahira.

She quickly grabs the Shamash shirt with them both barely evading the blast.

Once she lands, the dark creatures grapple her from behind, attempting to throw her to the floor.

"Hold on," Shamash yells. Zahira quickly grabs hold to a railing attached to a wall beside her, as does Shamash. He then smashes his charged fist into the floor and creates a chasm, destroying the floor beneath their feet and sending the creatures falling into an empty, endless abyss below.

Rearing back, Fazeem releases another blast, demolishing the wall Zahira and Shamash are holding on to.

As they begin to fall, they find new wall fixtures they grab hold to breaking their fall.

Zahira takes immediate action. She bolts off the side of the wall at Fazeem slicing into his energy form and landing on the flooring on the other side.

A loud shriek of pain is emitted from Fazeem.

"That sword, it burns!" he shouts.

Zahira smiles saying, "This sword was forged by the blacksmiths from the Nabatean regions. Forged from Kadmadyn and touched by the star. Refer to this blade as Nazaar, the gazer."

Another blast is fired from him, only to be blocked by her sword.

Zahira runs further between the towering pillars. She then discharges constant exchanges of energy blasts with Fazeem, but he successfully intercepts her emissions with his energy exchange.

Once finding shelter behind a pillar, she begins to access her situation.

"How can I defeat a being made of pure energy."

She noticed that she can cause him temporary pain when using the sword alone. But he recovers quickly, becoming more powerful than before.

She recalls from her training with the Muhas: "When circumstances seem to be phenomenal and unpromising, then seek the least solution to your dilemma."

As she meditates on these words, her countenance begins to change. The glow of energy that surrounded her dissipates.

Zahira lifts her sword and slowly steps from behind the pillar to confront her adversary.

"I see the rat has come from the darkness in order to once again nibble at death. Your scurrying has ended. Your shelter will not conceal you from the coming judgement that awaits you. Prepare to die!"

Without acknowledging a word of his boasting, Zahira charges at him, leaping into his bosom, plunging her sword forward and leaving it inbeded inside him.

Fazeem squirms, pulling desperately at the sword as energy shoot to every corner of the citadel. Eventually an explosion erupts and sends her flying into one of the pillars.

Large amounts of energy disrupt, lighting the entire citadel.

A very loud scream is heard throughout the corridors of the mountain and the large pillars start to collapse. Her sword eventually shoots from the exploding Fazeem into the floor. Running over to dislodge it and after many attempts finally pulls it from the floor.

Zahira runs to retrieve Shamash, who was finishing up slaying the dark shadow beasts. They run toward the flickering light seen earlier upon their entrance to the cavern; and there lay the Shard.

They retrieve it and flee the crumbling fortress by way of an underground tunnel that leads outside.

CHAPTER 24

The Uncovering of Nazaar

Because of their injuries, Zahira decides to set up camp for a few days before returning on the journey back to Azal. The road back will be long, and they will need all their strength to make the journey home.

"I can't explain what happened back there," Shamash states in shame, "I was caught off guard . . . If I would have seen that blast coming . . . well, you know me, I would have . . ."

"Shamash, there is no need to explain anything. We were both caught off guard. You are a powerful warrior, we just didn't really know what to expect."

"How were you able to defeat him Zahira?"

"He was energy and unless I was able to match or overmatch his energy level, my attacks would have no effect. I realize that my powers are still developing. Using the sword Nazaar, I suppressed my power and used it alone."

Zahira gazes at the sword and exclaims,

"This blade is very special, a bit more to it then the Muqarahein alluded to."

Shamash glances at Zahira with endearing eyes and a warm smile, and commends her like an older brother would,

"You've done well Zahira."

After thirty five days of travel they finally arrive back in Azal. Zahira approaches the council of Muhas and returns the Shard to its rightful owners.

"The courage and strategic skills you displayed has resulted in a successful mission. Congratulations." Ahura commends, "Let us celebrate your safe return and the safe return of our prized possession."

As the council disperses Ahura stays behind and Zahira inquires of him,

"Excuse me, Muqarahein. May I have a word with you?"

"Of course you may." Ahura responds, "What is it you wish to ask?"

"There was something more to this sword." Zahira exclaims, "It alone must have defeated the creature. I must know how it was possible without using my powers to assist it."

"My child, he was a product of the element he stole. He added it to his own power to become even more powerful. If the opposite element is reunited with him in his enhanced form, it will prove to be an aversion to him and will disperse his energy—"

"The blade I had was the opposite element," gleefully interrupts Zahira, "a negative piece of the Shard in which he stole. It, in effect, became his allergy."

"That is correct." Ahura smiles, "The blade possesses similar elements in which his new form was made of, with some opposing properties. Not only was it his power formation, but it also proved to be his downfall in the end. The mission was not meant to test the powers of the Whitestar, which you possess. This time it tested your physical and mental abilities, abilities that will preserve you alive, even if outmatched by an adversary possessing more power than yours. Quite simple, your use of common sense.

You must keep in mind Zahira, though you possess the power of your people combined, these powers remain latent and only a portion makes itself manifest when forced. Many of your past tests that you have embarked upon constantly calculate your power, pulling it further from remission. The fullest extent of its power can only be harnessed once fully matured. When this will happen, again, I have not the answer. But it shall come when you face that evil that powerful enough to do so."

Ahura smiles and looks unwaveringly into Zahira's brown eyes and says,

"Come, my child. Let us celebrate, for there is much to be joyful about."

During the festivities, Salasa pulls Zahira aside to speak on pressing matters. She states,

"Zahira, I am so glad you have returned. I have missed you dearly. But I really must speak with you."

They move to a secluded area and Salasa falls upon Zahira's neck hugging her tightly and exclaims,

"It has been three years since we talked about returning to Naldamak. I have become desperate. I need to see my family. There is no place for me here. I do not belong."

Zahira asks, "To be one that talks a lot you sure do hold a lot in?"

"I feared that if I expressed my true feelings that you would not want my friendship anymore. I could not chance losing that. It is the only thing that has prevented me from going insane here."

Zahira soflty pulls back from Salasa so that she can look into her eyes. She then places her hand on Salasa's shoulder and says,

"Our friendship was and never will be in question, Salasa. You do not have to share my desires to remain my friend. Did I not say many years ago that we share a bond that will never be broken? That statement holds true today and always will."

"If what you say is true, then return to Naldamak with me." Salasa states with tears pouring from her eyes, "We need not stay long. A brief moment is all I ask to make sure that all is well. We can leave while the festivities distract everyone. By the time we are missed we will be well on our way."

"Kimoni will be incensed when he finds we are gone Salasa." Zahira moans, "He has already been informed in the past of our talk about taking such a long journey and has warned me not to see these plans through."

"He was probably informed by that sniveling little Tegene," Salasa murmurs, "but what will be done to us? Are we not adults now, able to make our own decisions in life? He cannot hold us back. Please Zahira. You long to see your mother, do you not? Come with me."

Salasa pauses for a moment and then gallantly states,

"But if I must make this journey without you, then I will."

As Salasa turns to leave, Zahira hesitantly stops her and says, "Wait, Salasa . . . you will not go alone . . . I will go with you."

Salasa embraces Zahira overjoyed with tears flowing.

"Thank you. There are no words to express the joy in my heart this day."

While the compound indulges in the festivities, Zahira and Salasa quickly head back to their room and prepare their belongings. They then quietly saddle up two cammels and make their way to the Waters of Al Qalzam awaiting the ferryman on their long journey back to Naldamak.

CHAPTER 25

Pain and Loss

Upon returning to Naldamak, Salasa and Zahira shockingly find what appears to be a desolate wasteland.

"Zahira, have the many years away affected our sense of direction? This certainly is not the land of our childhood." Laments Salasa.

"Something is wrong Salasa." Zahira states, "I don't believe we've taken the wrong route."

They progress further towards their tribal village and notice that the homes are broken down and charred.

When closer, it finally becomes evident that the village had been demolished sometime ago by fire. The ground is covered with a carpet of burnt sand. They both dismount their camels and run over to get a closer look.

Walking among the ruins they see skeletons of family and friends scattered throughout and broken.

"Zahira, this can not be. I refuse to believe this." cries Salasa, "We must certainly have lost our way."

"If only that was true," Zahira laments with tears flowing from her eyes, "my sense of direction has always been one of my greatest strengths. This most certainly was the camp of our people."

Suddenly Salasa becomes motionless. Her heart starts to pound so that she wonders if Zahira can hear it.

Terror is present in her eyes as she looks around at the numerous piles of bones. She soon notices something shining on one of them.

186

She walks over and picks it up. She brushes off the ash and is startled. She recognizes the shining article. It is a hair ornament that belonged to her mother. Tears flow unceasingly from Salasa's eyes. She clutches the article in her hand and brings it to her bosom. At that moment, she cries out as if someone had plunged a dagger into her breast. Zahira runs to her side,

"Salasa! What has happened? What is that in your hand?"

Salasa looks into Zahira's eyes and begins to tremble.

"They're dead! My family is dead," she screams.

Zahira opens Salasa's hand and sees the hair ornament.

"It belonged to my mother," Salasa stutters. "She wore it all the time."

All of a sudden the tears in Salasa's eyes turn into flames of rage. She slowly turns to face Zahira.

"This is your fault. If we had left when I wanted to leave the first time we could have been here to help them. They suffered at the hands of those that were searching for you!"

Zahira reply, "If we were here for a certainty we would have shared the same fate. Your family knew this and that is why they allowed you to come with me."

Salasa screams, "I would rather have died at their side than stand over their remains alive!"

"Salasa, I feel your pain, but you must remember that my mother was here as well . . . you are not the only one that has lost."

Tears run down Zahira's cheeks. She than cry out saying,

"Please do not lay fault at my feet. I am not responsible for who I am. I too have suffered a loss, but I have suffered more than you have. My people, the people I come from, were annihilated at the hands of these evil beings that did this. An entire race was decimated. The privilege of learning from them personally was taken away from me. And now, now I have lost the only family I have ever known. My pain goes much deeper. I have lost twice as much, if not more."

Zahira's words cut at Salasa's heart.

"Forgive me, Zahira. I know you have suffered, too. The shock and pain of losing my family have caused me to speak harshly. I—"

"There is nothing to forgive," interrupts Zahira. "Pain makes us speak hurtful things at times. But what has happened can do nothing but strengthen our bond yet more."

As the reality of what has happened begins to sink deeper, Salasa falls to her knees and buries her face in her hands.

Zahira kneels beside Salasa and embraces her in her arms. Here they remain, holding each other.

A couple of hours go by bringing in the night sky. They decide to set up camp on the outskirts of what is left of their former home.

Salasa's cries of pain and sorrow continue until she exhausts herself finally falling asleep.

When she is sure Salasa has fallen asleep, Zahira returns to the decimated camp to search for the remains of her mother.

Her search is a long one, for there are many skeletons and singed clothing scattered across the village.

As Zahira continues her search, she comes across a gold band resting peacefully on a pile of ashes.

She kneels down beside it, discovering it still on the skeletal remains of its owner.

She removes the band to examine it, her eyes narrowing as she recognizes the markings engraved. She starts to tremble as it becomes evident as to where she last remembered seeing the band.

The day Romana informed her of her journey, she wore this band. She can see her mother's out-stretched arms as she summoned Zahira to her tent.

The tears begin to flow from Zahira's eyes.

"Oh mama, I'm so sorry I was not here for you. I am the reason you suffered such a fate." Laments Zahira.

Zahira puts the band on her finger and rises to her feet.

"I will avenge your death, mama. I will not rest until I have brought those guilty of this atrocity to a vicious end."

As Zahira rummages through her mother's remains near her home, looking for anything she can salvage, she comes across a squeaky part of the ground. She steps on it again and it cracks. She quickly kneels down and starts to rub the sand and dirt from off it to reveal a wooden trap door buried in the ground. It's locked so she breaks it open with her sword. To her surprise she finds inside an old leather wrapping. When she opens it she finds five sheets of expensive parchment decorated intricately with red and yellow markings. Written on them are ancient Azmarian writings. It speaks of a weapon possessing the power to annihilate an army of Blackdust users alone, only if activated by its rightful owner. It also speaks of companions who will aid her in finding this weapon and other pertinent information.

She quickly wraps the parchments neatly back into the leather wrapping and places it up under her arm. She then digs a grave and buries her mother's remains alone with Salasa's parents as well.

She looks at the grave made and sheds her final tear. She then returns to Salasa to find her still sleeping. Zahira makes a palate beside her and lies there until sleep finally overtakes her as well.

CHAPTER 26

The Restitution

The morning sun rise high into the sky. Zahira rubs the sleep from her eyes as the morning sun sends a warm beam across her face.

She turns to see if Salasa is still asleep, only to find her gone.

She leaves the tent and looks around vigilantly for her, but sees her no where. It finally occurs to her to return to the demolished village.

Upon arriving, she finds Salasa lying beside the grave of her mother Zahira made. She kneels down beside her to comfort her saying,

"Salasa, it is time we return to Azal, there we will find the strength needed to cope. The longer we stay, the harder it will be to leave."

"I am home," Salasa abruptly replies. "There is no place for me in Azal. The Muhas gratify the male species. I am only a woman there, with no special abilities. I would serve no purpose there. I will stay and die here. Leave me to grieve, Zahira."

"Do not speak of dying, Salasa. You cannot stay here. What purpose would you serve here? The land is a desolate waste. There is no sufficient food. In your state of mind, you will be dead in a matter of days. Pain can make one say and do illogical things. Return to Azal with me. The Muhas will assist you in dealing with our loss."

"The control you possess is one to be admired, Zahira." responds Salasa, "I am weak mentally and emotionally, I would only be a disgrace to the Muhas. They will see me as unworthy to spit upon."

Zahira begins to lose patience with Salasa's self pity and replies, "If you want pity you will no longer receive it from me. I have experienced a loss, too, or have you forgotten? The pain I have is deep in my bones. But I see the need to keep my senses about me. Nothing more we can do, we have to go back. We cannot stay here."

There is silence for a moment and then Salasa returns to her feet.

"Your words are harsh, Zahira."

"You know that's not my aim Salasa." Answers Zahira.

Salasa looks up into the sky and sighs,

"I wish I possessed your strength, Zahira. You honor not only your mother, but your ancestors as well. What pains me is not just that my family is gone, but that I am alone now. It frightens me.

Zahira puts her hand on Salasa's shoulder and gazes at her with comforting eyes.

"You will never be alone. I am your family. The bond we have is so strong that death itself could not break it. And even if there should be a physical separation, we will always be together in our hearts."

Salasa embraces Zahira tightly crying mornfully.

"I am grateful to have you as a friend. Only a friend such as you would continue to tolerate my foolish ways. Thank you."

CHAPTER 27

A New Hope

The journey back to Azal proves to be longer than the journey to Naldamak. The young women decide to take this time to enjoy each other's company, knowing that upon returning to Azal, Zahira's time would be focused on her intensive training.

When Zahira and Salasa finally reach the shores of Azal, they are met by Taye, Tahro, Tegene and Zere who are camped there waiting to cross the sea.

"Where have the two of you been," Tegene demands of them hysterically. "We have searched high and low for you. Kimoni has been through fits at your sudden departure. Do you not know that it's been over thirty days since the two of you went missing? You will indeed experience his wrath when he lays eyes on you."

At that moment Zahira sees Kimoni running towards them.

The words Tegene had spoken are indeed true; for when Kimoni reaches them his eyes are blood red with anger.

Kimoni glares at Zahira and Salasa as if daggers are in his eyes.

He screams, "You were commanded not to leave the compound! You defied my orders! You endangered not only your life, but the life of Salasa as well. This is an outrage! What were you thinking? Have you gone insane . . . its been thirty days since your disappearance, can you not imagine the upheaval you caused all in Azal?"

As Kimoni rages on, Ahura approaches and calmly asks, "Zahira, you have returned. Where did you go my child? You should have informed us of your trip."

"She was instructed not to leave," screams Kimoni.

"Kimoni now is not the time for your angry words," Zahira patiently interjects. "I need to tell—"

"You do not know the fear that went through my bones while you were gone on probably some foolish expedition," interrupts Kimoni. "I am incensed! I am outraged!"

Zahira then respectfully replies,

"Kimoni, I am grateful you care about my well being, but I must remind you that I am no longer a child. I am no longer your responsibility. You are relieved of your duties to look after me. My well being is my concern now. What perils come my way will be for me to endure. I have—"

"They're dead!" abruptly cries Salasa, interrupting Zahira's explanation, "Our families are dead!"

Salasa falls to her knees, crying feverishly. She looks up at Kimoni and continues,

"The camp lay in chard ruins. All around us were the chard remains of our people. The stench of death lingered in the air. So you silence your tongue, Kimoni! The only reason Zahira agreed to journey with me is because I threatened to go with or without her!"

"Our journey was not out of rebellion," continues Zahira, "but concern for those we left behind. I was able to locate my mother's remains, this trip was meant for me to take, it had to be, because under the ground where my mothers home use to be I found these rolled up parchments with an inscription written in the Azmarian tongue. It speaks of a weapon that can bring peace to the world if operated by a child of the Whitestar or misery if operated by a child of the Blackstar. It is in the land of Tanirta, protected by the Tanazart."

Ahura is moved by her discovery, he then asks, "And now you wish to go in search for that weapon?"

"Yes Muqarahein." Zahira answers with surety in her voice.

Knowledge of the deaths of the Beshari leaves Kimoni and his comrades speechless. Tears slowly start to run down their cheeks.

Kimoni laments, "Tafari was like a father to me. He took me under his wing when my parents died."

"This would explain the uneasy feeling I felt before leaving Naldamak," interjects Tegene, "I knew something terrible would happen to them."

"Their deaths will not be in vain," cries Zahira. "I will find the weapon, and I will return to the lands overtaken by this Blackstar that calls itself Rathamun. I will avenge those that died this senseless and horrid death. Rathamun will pay a heavy price for his wicked and vicious actions."

"Have you planned your journey, child," asks Ahura.

"I have." Zahira responds, "According to these writings left by my mother I must take a long journey to the north across to the great continent and pass through the land of Kemet, through the land of Batheria into Zehuma, the realm of the Zehumians and finally Tinitra. Tinitra is where the Koryan is said to reside. This is the destiny I have been chosen for."

"Who will accompany you on this journey?" asks Ahura.

Zahira glances back at the parchment instructions, she then answers, "According to the writings here, I will meet with two champions of the White Dust who will assist me in my journey back to Azmaria. They were chosen specifically by my father, for they too long for peace in the cities of Light and they seek to bring the reign of Rathamun to an end."

Before Zahira can utter another word, Shamash, who was also at the encampment with Kimoni and his men approach the meeting and shouts out, "I shall go with you. Battle and adventure is what I crave! I shall be your companion on this grand quest."

"To desert you now after many years of looking out for your well being would be the action of a coward," exclaims Zere. "I will accompany you as well; for I have experienced loss and desire to avenge the deaths of those taken away from us."

Taye, Tahro and Tegene also agree to accompany Zahira.

Kimoni approaches Zahira and admiringly gazes at her.

"I know you are no longer a child. But you are like a daughter to me and I wish no harm to come to you. I know I over-stepped my bounds and I need to release my grasp. It is your destiny. Go and establish peace upon the land. But know that I will accompany you as well."

"The time has come," laments Ahura. "It is time for Rathamun to relinquish the kingdoms he holds captive! The Chosen one will deal him a mighty blow . . . come, child."

Ahura now walks back to the tent he stayed in and brought back out of it a satchel. He approach Zahira and opens it, inside is the Shard she reclaimed from Fazeem. After handing it to her he states,

"Your abilities will be enhanced if you possess the Shard. Join it with the Koryan and with it the finality of your matured powers; you will be able to face the feared Rathamun."

Ahura then gives her further instructions, "First, you are to head to Bahat just ten miles from here and find the Mabinti Ya Bahati, the Daughters of Destiny. They will be able to direct you more precisely than the written instructions you received. They know of your coming and have waited even before your birth. During the crescent moon of your birthday they sung songs of your coming, 'the dawn of the female knight'. They are the age of your great grandfather, but this you will not know for their skin is as smooth as an infant's; their eyes are as sharp as a falcon's and their hair black as ebony.

The power of the star has given unto them unnatural long life. Seek them out in Bahat and they shall answer further questions to your quest and they will give you a gift that will help in your travels."

After that all of them pack up and head back to the confines of the school. On arriving it is night, the trip back takes two days. Zahira and Salasa quickly head to their home. Zahira enters Salasa's room to speak of her departure,

"How are you feeling?" Zahira asks.

"Despite everything that has happened, I am holding my own. I have not completely fallen apart." Salasa laments.

Zahira continues saying, "That is good to hear. You know of the journey I must take."

"Yes . . . I've heard." Salasa answers with her head held low.

"I will have to leave you once again." Zahira exclaims, "It is not possible to take you with me, but I will return for you once I have reclaimed the kingdoms from Rathamun. I promise. I will return for you."

"I know you will. You have never let me down, at least entirely. I will wait for you." Laments Salasa.

Zahira kisses her on the head and says, "I will leave you now. You need your rest. Goodnight, Salasa." Zahira then leaves into the larger living room.

Looking out of the window into the night sky she heaves a heavy sigh. Now alone she turns around and looks peculiarly at the deer skin carpeted floor. She then drops to her face, prostrating in deep prayer, to the one God that was taught to her when but a girl, the new understanding of this one that gradually increases throughout the lands. She starts to pray deep and hard, but her voice starts to shake. Sweat poors from her head, fearful of this one powerful being, unsure as if he even notices her. She finally collects her thoughts and respectfully prays,

"I have never prayed to you before, for the understanding of you in our land we are still learning, thus, I don't know how. The mystery of you even tests the knowledge of the Muhas. However, your greatness is seen throughout all creation and in time mankind will learn the proper way of worship to you and only you. I wish to see that day, where man will no longer prostrate to gods made of altered flesh but will worship you alone.

I long to see that day, when the knowledge of you will permeate our minds and hearts and we start to live our lives accordingly to the laws you have provided. Though, if I do not live to see that day, do accept my obeisance to you now, for I do fear and love you. For your signs abound with your glory and majesty, all acts of worship belongs to you and you alone.

I beg that you see us safely on this trip, and provide me the necessary courage and strength to undergo the trial that face me. This along with all that I have encountered are merely tests and I would presume that they are lessons for me to learn by so that you will become dearer to me in harmony with that I give for its sake of sacrifice and burden. Those that live by worthless beliefs and the fear of the dust users, which requires no sacrifice from them will not delay to dispose of their beliefs at the first sign of hardship, this I have seen with my own eyes. So, it is the personal price that I must pay so that this belief in you becomes dear and priceless in my heart before it becomes dear to the hearts of anyone else. Guide me and protect me . . . all of us. Please."

After that, she rises to her feet and head back over to the window, she then declares,

"I will not return to this land until I have avenged the death of my people, by your willing great deity. Your days are numbered Rathamun. I will bring you to your knees and bring an end to your sadistic rule."

CHAPTER 28

The Daughters of Destiny

After a few days, Zahira and her band of warriors leave Azal with many supplies, hardy camels and blessings from Ahura and the other Muhas.

They travel for a sum of fifteen days, camping every night and rising the following morning to journey until the next night, covering many miles.

Finally, they reached the region of Bahat. Bahat is a wooded small region on a flat terrain. They set up camp near an abandoned cave that night and enjoyed the company of one another, talking and eating cooked rabbit over a warm camp fire. Soon faint noises of people struggling can be heard in the distance of the forest.

Shamash rise intent on finding out the source of the distant commotion.

"Do you hear that?" he mutters looking into the dark forest.

"I do." Zahira replies.

"Perhaps it is the Bahati." remarks Taye.

Kimoni slowly stands and says, "It sound like women crying, and men laughing."

Zahira and her companions gird their weapons and creep towards the direction of the sounds. Taye is left behind to watch their supplies and camels.

On arriving to the source of noise they can see a burning campfire in a cleared out space of the forest. They also notice what looks to be over thirty men dressed in dirty rags behaving strangely, performing some form of tribal dance.

The men rejoice, dancing in the night around the small camp fire over their captured prizes, ten young women, all later identified as the Mabinti Ya Bahati, Daughters of Destiny, the very ones Zahira and her friends were instructed to find. The women are tied to trees with thick ropes encircling the fire they face. They tremble feverishly as sweat pours from their faces like buckets of water.

Zahira and the others observe the men running over to the captured women, grabbing them by their hair and kissing them insatiably. Afterwards, the will spit on their faces and slap them, all the while laughing and singing songs of foul romanticism.

Hiding behind the dense foliage and cringing in anger, Zahira and her companions watch in horror as the women's frantic cry for help at long last simmers down due to exhaustion. Zahira plans her strategy to help the women, but Shamash patience is wearing thin.

The leader of the sadistic men starts to announce loudly in a hissing voice, "We have women, the Bahati. We will breed and become more, possessing their powers of foresight. We will lust and bathe in their bosoms!"

The men look toward the sky and bellow to the moon. They strip the rags from their bodies and dance naked around the women, laughing and harassing them over and over again.

One of the men crawls up onto one of the women and forces her mouth open with his hands. He then places his face right before hers; and when he opens his mouth three intertwined serpent tongues slither out, licking her face.

Just before he puts his tongues into her mouth a large scimitar comes hurling through the air from the forest plunging into his back. Fluid from his mouth spurts into her face as he slides to the ground dead.

The men scurry around frantically, trying to ascertain the nature of the attack. Again another attack is made, this time with arrows flying from the darkness, each hitting a different man.

The enraged men scream amongst themselves, scampering for their clothing and beating their chest.

Suddenly, Shamash, followed by the others, emerges from the darkness with their battle cry.

In a blind fury Shamash runs in severing heads and body limbs. He then approaches three larger ones, slicing one in his side while kicking another in the abdomen. Immediately he withdraws his weapon and hacks into the shoulder of the one he kicked.

The third man runs toward him with a large spiked club, screeching deliriously.

Shamash falls to the ground and rolls toward the attacker, causing him to lose his footing and crash to the ground.

Shamash then stands over the fallen creature and plunges his long dagger into his back, pinning him to the ground.

The others fight just as well, cutting the creatures down to the earth. Zahira quickly runs over to the tree bound women and cuts them loose. She then leads the women toward a path leading out of the woods.

She calls out to Shamash and the others, "Come, we must go now, something is not right here."

The others relinquish their fight and quickly follow her. As for Shamash, reluctant he pulls away and follows still lusting for combat.

As they run through the forest, growling and eerie cries can be heard echoing behind them.

The women of the Bahati scream in a panic as they clumsily run behind Zahira with the others serving as a shield from their pursuers.

Kimoni then commands his men to get the women out of the area, while Shamash, Zahira, and he stand behind to keep the approaching danger at bay.

"Go! Do not wait for us," screams Zahira to the men, anticipating another attack by the pursuing creatures.

Zahira readies her sword and positions herself next to Shamash and Kimoni while awaiting the enemy.

By now dawn starts to gradually ascend and a faint light attempts to pierce the denseness of the forest.

When the pursuers finally catch up to Zahira and the other two, the odds prove staggering. Now the enemy has tripled in number, there appears to be at least a hundred men racing in from the forest.

They no longer bear the resemblance of men, but now have taken on the appearance of beasts, half man, half beast, beasts of an unexplained nature. They progress towards the warriors with some swinging from the trees while others ran on foot.

Shamash shouts boldly, "Fight! Fight! Intoxicate yourselves with the drink of battle . . . let them come and taste cold steal."

With that the three warriors brace themselves and are back to back awaiting the charging horde. However, Shamash anxious for combat breaks the formation and runs right into the charging horde, slicing into the lead creature and severing him in two.

The other two stand and brace as the beast run right into them. Soon a vicious fight ensues.

With great speed the three slaughter a great number.

With every swing and thrust of their weapons bones crack, flesh tears, and blood spills.

A fury never before seen amongst Zahira and her companions comes upon them like a black shadow.

Shamash, the strongest, uses two swords with great skill and precision.

One beast runs to him and meet his sword with its chest, while another run into another blade with its head.

Shamash pulls the weapon from the skull of one dead creature and swings it behind him, hacking into a creature's neck that had attacked from behind.

Many that comes upon him he pulls his sword from each slain victim only to meet a new.

Eventually, many of the creatures charge into him knocking him onto the ground. They pile upon him like a large heap mound. While beneath the pile the energies inside him become operative by his savage rage.

Then suddenly, the crowd of attackers burst off of him like an explosion. His energies begin to activate through the bands he wear upon his wrist. There he stands with his eyes glowing intensely, free of the mob that engulfed him.

This battle continues for hours when finally Shamash, in a berserk rage cries out, "Die you blood sucking maggots!"

However, Zahira can see that Kimoni is starting to tire substantially. Even though he is a great warrior he is only human and the reality of his age begins to encroach upon him.

Though the beasts are not very skilled fighters, their sheer numbers causes strain on Zahira and her companions. Later Tegene, Tahro and Zere join Zahira and the others after leaving the women with Taye. Hearing the commotion Taye met the men at the end of the forest with the camels and supplies.

The numbers of the creatures grow and grow, pressing in hard on the warriors. Zahira is now concerned that they will not be able to continue to ward off this relentless attack. Even she begins to tire out and fight clumsily. Just when it looks as if Zahira and her group are about to fall the sun make itself fully evident in the sky right above the forest. Its mighty rays pierce through the trees, speckling the grass floor of the forest.

Suddenly the creatures begin to cry out loudly and then run for shelter from the growing sunlight, disappearing into caves and hill crevices.

After the beast leave the area, Zahira and her companions fall to the earth totally exhausted. They are baffled over the sudden retreat of the creatures.

Amazingly, no one is seriously harmed but all suffers from scratches from the beast claws.

"Are you ok," Zahira asks the others.

Zere quickly replies, "We're fine Zahira. We will make it."

They now leave the battle area and head out of the forest towards the direction where Taye and the Bahati women were. When meeting up with them Taye runs toward them anxiously stating,

"I didn't know if I should have stayed or join you."

"You did what you were told . . . and that is what was expected of you," the exhausted Kimoni replies.

Zahira stumbles over to the ten women that sit huddled together by the fire, shivering from the night's ordeal. She kneels down and sits beside them. She then assures the women,

"Whatever it is we can do for you, please, do not hesitate to ask."

"No, you have done plenty," one of the women responds. We are indebted to you."

Immediately one of the women notices a piece of Zahira's stark white hair from under her scarf, she then rises excitingly saying, "It is her! It is her!"

The others rise as well; their eyes open wide and pointing at Zahira with excitement.

"It can't be. After all these years the light has finally come to our land. Are you not the daughter of King Zada, once ruler of Azmaria and prince of the Whitestar?"

Zahira humbly rises and nods in agreement.

"Finally," screams another, "you have come and now the land shall see light once again."

Attempting to explain the purpose of her and her companions, Zahira begins to open her mouth when she is interrupted by one of the women.

"You need not tell us why you are here, for we know. Ahura has sent you to us. You were commissioned to come here and receive information pertaining to your travels. Listen well young Star, for there is much to tell regarding your journey."

After that Zahira, Shamash, Kimoni and the others all sit and begin a lengthy discussion about the many dangers that they will confront on their journey.

After many hours, the head of the Bahati women gives her final statement concerning their safe travel saying,

"The route given to you by your father is the safest route for your journey. Do not deviate from it by any means, for you will put yourself in harms way. The champions will not receive you well from the start, but soon your mark within will shine bright and will speak for you. When you reach the land of the Tanazart do beware. Their passion is strong towards evil and may believe you to be the very evil you wish to destroy, but know this, they will be your greatest allies in the fight against the Blackstar, only if you are able to win their allegiance and trust."

Kimoni humbly interrupts asking, "Zahira will be victorious once she gains control of this Koryan and face Rathamun, right?"

The head of the Bahati looks directly into Zahira's eyes and answers slowly, "Rathamun has grown wickedly powerful. Do not be overconfident in your gifts for only with the aid of the Koryan may you face him. But it is possible that you will not destroy him . . . or even you may lose your own life."

"Then we are walking Zahira to her possible death." Shamash abruptly interrupts.

The Bahati responds, "Possibly. But know this; such a sacrifice will not be in vain. If she dies, then he will die as well, they are connected. The power of the Koryan and Whitestar together will bring the Blackstar to an end along with them."

Shamash rises and places a blanket around the shoulders of Zahira who is intently listening to the women, for the air grow chilled with the setting of the sun.

Shamash then grunts, "So, in order to destroy the Blackstar she must die? I welcome death, but I do not bring my joy for the afterlife to my companions. I am with you Zahira, no matter what you decide . . . yes, even if it means my death in your behalf, for I will not allow you to taste it . . . not yet."

Zahira smiles and pats Shamash's knee without saying a word, but remains in deep thought.

The head Bahati then states, "We will now take our leave and wish many blessings upon you and your journey. But before we go there is a gift that we are to give you, sweet princess."

She then walks over to Zahira and gently places her hands upon Zahira's head.

Suddenly, light begins to flash from both Zahira and the Bahati's eyes, with both momentarily becoming still as statues. Zahira's companions rise in awe over the transfiguration.

After the brief ordeal they both return to the way they were. The Bahati states, "I have given you the fluent gift of the Azmarian tongue, your people language."

"Zahira already knows Azmarian," states Kimoni. The Bahati answers, "what we have given her is the ability to understand the Azmarian dialect that preceeds your father and his father. It is a language now dead but will be needed once you confront the riddle of the Whitestar."

Zahira rubs her forehead confused over what just took place.

The Bahati face takes on a serious nature and she warns.

"Know this Zahira, the power of the stars carry with them a riddle, you must learn their riddle Zahira you must know it, for only with this knowledge shall you be victorious."

The women then rise and bid them all a farewell.

"Is that it?" Ask Shamash with disappointment in his voice. "That is what we fought so diligently to hear?"

Kimoni then concerningly addresses the Bahati women, "Will you be ok? Danger still lurks here."

"Worry not for us for we will find our deliverance." They reply, "They will not come here any more. They have sensed the presence of the Whitestar and are now deathly afraid of it."

"What were they and what did they want with you," Tegene asks.

The Bahati answers, "They are the 'Majoka Wanaume', the serpent men. They wanted the energies within us, feeling that if they copulated with us, we might pass our gift on to them and their offspring."

With that The Bahati women once again bid their farewells and leave. Zahira has much to think about and many burdens she carries.

After that they are quick to bed, for the next morning they will continue their journey, first to the town of Ruheiba.

CHAPTER 29

The Forgotten Stallion

Rising that morning, they set out on their long journey to the flourishing town of Ruheiba, a five day trek from Bahat. It is night when they arrive. They set up camp outside of the market-square tying their camels.

When morning breaks, they head toward the small market-square to purchase goods for their travels. They buy fresh fruits, new baggage and replenish their water reserves, a most precious commodity.

They then head back to their camels and begin to pack up for their next destination. On their way back they are spotted by a merchant wearing a turban and an expensive robe in the square that follows closely behind.

"Your camels look tired," the merchant yells out to Zahira and her companions.

"They are tired. But we shall rest and allow them time to regain strength." responds Zahira.

"The way you and your companions are stacking, it looks as if you are headed quite some distance," replies the merchant.

No one utters a word, only nodding in agreement as they continue to prepare for departure. Persistent the merchant states,

"Let me introduce myself. I am Sazzid. I have lived here for about ten years. I am well known for having good merchandise, whether it is frankincense, myrrh, silk from the orient and genuine cotton, the

finest to be found. I have the best of what you need, and I think I have
something that could greatly benefit travelers of your kind."

Looking around suspiciously to see if they are being followed he
whispers, "Are you bandits?"

"Bandits," abruptly yells Shamash. "We are from noble blood,
you insolent dog!"

"My apologies, large one," quickly apologizes Sazzid, "come
to think of it . . . that blade you carry does resemble Sabaean
craftsmanship. The term bandit was only used to describe the small
war-like band of travelers, which would—"

"Silence fool," yells Shamash. "We wish not to entertain your
snake tongue. Ask what you wish and be silent . . . or silenced."

Sazzid casually looks around Shamash's broad shoulders and
address Zahira sayin, "I have something that could benefit you
greatly on your journeys . . . a Quaggia."

"Quaggia?" Shamash asks puzzling.

"Yes, large one, a Quaggia." Smiles Sazzid, "the young lady
knows exactly what I am referring to."

"I've never heard of them . . . you Zahira?" Shamash asks Zahira.

Zahira remains silent,

"Quaggias," she thinks to herself. "These are the stallions upon
which my people once rode in the time of their being. Can it be that
one of these stallions that far exceeded the speed, strength, and
endurance of camels or horses still exist? I remember reading they
were the life-line of my people."

"Come with me, all of you," utters Sazzid. "I shall show you the
legendary Quaggia of the plains."

Although wary of his intentions, they equip themselves and follow
the merchant to his home.

After walking one mile outside the town-square, they finally come
upon bushy terrain littered with small baked clay homes sporadically
arranged in the vicinity.

As they come closer to Sazzid's home they can hear the sound of
stumping and trotting, followed by the vigorous snorting of a horse.

"Wow," Sazzid laughs, "he has never acted like that before, whats going on back there."

Zahira pauses and falls to her knees, as if losing all strength. Sazzid turns and smiles at her realizing her sudden emotional state. He states,

"You, my friend, seem to have a natural awareness of this beautiful beast. Come, for what you are feeling right now will only be enhanced once you have actually seen this creature."

As they continue, Zahira remains on her knees. Shamash continues to press forward with Sazzid, while the others remain with Zahira, inquiring of her behavior.

Shamash follows Sazzid into his home. They head to the back of the house and Sazzid opens the back door facing his gated back yard. To his astonishment, before Shamash stands a large white stallion, perfect in appearance. He is striped like a zebra from his head to his shoulders, large wide striping. The remaining half of his body from shoulders to tale is completely white with no striping. He possesses a sleak and muscular build. His mane is very short and bristly and he has a large muscular head with wide nostrils.

"This is the last known stallion from the city of Sagala in the land of Azmaria." States Sazzid, "There are none like him today. He—"

But before Sazzid can finish his statement, the great animal gives out a loud snort and rakes the earth with his front hooves. He then looks up eyeing both Shamash and Sazzid intently.

"Oh boy," warns Sazzid. "He never did this before. Asaryn looks—"

No sooner does he utter those words, the stallion gallops toward the men with great speed as if charging into combat.

Sazzid leaps out of the way where Shamash keeps his stance, as if challenging the stallion, but the stallion does not falter in his gallop, causing Shamash to evade his progression at the last minute.

He gallops through the house madly towards the front door, knocking over tables and other things inside. When exiting the front door of Sazzid's home, he lowers his head and gleefully trots outside, as if celebrating his freedom.

He soon spots Zahira and races over to her. Kimoni and the other men bare arms to confront the horse but Zahira tell's them to let him by. He trots past her companions slowing his gait when approaching Zahira who is still kneeling and gives a mellow snort to her head. He then gently lays his powerful muzzle upon her shoulder, relaxed and satisfied.

Zahira rises to gently embrace the large stallion's neck.

"I can't believe what I am seeing." exclaims Shamash baffled over the experience.

Sazzid smiles and states in reply, "Oh believe it big guy, these two are bonded. The Azmarians once used these horses long ago in their wars. These horses carry a special link with them and only found amongst them."

"How did you know Zahira was Azmarian?" grunts Shamash.

"Ummm, let's see," replies Sazzid in a cynicial manner, "I don't see any other young women her age with a head full of white hair. I could see some of it sticking from under that nice gray scarf she is wearing."

"Well then, she likes the horse, lets talk business . . . seeing that's why you brought us here." states Shamash.

Shamash and Sazzid join the others.

"It looks as if he has already taken a liking to you Miss . . ." Sazzid ask coyly.

"Zahira." She softly replies while still rubbing the Stallions neck.

"Oh yes, Miss Zahira. Do you like him?" Sazzid ask.

"Like is an understatement, Mr. Sazzid. He is wonderful." Zahira replies.

Sazzid then states while rubbing his hand, "Then I guess you would not mind owning such a beauty."

Zahira remains silent.

"Now, I am a businessman." Sazzid continues, "I make honest money while providing you with a product you will benefit from. He is a fine steed as you can see. He was brought to me by a group of children who befriended him in the hills of Afa, far northwest into Batheria. Well, at least this is what they told me. I bought him for a good price off the little ones and sent them away with plenty of money to help their poor families. I can see you like him, and it looks as if Asaryn likes you as well. Ummm . . . are you carrying deben coins?"

"Of course," Shamash replies irritably.

"Good . . . so, I am willing to sell him to you for . . . ummm . . . twenty cut debens and I will include a saddle and strap. An awesome price for such a rare animal, what do you say?"

Sazzid steps over to the horse Asaryn and strokes his side. He then places his ears to Asaryn's rib cage and joking says,

"What was that boy? You like her? Oh, I think she likes you too. As a matter of fact, the big guy likes you as well."

Kimoni pulls Zahira to the side and speaks to her in private.

"How is it that this horse moves you so?"

"It is no mere horse Kimoni, it is the mental bond that has been cherished between steed and Azmarian for a thousand years. These animals ran with my people in combat, and were cherished as a national monument. He is a true Quaggia, the stallion of the Azmaria plains. I learned of this in my studies of the Ged'i. I thought they all died out with my people, and they did, but here is the legend in the flesh, possibly the last one. I knew right away without even laying eyes upon him. I felt the aura which was explained in the Ged'i, the aura of attachment between the two of us, stallion and Azmarian. Im not sure how Sazzid got his name, but his name is even Azmarian, it means, 'Strider'."

"Are you sure of this Zahira," Kimoni implores.

"I am more then sure." assuringly answers Zahira.

"Then I know the answer." smiles Kimoni. "The gleam in your eyes tells me so. We will buy him. We won't have much money left afterwards, but our journey will surely call for his assistance . . . seeing that he is as great as you mention."

Kimoni then turns to Sazzid and says,

"We will take the stallion, and at the price you requested."

As Kimoni hands Sazzid the money, a smile of gratitude appears on Sazzid's face. He then replies,

"You are a very shrewd businessman, my friend. You have purchased a remarkable animal."

Sazzid thinks to himself, "This is the largest sale I have ever made."

After payment is made the group pack up their camels take their leave with Zahira and the horse Asaryn walking side by side. Shamash lingers behind. He then approaches Sazzid who is happily indulging in counting his money. Shamash tightly grabs hold to his ear and yanks him closer whispering,

"The price you extracted was without a doubt, outrageous. You are nothing but dung like the rest of the merchants in this forsaken town. I could have easily skinned you alive, fed your rotting corpse to the fowls of the air and taken the horse at no cost to us. Consider yourself a fortunate soul . . . fortunate that Shamash felt not spilling blood this day."

As fear and pain enters Sazzid's body, he unintentionally relieves his bladder in his clothing.

Shamash throws the merchant to the ground. He then releases a grim laugh and leaves to join the others.

Zahira and Kimoni are engaged in conversation when Shamash reaches them.

"He is a magnificent specimen, I have not seen another like him." exclaims Kimoni.

Zahira then says,

"How this breed managed to survive the horrific destruction of my people is amazing. He is very special. It was meant for us to find one another. It was an instant bond. Everything said in the Ged'i about this special bond was true. Had I not experienced it for myself, I would have always thought it to be a myth."

"I am glad we did not let our uncertainty of Sazzid prevent us from coming to his home. Otherwise, we would have missed out on this magnificent find." states Kimoni.

"I believe that at some point in our life our paths would have crossed. As I said, it was meant for us to find one another." Zahira replies.

"You amaze me, Zahira."

"Why is that, Kimoni?"

"Most young women your age would be more concerned about being married and caring for a family. Do you not long for these things, at all?"

"I am not most young women dear Kimoni. My destiny was planned even before I was conceived. My whole purpose in life is to find the Koryan and bring peace to the land. That is the only desire I possess."

"Those may be your feelings now, but what about the future."

Zahira laughs, "I can ask the same of you, Kimoni. Why is it that you never sought the love of a wife? Did you not desire a wife and young children for your name?"

Kimoni smiles rubbing his beard and responds, "I had an obligation to the clan. I could not very well carry out my duties in an efficient manner if I were weighed down with the concerns of a family."

"Interesting Kimoni, I had always wondered why you stood alone." Zahira states rubbing her earlobe, "besides, Kimoni, I have an extensive family to comfort me. You have been like a father to me. Salasa is like my sister. I have known the love of a mother. Now Shamash is like an older brother. What more could I ask for. I have been blessed with a wonderful family, to name only a few." Kimoni stops and looks Zahira up and down with admiration, he then states,

"Your maturity is amazing. But I guess you have had to face a many adult situations in your early years to speed that up."

"That is true." Laughs Zahira, "But I consider it an honor to have been blessed with the task I must face. Despite the many dangers I am sure to face, I do not regret being chosen to face them, at least anymore."

As the travelers move along for some hours they soon notices, against the horizon along the sand dune chains, ten figures sitting on camel backs dressed in black garments with black turbans and draw scarfs over their face revealing their eyes only.

"Who are they," asks Tahro.

Shamash slowly starts to draw his sword and commands the others,

"Draw your weapons!"

"Shamash lets take this one easy," exclaims Zahira, "although it is wise to always be prepared for battle, a hasty attack could prove to be more disastrous. It looks as if they are only observing . . . let's just continue cautiously."

As they continue on their way a strong wind suddenly gushes in front of them raising the sand and temporarily hazing their vision. Once the winds and sand subside the elusive men vanish.

"Where did they go," shouts Shamash. "They were probably spies, we should have struck quickly."

"Shamash, you should not be so quick to jump into a conflict." exclaims Zahira.

"But this is who I am and how I am, I take no chances." Shamash boldly replies.

"Have you not learned anything while in Azal. Let's just remain cautious and keep our wits about ourselves, no need to bring unwanted trouble."

Angry and frustrated, Shamash replies, "You trust too much and react too slowly Zahira. That will be your downfall."

"No, I desire not to pass judgment on someone or something just because I do not understand it or can not explain it, that's all. I like to try and analyze first then react later. Again, that was and is our training. I thought this was a trait of men . . . something I would have thought you could understand."

"So you are trying to be a man now?" laughs Shamash sarcastically, "leave reason to us men and you continue to coddle emotions woman."

"I didn't say that I was—", but before Zahira can finish her statement Kimoni interrupts,

"That is enough! You will cease this conversation at once before it erupts into an argument. We need not create problems for ourselves. We have enough enemies breathing down our necks. Let us just hope we have seen the last of our mysterious friends and continue our travels."

Once Zahria and her companions past the region, unbeknownst to them the mysterious men in black appears once again. They intently watch Zahira and her companions unseen. Finally they turn and gallop away.

CHAPTER 30

Children of the Fang

It is night when they enter Sekht'mn. Sekht'mn is indeed an uncanny place. It is located on a hilly terrain with sporadic trees and open bush land. Its location is just outside the great land of Kemet, their next passageway. It is often called the tomb of Jackals.

They set up camp near an abandoned cave surrounded by dead trees and rest for the long journey that lay ahead of them. Zahira takes her horse Asaryn to a nearby stream for a drink and to gather her thoughts alone. As Asaryn laps up water voraciously Zahira sits under a large tree nearby rubbing her ear lobe, and pondering over their journey.

Once Asaryn finally gets his fill he becomes impatient and nudges her shoulder, snorting, attempting to get her attention about leaving and heading back. Just before leaving to join the others, she hears the rustle of leaves above her head.

She quickly stands up looking up into the branches for the source of the sound. Again they rattle. She than slowly sits back down and lowers her head so as not to cause any alarm to whatever it is.

"Whoever you are, your presence is welcomed." She invites reassuringly, "I am a stranger in these parts seeking peace and rest only."

From the tree, the voice of a young boy asks,

"Who are you?"

"I am Zahira. I come from the south. I mean you no harm."

216

With great swiftness, the boy jumps down from the trees and lands behind her. He looks to be about twelve years of age. His clothing is worn and soiled and his skin is black with piercing jaundiced eyes.

"Why you and your friends here?" He demands.

"Again, we are just passing through and wish to rest momentarily," Zahira answers reassuringly, "for we have a long journey ahead of us. Do you live in this area?"

"Yes." He answers.

"Where are your guardians? I would hope a young boy like you would not live in this murky land alone. Do you have a home?"

"This is my home!" he snaps back, "and I don't need a guardian. I have friends, brothers and sisters of the pack; and that is all I need. You are a stranger. This place is not for you and your friends. You must go now."

"What dangers have we to face?" Zahira asks.

"There are many, too many!" he growls.

"Ok little sir," Zahira responds smiling, "by dawn we will rise and continue on our way, but now we have to get some rest for our long journey. Perhaps you might come with us and we can find a better home for you . . . what do you say."

The child's countenance begins to fall he becoming more urgent in his demands. He hits the side of the tree with his fist and growls,

"No . . . you go now . . . we do not want you here!"

The boy now starts to shout and curse at Zahira. She shakes her head in disappointment. She then turns away ignoring him, grasps hold of Asaryn's rings, then leaves back to her companions.

When Zahira returns to the campsite, she sits by the tent and engages in deep thought.

"Did I hear the voice of a baby screaming in the night," asks Shamash.

"Yes you did. The child looked to be homeless and quite confused." Zahira relates, "Judging from his appearance, he must have lived in these woods for quite some time. Needless to say, he was not too happy about our being here."

"Is this his families land?" Shamash inquires with a grunt.

Agitated Zahira replies, "Shamash . . . I do not know."

They eventually all fall asleep by the fire. As time elapses, Tahro rises out of his sleep to get a drink of water at the stream. On arriving at the stream he lowers down and washes his face and hands up to his elbows. He then takes a drink.

The night is still and quiet with the exception of the mating calls from crickets and an occasional Owl call.

While sitting there for some time he soon hears leaves rustling behind him. He quickly draws his sword and quickly turns, but sees nothing. Nevously he calls out the names of his companions, seeing if it was one of them. After no answer he concludes that it was merely the wind.

When he turns back towards the stream, there standing in the water is a large seven foot monstrous beast covered with black fur and salivating profusely from the mouth. The creature has the body of a man but the head and tail of a panther, bearing his long k-9's as he growls menacingly. Tahro quickly attempts to draw his sword but he is not fast enough, the beast is on him before he can do so. The killing is swift with a brief yelp from Tahro.

After killing him, the creature holds his head back and roars into the night air. Soon his call is accompanied by others.

"Lions," guesses Tegene.

Zere then asks, "Where is Tahro?"

"He probably went to ease nature, or perhaps to get a drink of water," replies Kimoni.

"How is it that—"

But before Zere can complete his statement, one of the beasts rush into the middle of their encampment and attacks the closest person, which is Zere. The beast leaps upon him, breaking his back instantly, killing him.

After that they are surrounded by twenty of the black beasts. Snarling and grinding their teeth anticipating a night meal. Zahira and the remaining companions quickly stand arming themselves to face the creatures. One of the beast growls,

"You do not belong here, go back to where you came from . . . but your animals will stay with us!"

Zahira responds boldly,

"We came here only to rest, but in light of the loss of our fellowman, we shall now make you pay for this . . . with blood. And after we have finished with you we will then leave, and our animals will be the ones to carry us out."

"No," the beast screams.

At that moment the beasts rush in at Zahira and her companions.

Shamash charges at one of the creatures with such force that both crash into a tree, uprooting its foundation. The impact renders the beast unconscious, but unknownst to Shamash, another slashes at him from behind.

"Arrgh," cries Shamash.

He then draws his sword and plunges it into the beast chest.

Five of the beasts close in on Zahira, snapping and slashing at her as she blocks diligently each attack.

Kimoni and his men, though highly skilled fighters, are greatly pressed by the beast's relentless assaults. Their strength proves far more superior to Kimoni, Taye and Tegene, seeing that these men are merely human beings, not touched by the power of the dust.

One of the beasts grabs hold of Kimoni's hood to his garment and yanks him to the ground. The force of it shakes him so that he relinquishes his weapon.

"How does it feel, old man, to know you are about to be eaten alive?" the beast growls, as saliva oozes from his mouth onto Kimoni's face, "You shed no tears yet, but soon you will be screaming and pleading for a quick death."

Kimoni struggles with all the strength he can muster, but to no avail.

All of a sudden, Tegene and Taye both simultaneously plunge their scimitars into the back of the beast holding Kimoni.

The creature swings his large arm in back of him, which misses Tegene, but strikes Taye, sending him into a large rock and killing him.

Shamash runs over to the beast that has Kimoni pent down. He takes hold of sparse mane of the beast from behind and then hurls him into a tree. He then helps Kimoni to his feet.

"The creatures are invulnerable to our attacks." Exclaims Kimoni exhaustingly, "there must be a way to defeat them."

"There is a way." Shamash states. After helping Kimoni he runs over to assist Zahira who herself was warding off the attack of eight beasts.

"Zahira, where is your sword Nazaar . . . why are you using that stick?" Shamash asks cynically.

Zahira is engaging the beasts with one of the normal steel scimitars they have with their supplies. Her sword is sheathed and tied on her horse away from them where they tied the animals.

"The sword Nazaar from the Muhas, get it!" Shamash demands. "Don't charge it, use it alone. Remember the element it possesse . . . Im thinking these things are like Fazeem, from the same dust."

Asaryn is already struggling with his restraints, trying to break away from the tree and assist Zahira. Zahira manages to break away from the fight and head over to Asaryn. She quickly unties him from the tree and mounts him.

The two gallop through the beasts, breaking through them until finally coming to a complete stop in a clearing. Zahira removes the sword Nazaar from its sheath and places it before her eyes, planning her pathway to strike. She then taps Asaryn with her heels to his side and he bolts toward the beasts in a full gallop. On passing into the mob of beasts she swings her sword from side to side striking them as she passes by.

A great cry of pain echoes through the forest as the beasts fall dead to the ground. The effects of the sword are horrific to their biology.

The alpha of the pack sees that his fellows are falling to Zahira's sword. He then turns and runs away from the scene, accompanied by another beast.

Zahira notices them and taps Asaryn who turns and chases them. The beasts run so fast that it is even hard for Asaryn to keep up with them. However, soon they catch up to them and Zahira strikes the lesser of the two in the back, sending him to the ground.

When almost upon the alpha, the creature turns, facing Asaryn. In a last desperate action he leaps forward at Zahira and Asaryn with claws stretched out. Asaryn quickly evades the attack and Zahira severs the creature's foot off on its passing.

Upon landing, the beast utters a cry that pierces the ears of all in the vicinity. Right before her eyes the severed foot transforms into a Childs foot.

Zahira dismounts her horse and cautiously approach the child.

The child hisses at her and limps away into the night, disappearing from their sight into the foggy woodlands.

Zahira heads back to her companions, who are recovering from the battle. Left remaining are Kimoni, Shamash and Tegene.

Shamash shouts in disgust saying, "This massacre is outrageous. Three of our men have perished and now only four of us remain. We have many months yet to cover before we reach our destination?"

"This journey is quite dangerous, but you and Zahira have a big advantage over us." Kimoni answers, "Tegene and I may be great warriors, but we are as children when faced with those touched by the stardust. However, I will not stop. My journey will only be complete once I have traveled the distance with Zahira."

"We are only human," remarks Tegene to Kimoni, "our abilities as you stated, are futile compared to the many atrocities that await us. You are well on in years and I am not sure you can continue."

"I will do what I must do, Tegene. It is my duty." Snaps Kimoni.

An argument erupts between the three men concerning the journey and the attack upon them that night. Rubbing her ear lobe Zahira pauses, seriously pondering the matter.

"We will never reach a solution this way." She finally intervenes, "Do you not see that we have lost those dear to us?"

Grasping Kimoni's hand firmly, Zahira continues,

"Kimoni, I love you dearly. You have been my guardian and like a father to me. Because I love you I must do what I think would be in your best interest. Perhaps you shouldn't continue this journey with us. This is—"

Angry Kimoni interrupts, "I am here to guide you and assist you. I promised my allegiance to you. I have sworn to protect you with my very life."

"I am aware of the oath you have sworn." Zahira responds, "I am very grateful. But alas, you are not the man you were when you made that oath, and I am not that same little girl anymore. I have lost too much, and I couldn't bear losing you in this journey . . . I am no longer strong enough to lose more family like this."

"You can not face Rathamun alone." Kimoni snaps back, "He will devour you. You need as much support possible if you are to be successful on this mission, don't worry about me, I have fought many wars and well seasoned."

Zahira sees that she is getting nowhere with Kimoni and his stubborness. She knows now that she will have to be blunter with her words.

"If it was not for Tegene and Shamash we would surely be burying you right now!" She tearfully shouts. "You would have shared the same fate as the others, which is hard enough bearing their death. I will not be able to focus my attention on Rathamun if I am constantly concerned about your welfare in the battle with many more altered beings, far more powerful then what we met here. Please . . . hear me, as a daughter to an old father . . . I beg for your ear. Please do as I ask . . . and go back to Azal . . . please, go back to Azal."

Kimoni gazes upon Zahira, who stands erect staring at him with tear soaked eyes. He makes his last attempt for his defense, calmly stating,

"Any of us could have fallen at the hands of those creatures. Do not use my advancing age as your defense, Zahira. I am still a great warrior."

Zahira reply, "Oh father . . . that fact was never in question. But do you not agree that one who has youth on their side has an advantage over one advanced in years? Can you in all honesty say your vigor is the same as it was when we left Naldamak?"

There is a brief moment of silence. Kimoni lowers his head and replies, "How are you to fight a force like that of Rathamun with not even a handful of men, child?"

Zahira gazes at Kimoni and smiles,

"Have you already forgotten the purpose of our journey? Once I possess the weapon then victory is at my feet. Once I have engaged the assistance of the champions my father spoke of, we will become a force to be reckoned with. And once peace has been restored, it is then that I will need the guidance of one that possesses the wisdom that comes with age . . . which is you, only you."

Kimoni gently kisses Zahira's hand.

"I am honored to have had the privilege of seeing you grow to become the beautiful and remarkable young woman you are. If I had been blessed with a daughter, I would hope she would have been a lot like you. But alas, I do have a daughter."

Kimoni tightly grasps Zahira's hands.

"As hard as it will be, I release you to continue this journey and I will await the sound of your victory."

"When I return, father, by the will of he that guides all things I will bring with me peace and you will live out the rest of your days in comfort."

Tegene interrupts the emotional farewell.

"If it pleases you, I will stay with Kimoni. It is not safe to journey alone."

"By all means, Tegene," Zahira replies gleefully, "Thank you so much. Shamash, Asaryn and I will be fine".

After that, they clean and wrap the bodies of their dead, make prayer and burry them into the earth. They stay with each other over night, enjoying each others company before Kimoni and Tegene leave back to Azal. That next morning they all bid one another a heartfelt farewell and Zahira atop of her stallion Asaryn with Shamash atop of his camel, along with an extra camel head further east off track. Kimoni and Tegene leave south back to Azal.

Zahira and Shamash journey starts out with an uneasy silence. Noticing Zahira's grief, Shamash breaks the silence asking, "Are you okay?"

Wiping her eyes she replies, "Yes … I'm fine. It just seems like I am always saying goodbye to those I love, never to see them again."

"You will see him again." Shamash consolingly states, "And you will be shining in your glory when you do."

Zahira envisions the night she embraced her mother for the last time. She is determined not to have the same experience with Kimoni.

She quickly shakes the visions out of her head and focuses on their next destination, the city of Uruk.

CHAPTER 31

The Wonders of Sumeria

As they leave Sekht'mn, they leave off their route heading 400 miles back East to the large city esteemed as Uruk, a trip that takes over 15 days. This they do in order that they might fully equip themselves with the proper nourishment needed for their long trip to Zehuma and to introduce Zahira to Shamash's people, who with their wealth will be able to provide more than enough for their journey. Shamash also need to inform the rulers in Uruk of his delayed duties for the city in joining with Zahira on her journey.

Uruk is a wondrous city of beauty in the land of Sumeria. The city is heavily walled for protection, surrounded by protective canals from long rivers. It is in the city of Uruk that Shamash was born.

"Here we shall have a bounteous welcome. These are the gates of Kiengir, the land of the lords of light", Shamash exclaims proudly.

"So am I correct in assuming they are quite welcoming?" Zahira giggles.

"Oh yes! We are the Saggiga, the dark haired peoples that are prized for our generosity and feared for our savagery in warfare. Now you will see what it really means to live well and be joyous. I guess you never really new that, eh,"

"There is never a dull moment with you Shamash." Zahira laughs, "Why would I expect any less from your people."

As they approach the gates of the city, little boys who catch sight of them start to run out to meet them in song and jubilation.

"It is Shamash! He has come back, savior of Uruk, mightiest of all men."

"How do they know who you are?" Zahira whispers.

The children race toward the two with intense happiness leaping from their faces.

"Whoa, young lions, you race as if to battle." Shamash states in loud laughter, "The glow upon your little faces brings gladness to my heart. Does Lord Shadaram still dwell here?"

"Yes, he stays in the house by the spring-well of Antu."

"Then why do we pause? Let's go," laughs Shamash.

The children begin to sing and cheer as they enter the city gates. Shamash turns to Zahira and answers her,

"Lets just say, our visit was already planned."

"You big sneak." Zahira states pointing her finger in an angry joking fashion.

They are welcomed by the watchman and captain of the guards then they are brought into the city and head to the house of Shadaram.

The entrance doors open slowly to reveal a beautiful city, with round, stone houses and many fountains. The ground is paved in what appeared to be granite, pure white.

The mighty temple is large and steep, much like a rounded pyramid with the inner floor encased in marble. To both sides of the temple stand strong golden statues of human-headed lions with wings of great eagles.

"You have to excuse the idols," grunts Shamash, "the training we got from Azal has not reached my people yet. They are still worshippers of the many gods."

Zahira sneers looking around and responds, "That I can clearly see."

The house of Shadaram is beautiful as well, and from it emerges an aged man, frail in appearance, clothed in long brightly colored garments.

"Behold, the warrior has returned!"

"Shadaram, it is wonderful to see you again. Is all well with you?" Shamash asks.

"I am only affected by the ravages of time, my fine warrior. And who is your lovely companion?"

"This is Zahira, daughter of the great Azmarian general Zada of the south near the lands of Kush."

"Ahhh, Zada Talat. Fine general, he was. You should be very proud, to be the offspring of such a mighty warrior. His life was taken far too soon. But at least we have his offspring to carry his legacy. Welcome to Uruk. There shall be dancing, drinking and singing. Let the merry-making commence!"

Shadaram summons the servants of his palace so that provisions can be prepared for the festival.

While preparations are being made, Shadaram takes Zahira and Shamash on a tour of the grand palace.

Pure stone-marbled pillars line the hallways with meticulous paintings of god-like creatures possessing wings, lion's bodies and human heads with the traditional thick long curled beards of royalty.

Zahira whispers to Shamash sarcastically asking, "And why isnt your beard that luxurious young man?"

"My work on the battlefield speaks volumes of my luxurious nature woman." He blurts.

In the middle of the foyer is a fountain that houses numerous species of large fish, clothed in the colors of spring.

There is a winding staircase crafted in marble with gold and silver railings.

Shadaram looks at Zahira and smiles saying,

"If you continue with your mouth open, the flies will set up residence."

Zahira quickly closes her mouth and replies,

"Forgive me . . . your home is truly magnificent. I have never seen such beauty. I am at a lost for words."

Shamash interrupts jeering, "You at a lost for words . . . that would be impossible."

Zahira turns a quick look at Shamash who smiles at her.

"Leave her be, Shamash." Shadaram states laughingly, "She has reason to be fascinated. I have lived here for years and I still find myself mesmerized at the beauty of this place. But you need not be so mesmerized, for the Azmarians possessed such wonderment within their cities. Volumes of literature speak of the beauty of your land. Now come, I will show you my gardens."

Shadaram escorts the two warriors to the gardens. Gorgeous flowers carpet its floors. Among the flowerbed stand towering trees and an astonishing array of plant life surrounding the thunderous waterfalls.

The melodious songs from colorful birds echo through the air.

"Shadaram, to have beauty such as this to greet you every time you open your eyes—"

It is a grand privilege, indeed," interrupts Shadaram.

"Your gardens remind me of parts of my home in Kush . . . before it was decimated." Zahira remarks.

"Yes, at the hands of Rathamun, no doubt." He states, "Such a savage and unnecessary loss of lives, indeed. You have suffered a great deal, child. I am truly sorry."

As they continue their tour of the palace and its grounds, the captain of the guards approaches them.

"Lord Shadaram, the provisions are being arranged. In three days as you requested the festival shall commence."

"Wonderful, wonderful!" declares Shadaram, "Come, there is much rest needed from this arduous journey you have made. You must eat and refresh yourselves; I have much to talk about with the elder council."

During their stay, both Zahira and Shamash are treated well by the Sumerian people. Zahira is treated just like an extended family member. On the third day, Shadaram comes toward the two, who both are sitting along the Tigrith River talking amongst themselves about their journey ahead of them. He then shouts,

"Let the merry-making begin!"

As they head over into the city, everyone is dressed in their finest garbes with the women being clothed in colorful garb from head to toe. Zahira is awe-struck.

Shadaram looks at her and remark to her surprise,

"Relax, my dear, and enjoy. This festival is for you and Shamash. Our mighty warrior has returned to the city of his birth and he has brought a lovely companion with him. He will protect us from all evil that find its way to our gates. This indeed, is a blessed day for us . . . a gift given back by the gods!"

Zahira gives Shamash a disturbing glance, who responds with a look of assurance. There are tables lined with all the delicacies of Sumeria.

It had been a long time since Zahira enjoyed a tasty meal; and she is not about to let this opportunity pass her by.

A rich red wine is brought to her and Shamash by the servers. Zahira respectfully refuse for them both saying,

"No thank you . . . we do not drink wine, but we will be glad to have milk instead."

Finally, after a few hours the festival simmers down a bit. Zahira pulls Shamash to the side saying,

"You most certainly spoke the truth about your people having such a welcoming spirit. I can see why you possess such enthusiasm about returning home."

"Yes, I am very proud of where I come from. The very reason for my training with the Muhas in Azal was so I could return and serve as protector of this city. I swore I would not allow what happened to my parents to be the fate of this glorious land."

Zahira lowers her head saying,

"Shamash, do not feel you must continue on this journey with me. I will understand if you wish to stay. This battle is mine to face, not yours."

There is a brief moment of silence.

"I thought you knew me better than that woman," Shamash responds indignantly, "but it is obvious you do not if you think I would desert you in your time of need. Besides, there will be no Sumeria to protect if Rathamun is not obliterated. We must dispose of the diseased limb before there can be a complete healing of the entire soul."

"You are indeed a true friend Shamash. I was only saying that—"

"I am aware of what you were trying to say woman." Shamash abruptly interrupts, "But to desert you now would be an act of treason. That, I will never be guilty of."

Interrupting their conversation, Shadaram approaches the two asking, "Why do you isolate yourselves? Join in the festivities!"

"We were just discussing our mission, that's all." Zahira explains.

"Mission? What is this of a mission?" he asks confused.

Shamash then interjects saying, "We are in search of the Koryan, the weapon said to bring peace to the world."

"I have heard tales of this weapon; how it must be powered by one of the light or one of the dark." Shadaram relates. Then looking at Zahira with pity in his eyes Shadaram continues, "A tremendous task you have undertaken."

"But a task I must carry out. It is my destiny." She boldly declares.

"You possess strong will." He states, "But enough of this talk, let us join in the festivities."

After everyone has devoured the delicacies of the land, they commence to dancing. The musicians enter with their large duff drums and begin to pound a heart throbbing beat.

Shamash puts on a show as he shows his people he has not forgotten their native dances.

Zahira laughs as Shamash almost falls into a crowd of singing women.

Shamash approaches Zahira and motions for her to join.

"I will not be the only one making a fool of myself." He laughs.

Zahira shy away saying, "I'm not familiar with your dances."

"Then you must learn. Come, I will show you." He shouts.

Hesitantly, Zahira agrees. She points at him demanding,

"I know you Shamash, don't touch me . . . I can do this myself."

The women join with her and she learns quickly suddenly becoming the life of the festival.

Flashbacks of the festivities she enjoyed in Naldamak appear in her mind. Shamash continues to cheer her on.

The moods of the people light the city. There is not a sad face to be seen. From infant to the elderly, everyone engages in the celebration.

Finally, Shadaram pulls Shamash to the side in private to converse with him.

"Your friend, she is very lovely. It is a shame she will have to make her search for the Koryan alone."

Shamash's expression changes from happiness to a look of despair. He boldly replies,

"She will not be alone Shadaram. It is my intention to continue with her."

A look of shock comes over Shadaram's face.

"You will continue with her? What of your duties to this city?"

"The protection of this grand city will always be my concern." Answers Shamash, "But we must first eliminate the evil that is bearing down on us. That is why I must assist Zahira in her mission."

"Before I can bestow my blessings on your journey, we must first bring this matter to the high council." Balks Shadaram.

As the festival starts to wind down, Shamash approaches Zahira.

"Let us walk woman. We must talk."

"Of course, Shamash, is something wrong?" She asks.

"I must meet before the high council. It was believed I would stay behind on this visit and serve as protector to the city."

Curiously looking at Shamash, Zahria ask,

"I have not caused you trouble . . . have I?"

"No, no." he assures her, "I intend to fulfill my role as protector here, but first things, first. I will explain my reasons for accompanying you and that will suffice. There is no need for you to worry."

Shamash leaves Zahira secretly bewildered over what would transpire before the council.

Shamash reaches the palace where the high council is waiting for his presence. When he enters the room there is complete silence.

One of the council members begins to speak.

"It has been brought to our attention that you wish to continue with this Zahira as she searches for this ... Koryan. Your reason for being sent to Azal was not to go on some blind reckless missions, but to serve as protector of our city."

Shamash replies, "I am aware of my duties as protector of this city, and I intend to carry out that service. But it is imperative that we do not undermine our efforts by allowing Rathamun to continue his reign of terror. If we do not eliminate this enemy now, his evil will assuredly spread to even this glorious city."

The elder impatiently responds, "Your enthusiasm is commendable, but right now we are concerned only about the welfare of our land. It is lacking superior protection from the twisted, mutated creatures that roam the lands. That is why it is imperative you remain in Uruk and tend to your duties ... at once!"

The veins in Shamash's neck begin to bulge as he tries to hold back the anger that starts swelling inside him.

"This is pure babble, no rationale to this logic . . . I have not refused my position as protector of Uruk. I am only asking that I be allowed to finish this mission started. Do you not agree that one should hold true to his word? I remember being told by a member of this high council that 'a man of his word is his strength, loyalty and honor'.

Shadaram lowers his head, knowing that he is the one that Shamash is referring to.

"And now you say I should not keep true to my word—"

"You were not to make such an oath with this woman, knowing your duties here," interrupts one of the elders. "What is the Muhas teaching their students now ... too rebel against their duites assigned to them when leaving Azal, to defend the land of their birth? Even your disrespect is shown in you not referring to even the king as lord. You have left reason and have joined with madness."

Paying no attention to what is said, Shamash continues, "I have never been one to refuse an order from my superiors, but in this case I will. Your narrow minds will not allow you to see the bigger picture here. I have sworn an oath to protect the city of Uruk from the Blackstar. This will only be possible if Rathamun is annihilated. I have sworn an oath to carry this mission out and I intend to see it through. It is only after I have completed this mission that I will return to Uruk and resume my duties."

Another elder screams, "Your mind has been contaminated, sullied. You have disappointed us deeply!"

Shamash walks over closer to the enraged elder and says, "No, not contaminated, but purified. I think no longer of my own interest, but that of others. I'm working for the future of this city."

Another elder remarks, "We are very much aware of the future of Uruk, but we cannot concern ourselves with the future of all man toiling for help. You can not promise you will return. Life is a gift and that gift can be taken away. Death has mercy on no one. You're not exempt. The South will have to deal with Rathamun in its own way. Our land has been blessed with beauty from the gods. If we are to keep these lands in their beauteous splendor we need the protection of our mighty warriors, which you were trained to be. That is the purpose you will serve. We will not give you our blessing if you continue with her. You will remain in Uruk and begin your duties!"

Enraged Shamash slams his fist on the council's table causing it to split in two. They pull away out of fear. The guards ready their weapons and head over to Shamash, but Shahdaram holds his hand up halting their progress. Shamash then yells, "Rathamun may have his sights on Uruk as well. When he march his black armies to the gates of this city then you and all your sick glory will realize the stupidity of your ways."

The heated argument continues with neither side giving in.

When it becomes clear he will not convince the council otherwise, Shamash decides to bring the futile argument to an abrupt end.

He finds his state of calmness and declares, "I have spoken of this city with pride in my eyes, but now that glimmer has faded. You say I have disappointed you; well you have disappointed me. I am a man of my word as was said before. I will return to begin my duties after I return from this mission. But if you say no, then may your bones melt in the burning flames of Tiamat . . . thus what your falsehood has lead you to believe."

Upon completing this statement, he storms out of the palace, slamming the door behind him, loosening it from its hinges.

On exiting the palace he diligently searches for Zahira. He finally finds her sitting in the garden, resting peacefully.

Pausing for a moment he turns and looks in the direction of the palace with a brief sense of longing. He then heads over to Zahira.

He states, "It is time for us to leave this place."

Rising anxiously Zahira asks, "What was the decision of the high council?"

"Their decision does not matter to me woman. We have a mission to carry out, and so we shall."

"Your expression tells me things did not turn out the way you had hoped." She sighs.

"Perhaps!"

She then states, "And so now you wish to leave. We can't leave with you in this state of mind . . . its not right to you or them. We can stay a few more days to give you time to consider the matter before making a hasty decision."

Growing restless Shamash replies, "Time is not needed. I have taken the matter into consideration. The high council is not interested in the welfare of others. They are only concerned with themselves. I must admit that I once shared those feelings. But those feelings no longer exist. I gave the council my decision and I am sure it was the right one."

"I am sorry your return to Uruk has to end this way." Zahira regretfully responds.

"You have no reason to feel sorry woman."

Shamash and Zahira gather their belongings, load their animals and head towards the city gates.

As they prepare to leave, a young child runs up to them.

"Shamash, Shamash, why are you leaving?"

Zahira looks at Shamash, awaiting his response. He places his hand on the childs head and says,

"There are evils that need to be reckoned with. Once I have exterminated the evil, then I will return. I am a man of my word."

Shamash hands the young child a necklace he made from dazzling smooth stones found in Azal.

"I want you to hold this for me. I will return for it."

A look of amazement comes across the young child's face. He takes it and runs back toward his home skipping happily.

The leave the city and travel west toward Avdat back into Kemet.

CHAPTER 32

Realm of the Elementals

After 45 days of traveling, they finally enter the northern realm of the great continent. Many stops are made along the way.

They first stop in Kemet. Here they set up camp for a few days and stock up on more supplies from traveling Hittites, traders and sellers. Afterwards they continue their long journey toward their next destination, the land of Batheria in the province of Zehuma.

A beautiful land abundant in long high mountain chains, trees and velvety green grass, a far cry from many of the other areas they traveled nearer to home.

The snow-capped mountains in the farthest part of the north are as white as the clouds above. The birds can be heard chirping in the surrounding dense trees. Albatross of different species sing loudly and soar through the air lunging toward the great sea for fish.

As they walk through the vast fields deep inland they spot in the distance exotic wildlife never before seen by their eyes. The great four tusk elephants, herds of large spotted equines and giant tree sloths that spread across the landscape.

The sun shines and crystallizes the flowing streams beneath, adding even more luster to the land.

"I have never seen anything so beautiful in my life," exclaims Zahira. "The land seems to chant peace in the air. This must certainly be Zehuma, the untainted parts that escaped the knowledge of Rathamun."

"I have never been to this area before, but I have heard much of its beauty." states Shamash.

"Here is where we will meet Sayda, ruler of the Zehumians." state Zahira.

"I hear he is not a friendly fellow," smirks Shamash, "These Zehumians are obsessed with the purity of these lands, fanatics, if you will. It has been said he kills all outsiders and claims this land to be one of the last frontiers of hope and light."

Courageously Zahira declares, "I am Zahira, born and chosen by the Whitestar to once again establish peace to the once radiant kingdoms. He will soon learn we mean no harm to him or his people. On the scroll left by my father, this Zehumian will join us."

The two continue until finally coming upon a mountain with rich green vines draped around a large hole carved into its base.

Peeking into the dark whole they can only see an unending darkness.

All of a sudden, the earth beneath their feet starts to tremble.

The trembling is so devastating it throws them to the ground.

Then, at that moment, ten figures grow from the ground like shoots of new grass right before their eyes.

A moaning sound resonates as they emerge from the ground. Once cleared of the soil from the earth, their appearance becomes more evident, five men and five women.

They wear long loose robes. Both men and women are devoid of any hair. They are of a cornsilk complexion and their eyes radiate a glowing light that is a rich green in color, showing their connection to the earth.

On their bodies are various symbols painted on their arms, backs, chest and faces. Each symbol is different from the other, speaking of their positions and titles.

There is one that stands in front of the others. He comes forward and in a reverberating voice asks,

"How is it you come to these lands? Beware, stragglers, for we are the keepers of these lands and have sworn to protect the earth from all mortals and stardust children alike."

"You will condemn the good with the evil?" asks Zahira.

"Good no longer exist on this earth." answers the man, "After the collision of the star, earth was changed. Evil spread to all men; those that claimed dark and those that claimed light. None are to be trusted. Much of the land has suffered greatly by the greed of man and his lust for power, riches and territory, thus man is criminal and foolish in nature."

Another speaks threatening, "We shall indulge you no longer. Your presence is not welcomed. Regardless of what you claim, you are from the south, the lands of shadow and you must die."

"Must die?" shouts Shamash. "We come here for your assistance. We have traveled a great distance from Azal. The woman with me is Zahira, a child of the Whitestar from the people of Azmaria."

At this point Zahira becomes more urgent in her request.

"Protectors of Zehuma, who made you judge over the world? We come not to fight. We seek the presence of Sayda, your ruler."

"Sayda! How have you come to know of Sayda?" inquires the man.

"My father Zada Talat, the great general of the Azmarians left for me instruction to seek out Sayda, for he is one of the champions who will assist me in the overthrow of Rathamun."

"Be gone woman! Take your beast and leave." demands another of the group, "There is nothing here for you, but death."

One of the female Zehumians in the background then maliciously accuses them saying,

"Scouts of Rathamun . . . you have come to spy out our land."

Before the two can react to the comment, the woman raises her hands and the earth in which they are standing forms into hands made of soil and rock and grabs hold of both Zahira and Shamash.

They are then swiftly lifted high into the air. As they are taken upward, more foliage continues to add to its substance, strengthening its grip. Once they reach about thirty feet in the air the earth bindings stop its growth.

In a rage, Asaryn begins to gallop toward the Zehumians in an attack charge. But before he can come within six feet of them, vines of the earth raise and entangle him.

"Zahira, can you reach your weapon," grunts Shamash while gasping for air.

"My arms are bound too tight. I can not move an inch." She bellows, "But we will not fight them. Once they learn of who we are they will cease this ridiculous battle."

"Are we to wait until we die before they come to this understanding," asks Shamash.

"We will not die. Be patient and have faith in my words, the spirit of truth is on our side."

Then suddenly, amidst all the chaos, from the opening of the mountain comes forth another, fully clothed in flowing garments with the arrayment of the forest.

"Who are you and where do you come from?"

"I am Zahira," she shouts down, still struggling from the grip of the earth, "heir to the throne of my father, Zada Talat, general and ruler of the Azmarians. We seek Sayda . . . he is one of the champions my father wrote of.

Doubting her claim the man replies, "Enough! You speak foolishly. There are none remaining of the Azmarians. All perished at the hand of Rathamun."

The man then walks around the mound of earth that continues to hold the two warriors high in the air.

As he walks, he rubs his chin in deep thought until finally ordering,

"Release them!"

The woman that entrapped them becomes indignant, questioning his orders,

"How have you come to this decision, whoever they claim to be is a lie. Why should we—"

"I said release them," shouts the man, interrupting her. Suddenly the grip of the earth begins to loosen and slowly crumbles under their feet, but keeps their footing that they might not fall, until finally returning both Zahira and Shamash to the ground unharmed.

Once to the ground they rub the soil from off their clothing and catching their breath from the pressure that the earth impended.

Zahira then looks over at her horse Asaryn, who is snorting and struggling to be freed of his entrapments.

"What of my horse?" she demands.

At that moment, the vines that restrained Asaryn begin to unravel and return to the ground.

After releasing Zahira and those in her company, the man invites them to follow him to the base of a different side of the mountain. As they come closer a small whole start to miraculously rip away form in the mountain side and grow in size allowing them to walk right through. Afterwards it closes behind them. The ground is very soft and a dazzling aroma of various plants fills the long corridor they progress through.

Continuing down the tunnel, they finally come to a bright light shining from a large opening in the cave.

Once entering the opening, they discover the most beautiful scene; a large palace, beautifully structured and decorated with the influence of the forest.

Two long tables sit parallel to each other in front of a large earthy throne. At each table sit a committee of twenty, ten men and ten women in all.

The man that led Zahira and Shamash through the tunnel motions for them to sit at the table.

He walks toward the throne and takes a seat.

He gazes over all in the palace and sighs. The expression on his face is as if pleased, yet disturbed.

"I know of why you come here and who you are Zahira."

After saying that, a woman steps from behind his throne where she is clearly seen. Zahira rears back in shock, for this woman is familiar to her. It is the woman of the forest she spoke with when she was but only a child. Zahira's facial expression of amazement peaks Shamash's interest.

"Are you ok Zahira?" Shamash asks, but the woman answers before Zahira can say a word,

"Yes Zahira, it is I, the one who spoke with you in the Ajulah forest."

"I thought we would never meet again?" Zahira inquires.

"No . . . this meeting was to happen, but I was not to assist you anymore during the time period I spoke with you."

The man sitting on the throne states,

"We sensed your arrival a day ago. I am fully aware of our planet's condition, its dying slowly, and through greed it has been pillaged and has been dealt many blows. We the Zehumians are one with the earth, and we have sworn to protect it at all cost. Our power gives me the ability to sense the power of the dust, either White or Black within creatures of this earth."

The room is suddenly filled with armed guards surrounding both Zahira and Shamash. Shamash smirks at their arrival, anticipating a good fight, but Zahira quickly grabs his massive arm so as to calm his defensive reaction. The man continues with a pleasing announcement,

"Behold . . . I am Sayda, King of the Zehumians."

Sayda then rises from his throne and proceeds to walk over towards the table where Zahira and Shamash are sitting with his loyal officials.

He gazes around at the grand palace and looks once again at the two warriors. He then walks ten steps away from them and turns back around and confess,

"Zahira, I fought with your father in the great wars of the South. It was a struggle of two great powers, that of the light and that of dark. Rathamun gathered a coalition, left the land of Mayota and proceeded to head north to the central plains of Azmaria. There is where your people resided in peace until this monster came and destroyed that peace. Rathamun lusted for power from all possible energies of the star. He conquered many of those of the stardust and incorporated them into his armies of darkness.

Your father knew of the power of the Blackstar. He knew that it would overwhelm the forces of good. Only with the help of the Koryan would one from the Light be capable of fighting Rathamun. Your father left you with the travelers with whom he was acquainted, and the woman he fell in love with after the death of your birth mother. Thus you were spared the fate of your people, hoping one day you would return, find the Koryan and reclaim the temple of Azwrala, the glorious cities in Sagala and the land of Azmaria."

"Why didn't my father retrieve the Koryan and destroy Rathamun then?" asks Zahira.

"Rathamun's attack was without warning." answers Sayda, "The Koryan was unoperable, as if waiting for its true master. So Zada had it taken far away and hidden in the north, protected by the two great lions. The Azmarians rode atop of their Quaggias to the place of battle not expecting the decimation they suffered. The threat was not perceived to be at its peak at that time, but they were all mistaken. The Blackstar was growing at a phenomenal rate inside Rathamun, feeding off of dust users and by the time the battle was fought, the combined energies of the dark kingdoms were at their peaks. Only then were you retrieved before the pillaging of the lands and taken to the people that raised you from infancy.

From these northern lands my people and I came and allied with the children of the light. We fought long and hard with your father, but were beaten back by the power of darkness. Many of my people died in that massacre, one of them being my son, Hamaat. I would search the face of the stars to have him back in my stay. I swore to Zada before his death that who so ever was his heir to the throne, I would fight along side them to my death in reclaiming peace for the known earth.

You, my dear, are the last of your people. I would only have dreamed of possessing the powers of the Koryan and reclaiming peace. But only one of the White or Blackstar can possess that great power. You are to retrieve this power before Rathamun learns of its whereabouts and claims it himself. If this happens he will be all-powerful. Nothing or no one will be able to stand in his way."

Sayda then smiles and approaches the distraught Zahira.

"You carry a heavy burden, young one. You have the weight of the world on your shoulders. However, I shall help you carry that burden. It is the promise I made to a dying warrior. I swear my life. I am at your service."

"I am honored to speak with you, Sayda. I know you are with me in this conquest." Reply Zahira.

Zura, one of the young Zehumian women sitting at the table quickly interjects, "Sayda, why are you agreeing to assist her? We must stay here and protect our lands. You are ruler over this land your greatness will be needed to help us fight off the Blackstar."

"Zura, this is the only way to insure peace for our land. We must go to this evil, face it on sacred land and dispose of it there. It needs not travel any closer north. Not only shall I go, but you shall assist me as well. The armies of the Zehumian elementals shall gather and once again prepare for war."

During Sayda's speech, Zura stares at Zahira with intense hate in her eyes.

CHAPTER 33

The Turbulent Soil of Hanaba

"We waist time coming into Hanaba, we could have gone west straight into Tinitra, and perhaps come back this route," Shamash complains as they arrived in the land of Hanaba, located south of Zehuma. It takes eight days to reach. However, they are thoroughly prepared for the journey.

"Shamash, I have to take time to meditate on our entrance into Tinitra. We must regain our thoughts and be mentally ready before entering into a land such as this, which I know you love doing," exclaims Zahira laughing under her breath.

Sayda, who now travels with them add.

"It has been said that here in Hanaba deadly vices surround the land. It is filled with evils unknown to our society. The Zehumians have never journeyed beyond Zehuma, so such legends remain to be seen. Zahira is wise in saying a plan must be accurately designed before entering Tinitra."

Zura then complains, "Sayda, are we to follow to the very end, this stranger?"

"The words she speaks are wise; and it is best that we follow such."

"Wisdom? Are we to be afraid of the Tanazart? Are they not our allies? Do they not seek the same goal as we? What is it to prepare for? Are we to have conflict with them?" Zura complains further.

"Oh, I see now, the strangers may cause us harm at the hands of the Tanazart. The presence of these strangers could surely mean our death. Our passage—"

"Enough Zura!" interrupts Sayda, "Your constant doubts and suspicions of our new associates irritate me. Cease your babble. Your bickering is only causing division. We are united in purpose and shall remain this way."

Zura loves Sayda dearly and adheres to his words closely. However, her distrust for both Zahira and Shamash will eventually lead to events that will astonish even Sayda.

When the travelers come into Hanaba, they set up camp and begin to relax. For three days they remain in Hanaba, pondering the trip and exchanging conversation about their journey.

Sayda then begins to speak of the Tanazart, whom they would soon encounter in the land of Tinitra.

"We will soon enter the realm of the Tanazart, warrior women who dwell in the twin towers of Tafukt, the tallest edifices in this entire vast continent. They are said to be the "keepers of peace" in the land of Tinitra alone, an untouched savage land with their edifices being the brightest light seen there. They are the gatekeepers to Tanirta. However, they are also the conquerors of men and sworn slayers of those touched by the Black Dust. Their army is strong and possesses an unflagging courage never before seen. If I am not mistaken, they originally migrated to Tinitra from Avdat, rebel women seeking a society of their own, breaking away from the servitude of man. Any more history beyond that remains bleak. However, they are born from the White Dust of the cosmic star. From the top of their citadel burns a light that symbolizes the last strong hold of hope in the land.

They only became our allies when our pureness was seen through the practice and care of the elements by our powers of the stardust. However, we do not trust them fully; for they will kill any, even allies, they consider a threat. Shrewdness is a must when dealing with these women."

Zahira laughs quietly and responds, "Then it would be in my best interest to be quick when attempting to convince them of who I am."

Zura quickly rises and abruptly interrupts, "Your jokes are not humorous. You take lightly whom we shall encounter. They are not like the inferior creatures you have fought. They are of pure elegance, might and abilities beyond your wildest nightmares."

"Woman, get a grip of your self," bawls Shamash. "Your hate for Zahira will be your undoing."

"You blundering mass of stupidity," shouts Zura, "I fear not you, nor your whore! I am the pride of—"

In a fit of rage and sheer exhaustion of Zura's insulting comments, Sayda rises from his sitting position, burning with a green aura. The earth beneath them begins to tremble, greatly.

"I said enough, Zura!" he shouts, "Silence your foul tongue!"

"I am greatly sorry my Sayda. I shall recant for my boisterous tongue. I am only concerned about—"

"Neither shall you be concerned of me nor of our new companions. You shall be concerned only for your own well being."

After that, all remain silent for quite some time.

At daybreak the four travelers rise and prepare for departure on their animals. They then start their ride northwest towards Tinitra.

On their way the scenery is very typical of the region. There are many mountains ranges and long streams. The air is fresh and life seems still, but vibrant.

Progressing further they soon spot what appear to be six cloaked silhouette figures mounted on horses in the distance. The figures pause briefly, as if waiting for them to come closer.

Zahira and her companions bring their riding beasts to a halt. They all seem quite puzzled at the presence of the figures in the far distance that watch them incessantly.

Then suddenly, the six silhouette figures begin to run toward them as if charging into battle.

Zahira and her companions draw their weapons and brace themselves for the attack.

Shamash grits his teeth and shouts, "If a battle is what they want, then a fight I shall gladly give!"

Before he continues at them he pauses for a moment and squint his eyes to get a better view of their attackers.

"Wait! Are those not the riders we saw back in Ruheiba?"

Zura sneers. "Put away your meager weapons. Sayda and I need not secrete a single drop of sweat. We know well these miscredents and will deal with them accordingly. Now witness the power of the Zehumians."

Raising her hands the earth in front of them grows agitated. Suddenly a large slab of earth breaks away and flings toward the dark figures. But the beings burst right through, as if it was only paper.

When the dark figures are just twenty feet in front of them, they throw out their hands and hurl to the earth what appear to be seeds.

Once hitting the ground, the seeds are immediately absorbed into the earth.

The beings continue galloping, violently breaking past Zahira and her companions and finally disappearing into the distance behind them.

Zura quite disturbed, comments, "The earth was not even able to stop them."

"They minions of Rathamun, they are not easily bested." replies Zahira.

"I do believe you are correct in your statement," replies Sayda. "They appear to be the dark minions of the Blackstar. It is said they were hand picked from mortal man by Rathamun and portioned residuals of the Blackstar to enhance their power. This is so that none can stand in their way of accomplishing their mission as his ambassadors. That mission, my dear one, is to seek out your very soul."

"Well, we welcome their challenge," Shamash shouts.

Not sure as to why they riders did not engage them in combat, they press forward cautiously, continuing their travels, when at that moment the quiet is broken by a loud roaring sound.

To their horror the ground around them start to produce what appear to be long plant like stems with hideous human like heads, with long muzzles filled with rows of silver sharp teeth. Their length measure over seven feet tall.

Glancing over the field hundreds of them grow instantly from the earth where the seeds from the dark riders were thrown.

With swift lunges the heads begin to strike at the travelers.

Zahira and her companions dodge the devastating strikes. The blows are so intense they leave large gouges in the earth.

"What madness is this," yells Zura. "The very earth, itself, has sprouted evil?"

Zahira responds, "This evil is not of the earth, but from the evil of Rathamun."

As the snakes strike the warriors severe their heads, but to no avail. Three more heads will grow in its place.

The heads seem to double in number, overwhelming the band of travelers. Soon the whole vicinity is sprouting these creatures.

Sayda and Zura's elemental power to manipulate the earth prove useless.

The travelers try to flee as fast as they can, but at every passage new heads immediately sprout up, striking at them relentlessly.

Shamash then shouts, "How do we fight off this attack? They continue to multiply."

At that moment, two of the snake creatures strike his camel, sending Shamash flying into the air, only to land in a mound of the growing serpents.

Their attack is horrendous, striking viciously and with great speed at Shamash, but his skills afford him the ability to hold them off. In a rage he slices and smash the attacking creatures that press in on him.

Zahira quickly comes to his aid, but the density of the creatures grows so thick she is unable to get through to him.

Swinging desperately at the creatures, Shamash grabs hold to three at one at a time and manages to dislodge them from the earth using his mighty strength, equipped with his bracelets of power.

Zahira finally reach Shamash, pulling him onto Asaryn's back with her.

Shamash then yells to his fellow travelers, "The root! Strike with your swords at the root of the creatures. They grow much slower than striking their heads alone; and they will not multiply!"

"Do as he says," yells Sayda.

Zahira interjects, "But as we do so, we must continue forward. We cannot continue this fight for long. They are too numerous."

As they press forward, they begin to lean on their horses, striking as close as they can toward the base of the creatures implanted in the ground.

Zahira then yells, "Sayda, Zura, see now if you can manipulate the earth under the snakes with severed heads!"

The two Zehumians' eyes begin to flow with green energies as they stare at the earth. Chunks of earth are then ripped up and the creatures whose heads were severed are dislodged from the ground, crumbling under the weight of the soil.

The earth consumes the creatures that are not cut by their roots as well.

Once the creature mounds have been cleared, Sayda then turns and lifts the remaining of earth in the vicinity of the creatures saying, "This evil shall not continue upon our leaving."

Zahira and the others race further away from the area. At that moment he compresses the earth that hold the captured creatures, crushing them under the pressure. He then returns the earth back to its rightful place.

"Impressive Sayda, the two of you have remarkable powers," exclaims Zahira.

Sayda replies, "Our power derives from the earth, as elementals we control the element the earth provides.

"Your skills with a sword are excellent, as well," interjects Shamash. "And might I add, your horse riding skills are not bad, either. The horses you choose to ride, they are truly different from what we are accustomed to."

"They are Zebrans, the mother to all Zebra," states Sayda. "We share a bond of brotherhood, much like your people Zahira once shared a bond to the animal you ride now."

Zahira then comments, "We must be especially alert now. Rathamun knows of our location and will attempt to spy out the location of the Koryan."

Exhausted, they continue their travels eighty miles more, which takes them further northwest.

There they set up camp and rest before their thirteen day journey to Tafukt.

CHAPTER 34

The Twin Towers of Light

"One thing I can honestly say about the northern regions, they are indeed mountainous spectacles. Every village and town we have visited thus far was landscape with many mountains." Zahira expresses her awe over the beautiful landscape of the north. They press forward, a thirteen day travel to this enigma land of Tinitra.

They reach a large hill and traverse upwards. After reaching the top, they look across the landscape to witness the most spectacular sight ever seen, grander than the homes and mountains of Sayda in Zehuma.

The city of Tafukt is beautiful. Its twin towers in the distance illuminate the whole land.

There is an abundance of lush trees. To the east of the city, large waterfalls plummet to the open river below that surrounds the towers.

"I am enamored by the beauty of your villages and towns. The north hold a beauty that can not be explained," exclaims Zahira.

Sayda responds, "'Tis the beauty of our world. We strive to keep it glorious."

The four travelers finally make their way down the sloping hill and start their track on one of the snow paths leading through the intimidating woodland towards the glowing city. The trees that line the path are centuries old. They are the tallest in the entire continent, reaching 400 feet in height and up to 30 feet in diameter.

After walking the path for some time they soon hear a swooshing sound above their heads. The thickness of the leaves and the height of the ancient trees prevent them from getting a clear visual of the peculiar shadows that soar above their heads.

Eventually, they reach the end of the path and enter an open landscape, which leads to a vast field of white grass.

Further in the distance a great gate, about a hundred feet ahead of them, stands tall and ever immense before their eyes connected to a wall measuring thirty feeth in height surrounding the two large towers.

No sooner do they take another step, two red blazes soar over them.

After passing by twice, the mysterious images land just thirty feet ahead of them.

Before their eyes stand two large red lionesses possessing large feathered wings, with a span of at least fifteen feet from tip to tip. Each lioness measures taller on all fours then a five foot man. And on each one rides a woman.

One of the women is dark golden rod in complexion and the other the color of white silk, they both are dazzling in beauty possessing straight flowing auburn hair. They are completely naked with the only articles of clothing worn being arm bands made of blood red leather strapped up to their elbows and a luxuriant long crimson cloak around their shoulders and dragging the ground. They use this long cloak to wrap around their bodies when still.

A long spear is carried across their backs along with a short sword with lion headed motifs held by a meager single strip of leather strap on their thighs.

The eyes of the women and their beast begin to glow like firebrick, while staring unwaveringly at Zahira and her companions.

Suddenly, one of the women addresses Sayda in the Tamajakor tongue, the language of the Tanazart.

Impatiently Shamash whispers to Sayda, "What is she saying?"

Sayda at once respond to the woman's statement. She pauses and starts to stare long and hard at the strangers.

Sayda and the woman continue their exchange of words until finally her expression becomes more welcoming.

She greets this time in the Sabaean tongue for the others to understand.

"Welcome . . . welcome to Tafukt! You have traveled a great distance. Come, refresh yourselves and prepare for your presence before our queen."

After that they follow the women towards the gates of the towers. As they approach there before them is a bridge plated in gold, reaching over the lake and to the gates.

When they reach the gates, the beautifully decorated gates open slowly echoing throughout all the forest. Each tower measures over 450 feet in height and are identical in structure.

Four more women come near, and the two women who escort the travelers tell the four in their native tongue to prepare the visitor's quarters.

The palace shines with a radiant light throughout. There are wide open windows in every corner that glisten with the rays of the sun.

Shamash looks at the well formed bodies of the women longingly. Noticing Shamash's roving eyes Zahira nudges him firmly on the arm with her elbow whispering,

"Shamash, calm yourself, we are guest here; we do not want to arouse any suspicion."

Once at the visitor's quarters Zahira and Zura are taken to separate rooms from the men to freshen up for their meeting with the queen. Sayda and Shamash too are taken to their quarters to prepare for the meeting.

When arriving at their rooms they are given clean garments to wear.

Zahira and Zura are clothed in gold satin robes that gleam, as if hand-made by the sun itself. A white velvet trim grace the edges of the robes.

On their feet are gold sandals garnished in the gems of the land.

The men are also draped in robes, brown in color, edges were trimmed in gold. However, Shamash robe proves a bit more snugged than Sayda's due to his bulky size.

There is a large bowel of fruit stationed in each room.

Zahira moans as she bites into one of them, the juices trickling down her chin. Never had she come across fruit that brought her so much delight.

The travelers are given time to enjoy the beauty of their surroundings before they are summoned before the queen.

The quarters themselves are decorated in elegant fashion. White leopard patterns carpet the walls, with each wall being framed in pure gold.

Marble statues of the queen and past ruling queens can be found in every room of the palace. Also, many tablets adorn the walls boasting of their accomplishments.

"The power these women possess," Zahira thinks to herself.

In the meantime, Zura gazes out the window of her quarters, she can only think of her hatred for Zahira. She thinks of how humiliated she felt when scolded by Sayda before the eyes of the strangers.

Suddenly, an evil plan starts to brew in her mind. Since she can not get Sayda to see the evil Zahira possessed, perhaps she can convince the Tanazart to side with her. She knows how the Tanazart feel about anyone from the South. It would not be hard to convince them.

A sinister grin comes over her face as she indulges her wicked thoughts.

She would have to speak with them before their meeting with the queen.

Zura has her evil plan figured out. All she has to do now is get to the Tanazart before Zahira speak with them.

The time finally comes for Zahira and her companions to meet with the queen.

The four women who escorted them to their quarters return to escort them to the queen's meeting chamber.

They enter a room where its walls are almost vacant due to the immense windows that surround every inch and the floors in smooth white granite.

Large plush pillows for sitting are scattered around floor level tables placed throughout the room.

Further into the room is the mighty lofty throne crafted in white marble and on it sits the queen of the Tanazart herself.

Next to her sits two great winged lionesses' pure white in color.

Four Tanazart guards stand at the bottom of the stairs that lead to their queen, who sits wrapped in her long golden colored cape on her enormous throne. She is very fair skinned with ebony black long hair, with streaks of auburn flowing through it. She holds in her right hand a long spear measuring seven feet in length and a flow of white light illuminates from her eyes.

"You have come far, Sayda," states the queen. "It has been a long time since our last meeting. Are your people in turmoil once again and in need of our assistance?"

Sayda respectfully replies, "My dear queen, the world lies in turmoil by the threat of Rathamun in the land of Azmaria. His powers are growing rapidly, much swifter than expected. His empire is flourishing and could soon be at the very gates of the North."

The queen positions herself in her throne forward.

"We, the Tanazart, are the sworn protectors of these lands and will kill any so-called Light or Black Dust that trespass. We swore allegiance with your people and your people only. Yes, Rathamun may be growing swiftly, but once he reaches these lands he will be cut down."

"Dear queen, we are at a loss in this battle," humbly interjects Sayda, "As you may know, Rathamun possesses the power of the Blackstar itself. This power is much stronger than yours and ours, but hope is not lost. The Koryan—"

"You know not of this Koryan," vehemently interrupt the queen, "and it is for no one to possess. Not even we can will it. However, we are its protectors and soon we shall find its secret to possession and harness its great power in battle."

"The secret lays here, now, before our eyes, great queen." Sayda hastily reply.

The queen immediately leans forward further, intently waiting for an explanation for his presumptuous statement.

Sayda continues.

"This woman we travel with is the answer to the dilemma we face. She possesses the power of the Whitestar. She is the one that might manipulate the Koryan that is in your charge."

Astonished the queen questions his claim. "Can it be; a survivor of the Light has come forth to claim the star which has been unbridled? Those of the Light were the Azmarians . . . they are now extinct. How is it she claims to be the last hope?"

"Dear queen, her very appearance speaks of who she is. I am of the Zehumians and our keen awareness of the earth gives us knowledge of all elements—"

"I know of whom you are," the queen interrupts abruptly. "Be silent."

At that moment, she rises from her throne and slowly strides down the stairs over toward Zahira, looking straight into her eyes.

After circling her a few times the queen finally puts her hand onto Zahira's shoulders and announces loudly,

"This day, I announce to all, a child of the pure Light has returned to us. Today, she becomes our sister and ally in the battle against Rathamun!"

A great rejoicing is heard throughout the palace.

The queen then turns to Zahira and asks,

"My sister, what is your name?"

"It is Zahira . . . but excuse me oh queen, your acceptance of me was rather quick."

"And you have an issue with this? Did you expect a dual to the death?" The queen laughs. "I too knew of your father, and he did send word to me by messenger of your possible presence here. One look into your eyes Zahira and I see your father Zada clearly. You are indeed his daughter. Now come with me. There is much to talk about, for your quest is not yet complete."

CHAPTER 35

The Uncertainties of Women

Amidst the rejoicing, Zura stands back in silence. She later heads back to her preparation chambers.

There waiting for her are eight Tanazart women, Kwella, Ijja, Damya, Dasin, Lalla, Dihya, Bahac and Menna. All resent and distrust Zahira and her companions from their entrance into their tower. Their heart proves one with Zura's.

Zura and the women meet in a quiet room in the palace where they plan an attack on Zahira and her supporters.

Zura addresses the women.

"All of us are fully aware of the menace that confronts us. In the region to the south of us Rathamun and his dark forces mount an attack on our pure lands. All those from the southern region have been corrupted by his evil influence, and such corruption will soon find its way to the northern lands if it is not stopped. This, Zahira, is part of that corruption. She is a spy sent by Rathamun . . . possibly even one of his secret ambassadors. Her plans are to form false alliances and trap us when we are at our weakest. If she is allowed access to the Koryan, she will surely wield its power and attack our people, increasing the power of her lord, Rathamun."

Kwella then interjects, "Me and my sisters are one in the fight against this severe menace, though the majority still remains loyal to the Queen. They follow Thiyya, blindly. However, we are very sure of our decision. But our numbers must increase. You are a Zehumian,

Zura. Why is it Sayda senses her as being from the Light, but you do not?"

"Sayda's senses have weakened due to age and his desperate hope for peace." Zura responds. "His desperation has led him to follow the first claim of hope that comes along, which is Zahira. However, you are correct Kwella; if he felt such a presence then I should have, also. I have not. So it must be a lie."

Dihya then speaks.

"A lie . . . Are you willing to turn your back on your master for the reason that you did not sense her as he did? Perhaps you are the weak one Zura."

"No!" screams Zura. "There is no weakness on my part. I am of the true elements. The White Dust has made my people and me who we are. For thousands of years we have lived and I am as strong as ever."

Ijja quickly interrupts, "Hold your tongue, Zura. You speak to Tanazart. Your enthusiasm and pride is pressing our limits."

"My sister, I do not wish to fight. I seek an alliance with our lands. There are others of my people who wish to join in this purification, as well. All I need to do is alert them that the time has come. They will be here in the twinkling of an eye. With our might combined, our armies will be unstoppable. We will then rid ourselves of this menace. Although we must act with guile, the pureness of our actions will become manifest."

"What is the plan my sisters," asks Dasin.

Ijja answers, "First and foremost, we must eliminate our barriers, Queen Thiyya and Sayda, the two so-called rulers and supporters of Zahira. But, of course, this must be done in secrecy, for there are many that remain loyal to them."

Zura looks at Ijja with a look of puzzlement, soon broken by a sinister smile.

She replies, "Music to my ears. I never thought you would sing it."

Menna looks at Zura and asks, "I still don't understand. You were known to have great loyalty to Sayda, even willing to give your life. This has changed?"

Zura turns and replies, "Sacrifices must be made for the betterment of our people and our world. Some times you have to accept the bad . . . to receive the good."

Time elapses and finally the women come up with a plan to rid themselves of Zahira, Thiyya, Sayda and Shamash.

"Sayda will send me back to Zehuma, in order to give word to the Zehumian armies of the union." States Zura, "Upon returning to Zehuma, I shall gather only those in compliance with us and return unseen to join you."

Ijja, leader of the eight speaks.

"I and my seven sisters will announce our desire to escort Zahira to the back mountains of Tanirta where the Koryan resides. We shall show full cooperation and agree to guide her to the Koryan. Once in the core of the terrain, we will attack, decimating her and her steed. We will then say the great Tanirtia ape, Gogoa, which dwells in the core of the area devoured her. After her death we shall feed her corpse to him. Bring your armies back and join us, then we will overtake the Towers of Tafukt."

"Sayda must die," replies Zura. "Even though he raised me from birth, he has become weak and may bring disaster to both our lands. I shall return to Tinitra with a thousand-fold, and with the help of you, my sisters, we shall become Tinitra's new rulers. Then we will bring about the peace that our lands long for."

"Is this to work? Have we covered all areas?" asks Kwella.

Zura replies, "It is sure to work."

In the interim, Queen Thiyya is in her armory chambers explaining to Zahira the task which is set before her in the mountains of Tanirta.

"Be careful on this journey, Zahira. Even though the land and its creatures belong to us, they know not of strangers. They will not harm Tanazart, but they will harm those who are not. The great silver backed ape, Gogoa, dwells in the middle of the realm. He is powerful and his race is giants. Even though I send Tanazart with you, you are still vulnerable. They will fight with you in order to assist your passage to the great mountains of Tanirta where you will find the Koryan.

Now, once you have reached the mountain your troubles will not be over. Two great lions guard its entrance, one as white as the snow atop our mountains and the other as black as night. Even we are not allowed to pass. The only one allowed passage is one touched by the Whitestar or the Blackstar. That one will enter unharmed. They will become like kittens, we shall than truly see who you really are. Be courageous and strong, for if you are truly a child of the Light, you shall succeed in your mission. Are you ready?"

"Yes I am." Zahira answers with great determination.

The Queen looks endearingly at Zahira and states,

"I believe in you, I know you will be successful on your mission."

The next two days, Zahira rests, preparing her mind and body for the final journey to retrieve the Koryan.

She rises from bed the last day and heads to Asaryn's stall.

She strokes his neck and states, "Asaryn, now is the time to reclaim what is ours. If it were not for you, I would not have made it thus far. We cannot fail. However, we must go alone. This trip belongs only to you and me."

That morning, Zahira wakes up quietly and girds herself with the necessary armament in preparation for the trip. She prepares Asaryn, as well.

Leaving her bedroom she heads toward the meeting room. She is abruptly stopped by Shamash; half dressed, running behind her.

"Woman what are you doing? Why did you not wake me? I will be ready to go with you shortly."

"There is no need for you to hurry so . . . Asaryn and I are going only with our Tanazart escorts."

Shamash screams, "Alone? Are you mad? Have I come all this way to the border of this great prize, only to be left behind? I think not. You are funny, but this is no time for jokes. We have a mission to fin—"

Zahira grabs Shamash's and sternly interrupts in a soft voice, "We will go alone, I tell you. This final part of my trip is not meant for you. Asaryn and I must go alone. It is our destiny. Only we will be allowed entrance by the guarding creatures of the star. Only I can wield the power of the Koryan. Your presence may cause unnecessary conflict."

"But I—"

"Shamash, you are perhaps the greatest man I have ever known. Your loyalty is unmatched. And even though you possess a few years over me, I am a big girl now."

Zahira smiles at Shamash and reminds him of their first meeting back in Azal, in "the circle".

"If I was successful in defeating you then I think I will be okay if I make this journey to Tanirta alone." She smiles.

Shamash gives a sarcastic laugh then states, "First and foremost, I allowed your victory and don't you forget that woman, I am a gentleman when need be. Go than you stubborn mule, and may all good fortune come your way. But know that I will always be there with you no matter what."

Zahira looks at Shamash suspiciously.

"Don't come following me Shamash. I—"

"Don't worry about what I will be doing woman, only worry about what you have to do."

Zahira and Shamash embrace.

Zahira begins to shed tears as she holds on to Shamash. He then releases quickly saying,

"Get going. No time for over dramatics!"

Zahira releases Shamash and then races toward the meeting room.

When Queen Thiyya spots Zahira, she immediately rises to her feet and introduces Zahira once again as the last of the Whitestar.

She then announces the trip in which Zahira is about to undertake.

She also announces the Tanazart women that will escort her to its location: Ijja, the captain of the guards and her loyal entourage, Kwella, Damya, Dasin, Lalla, Dihya, Bahac and Menna.

The warriors swear before the counsel to guard Zahira with their very lives.

After the announcements, Ijja approaches Zahira and puts her hand upon Zahira's shoulder reassuringly.

"We will protect you with our very lives. Trust us every step of the way."

Zahira puts her hand on Ijja's shoulder, replying, "I most truly appreciate your willing spirit. It is a strong and brave person indeed that would risk their life in behalf of one whom is really a stranger to her. I will also do what is necessary to ensure your safety. We are one. We all share the ultimate goal of peace. And we will succeed as long as we stick together. My prayers have been intense all night . . . im sure things will progress well."

They both embrace and proceed to prepare for the journey that lay ahead of them.

As the day advances, Sayda approaches Zura's quarters and knocks on the door.

"Who is calling?"

"It is I, Sayda. A word with you, please."

"Of course, come in."

Sayda enters.

"I want to commend you for the effort you have been putting forth to make peace with Zahira. Even though your feelings may not be truly genuine, you are at least willing to put them aside for the sake of the cause."

"I am deeply sorry for my past actions." Zura responds, "I have always looked to you for guidance and have always desired to be in your favor. My past actions have brought shame on my head that can never be taken away. I can only hope that one day I will be able to redeem myself and once again be in your good graces."

"All is forgiven, my child. But let us dwell on the past no longer. We must now commence with our plans. Return to Zehuma as was discussed and alert our awaiting forces to our imminent entry into Rathamuns realm."

"I will carry out your orders as planned. I will not let you down again."

"I trust that you will not. I will take my leave and let you prepare for your journey back to Zehuma. Be safe my dear."

CHAPTER 36

Betrayal

As Zura heads back to Zehuma, Zahira and her Tanazart companions begin their 150 mile journey to the mountains of Tanirta, which takes 12 days to complete. Tanirta is the land across the narrow stretch of the sea from Tinitra and is connected by an astonishing long wide flat bridge constructed by the Tanazart women over a century ago.

"Keep your wits about you, Zahira. We will soon enter the territory of the Gogoa ape. He is very dangerous and cunning. He will be hard to see in this dense foliage, perfectly camouflaged in his natural surroundings," Ijja exclaims, who is three paces ahead of her.

"Thank you for the warning. I will proceed with caution."

The Tanazart travel across on the backs of their lionesses, with Zahira traveling on Asaryn. Finally after many rest stops, they reach the core of the vicinity; the falling autumn leaves have slowed down.

The giant trees are colored various shades of red and yellow. The floor of the pathway they travel is blanketed with these fallen leaves.

There is a narrow stream in the middle of the area, rich blue in color. It seems cruel to disturb the tranquility of the meek quiet forest.

"It is quite understandable that the Koryan would be found here. I cannot find the proper words to describe what my eyes behold," exclaims Zahira.

"Do not be fooled by the beauty of this land, for once again I must warn you of the dangers to be faced," blurts Ijja. "The Gogoa guards the land and he is fierce. He will devour any that are not Tanazart. Despite our presence, you will still be vulnerable."

"I have been duly warned. I will take the necessary precautions. I have faced many dangers in my past journeys and will face this one, as well," courageously replies Zahira.

Indignant, Ijja states, "You have faced nothing compared to what you will soon be up against. The Gogoa are not to be taken lightly. Their powers are far superior to any creature you have ever come in contact with."

Zahira humbly remarks, "I am not underestimating the power of these creatures."

Ijja quickly replies, "See that you do not."

After some time in the center of the forest, Ijja starts to slow her pace. There are two trees facing one another, forming an oval shape.

"Do you see the two trees that form the oval shape? Enter among the trees and begin your journey to the Koryan," exclaims Ijja, knowing she is sending Zahira to her possible death.

About now, Zahira grows weary of the women that seem to not want to continue the journey with her. However, Zahira follows Ijja's directions and enters between the trees.

It appears as though she has entered into a denser part of the forest.

As she moves deeper into the brush she feels warm air whirling around her.

She brings Asaryn to a halt.

Before she can get down off of Asaryn to investigate her surroundings, she is suddenly knocked off of his back, landing hard on the leaf-covered ground. The impact is so great that her right arm is dislocated and her leg is badly bruised.

Asaryn begins to gallop toward Zahira so as to investigate the attack, only to be struck down, as well. The attack on Asaryn is so devastating that it temporarily stuns him.

With her remaining strength, Zahira props up against a crag and overlooks her surroundings seeing nothing but leaves whirling in the air.

As she struggles to reach Asaryn she is struck again, being sent into a tree. The force of the impact reset her arm.

A mysterious growl fills the air.

As she turns to see from what direction the growl is coming, she soon witnesses a frightening site.

Large beastly teeth seem to appear in mid air, salivating profusely.

Finally, the creature's whole body slowly appears out of camouflage.

It is an extremely large creature. It has two saber teeth protruding past its lower jaw, and in its hand it carried a large tree limb that is incased in a blue crackling energy. It is the Gogoa ape of the mountains.

The creature begins to speak in a language unidentified by Zahira.

It slowly approaches. With each step it takes the ground shakes violently.

Zahira quickly rises to her feet, disregarding the pain she is experiencing.

She draws her weapon and prepares to fight the beast.

The beast strikes at her with the tree club, missing her entirely as she dodges.

She quickly runs and leaps onto a nearby hill behind the creature and pounces on its back.

The beast screams and shakes violently in an attempt to remove her.

Zahira takes her sword and plunges it between its shoulder blades. She then jumps off its back, flipping and landing on a clearing fifteen feet before the beast.

The beast falls to its knees, snorting and moaning as it reaches to pull the sword out of its back.

It then hurls the sword at her, but she is able to grab its handle evading from being hit.

It swings the club once again.

Having faith in her abilities, she attempts to block its attack with her sword. The collision is so great that an array of energy shoots from the two weapons.

She is successful in blocking, though it pushes her backwards, she then leaps to avoid the next onslaught of attacks.

Avoiding the swings of the club, Zahira runs toward the creature, sliding between its legs.

Grabbing hold of the flowing hair between its legs she hoists herself up on the creature's lower back end and scales further up to its shoulders.

She takes her sword and plunges it into the wound she had made earlier, pushing it so deep that the handle finally disappears into the flesh.

The beast manages to flip Zahira off its back and falls to the ground, moaning in great pain.

Asaryn finally rises and runs to Zahira's rescue.

After mounting him, the two run toward the turbulent beast.

Holding Asaryn's strap she stands on his back.

Once they are fifteen feet in front of it, she jumps head on at the screaming monster.

Zahira then swiftly climbs on the creature's back once again and with her sword plunges it into the same wound, pushing it even further introducing the properties of her sword to its bloodstream.

A blue crystallizing energy begins to surround the beast in a circular motion, with it finally crashing to the earth dead.

Zahira walks over to the massive beast sorrowfully and retrieves her sword.

She looks at Asaryn as he gallops to her side.

She lowers her head and gives a long sigh, panting for breath, stroking his mane.

"Well . . . done, but it's a shame this creature had to die this way."

She now begins to look around in wonderment as to where the Tanazarts had gone.

"Where are Ijja and the others?"

Suddenly, Zahira hears the snapping of a twig behind her.

She looks around and notices eight silhouette figures emerging from the fog.

As the figures come closer out of the cold mist, she recognizes them to be Ijja and her Tanazart companions.

"Where did you go? You swore to fight with me and lead me from the path of the Gogoa. Instead you led me straight into its den. An innocent beast had to die today." Zahira fusses.

The women remain silent as they approach closer.

Ijja then walks up to Zahira and calmly replies, "You fought well, Zahira. We have underestimated your powers. You were able to defeat the Gogoa. We do mourn his death, but we will now complete the job it was unable to carry out. We shall succeed in ridding the world of this evil you possess. And once we have finished with you, we will finish off your master, Rathamun."

"Are you mad," cries the exhausted Zahira. "I am not one of Rathamun's puppets. My senses told me that you were not to be trusted. Your over-zealous, egotistical ignorance will be your downfall."

"The queen is weak; she is not with us in purpose." Ijja sneers, "She has been duped by Sayda the weakest of all, and has accepted you as the last child of pure light, our supposed hope. Weakness will not be tolerated. Queen Thiyya will be done away with and I, Ijja, shall rule in her place. I will bring true peace to the world. You shall not wield the Koryan, dark one. No one shall, but the Tanazart."

At that moment, Zahira in her weakened state draws her weapon in preparation for battle.

Ijja smiles and send charged expressions of her power pulsating through her spear. With the speed of an eagle she charges at Zahira.

The two weapons clash with great force, sparking spectacular displays of energy.

Ijja kicks Zahira to the ground and lunges at her with her spear.

Zahira rolls out of the way, tripping Ijja and sending her to the ground.

Zahira then rises and jumps on Ijja, striking her in the face with her fist.

Ijja kicks Zahira off of her, but Zahira flips to safety, landing on her feet.

Ijja regains her footing and charges Zahira with her staff held back. But Zahira blocks the attack.

At that moment the other women rush to assist Ijja, striking quickly at Zahira.

Zahira manages to block the attacks of all but one, Lalla, who manages to hit her shoulder with her spear.

Zahira falls to one knee, holding her damaged shoulder, the very one she dislocated and replaced when fighting the Gogoa.

Asaryn runs to Zahira's aid. But Bahac charges her spear and sends a blast of energy hurling to the earth beneath his hooves, causing him to fall in a large crater, unable to get out.

The Tanazart women then put their weapons down and start to strike her with knuckle armaments charged by their powers.

Zahira, although badly beaten and in excruciating pain, still tries to defend herself, but to no avail.

The women finally cease their attack as Zahira lay there in agony near death.

Ijja, who watches in the background, recuperating from her fight with Zahira, finally breaks up the fight and approaches the battered Zahira. She grabs Zahira's chin and holds her head in her hands.

With confidence she snarls, "Now, the evil of Rathamun shall end. It is the custom of your evil lord to cripple opposing ambassadors and send back to their masters as a warning. While it is true that you will be crippled, you will not be sent back to your master. We will kill you, make our army stronger and then kill your lord Rathamun."

Totally exhausted and badly beaten, Zahira replies, "Arrogant mistress of fools, I am not . . . and never have I been . . . a cohort of Rathamun, nor is he my lord. I have only one lord and God, he is the creator and sustainer of all life, and his ways far surpass this feeble planet and all life therein . . . whether White or Blackstar, but today . . . your blind cause and extremist views has become your downfall. Nevertheless, my soul is prepared today . . . how is yours?"

Laughing, Ijja responds, "Why should I prepare to die? You are the one that lies here in agony, awaiting your end."

At that moment a loud war cry fills the air above them.

When Ijja and her companions turn to investigate the cries, they witness twenty Tanazart on lioness backs led by the chief of the army, Silfa, followed by Tadefi, Tiziri and other Tanazart warriors, loyal to the Queen. And to Zahira's amazement, they are also accompanied by Shamash, riding upon one of the beasts with a Tanazart.

A great fear seizes Ijja and her renegade companions.

"This was not to happen," cries Menna, "We were assured the plan was full proof. We have been betrayed."

Ijja then yells, "Fight! Fight with your lives in the name of Tinitra!"

The renegade Tanazarts fight, but to no avail. Lalla, Dasin, Menna, Bahac and Dihya, the strongest of the band, are the first to fall. Damya and Kwella are taken captive.

After the attack, Ijja stands with her glowing spear held outward to the rescuing band. Silfa, Tadefi and Tiziri dismount their beasts and cautiously walk over to her.

Tadefi speaks softly, yet firmly, "You were one of the most trusted in the court, part of our special band, and the personal guard to the Queen. But now that privilege falls upon me because of your treacherous betrayal sister."

"Treachery," screams Ijja. "You, my sister, have become weak and treacherous! You welcome outsiders blindly. Proof was never given of this woman's identity, and you along with the others did not seem to care about this important detail!"

"You did not allow time for such proof, Ijja."

Ijja then screams, "If she is from the Blackstar and she wields the Koryan she will destroy us all! Join me Tadefi. Join me in rekindling the light of our proud city. Help me to rid our world of the treachery that has found its way to our very gates."

Tadefi looks down toward the earth then slowly looks back up at Ijja regretfully, staring straight into her eyes.

"Ijja, my sister…you have become the treachery and embarrassment in the land of Tinitra."

At that moment Silfa and Tiziri quickly slay Ijja with their daggers.

Tadefi then turns and announces to those with her, "The evil done by our renegade sisters has been removed. They shall serve as a warning to all that dare defy the Queen. Take the prisoners back to Tafukt. Tala, Tiziri and I shall accompany Zahira in continuing her journey in claiming the Koryan."

As Zahira recuperates, Shamash helps her free Asaryn from the crater.

"Did I not say that I would be with you?" He grunts.

Zahira smiles, placing her hand on Shamash' arm and states, "Thank you for not listening to me."

She mounts the back of Asaryn with Shamash's aid and a warm cloak is placed around her. Shamash walks beside Asaryn guiding his bridles for her as she takes her rest.

They then make their way to the great mountain that housed the Koryan.

CHAPTER 37

Koryan

Zahira is very much fatigued at this point and has lost a lot of blood from her wounds.

They finally reach another bridge, which spans over a deep canyon.

On the other side of the bridge, a radiant light glows ever so brightly at the base of a large snow-capped mountain.

"This is the mountain she is to go into," states Tala. "If she is accepted by the Koryan her wounds will be healed."

All of them dismount their animals and begin on foot to cross the narrow bridge, with Tadefi leading, followed by Zahira, Shamash, Silfa and Tiziri. Shamash carries Zahira in his strong arms.

When they reach the end of the bridge, there before them is a large tunnel carved into the base of the mountain.

Upon the brim of the tunnel are the written words, a riddle, of the ancient Azmarians, the dialect the Bahati women gave her the ability to speak.

Surprisingly Zahira seems to instantly be renewed with vigor and steps down from Shamash's arms. She limps ahead toward the writing on the cave.

Falling to her knees, she utters the words written; it is a riddle and only the one able to read it may gain entrance.

"Into the darkness the light, and out of the light comes forth hope. Into the light, darkness, and thus all hope be lost. The child *is born of light or darkness, but approaches from the unknown. Light walks to the mouth of the lion, darkness devours the lion, and darkness dwindles in the chaos of prominence. The division of both is mysterious, yet different but the same, both come to the missing piece but yet only one will wield its power and shall have no shame."*

She continues to utter the words faster and faster. Soon she zones out, as if in a sleep walk.

While she is doing so, the ground begins to tremble under their feet.

Shamash and the Tanazart women cautiously step back not knowing what will happen next.

As the tremors increase Shamash then jumps forward attempting to grab hold of Zahira, but Tadefi grabs his shoulder to restrain him.

Suddenly, from the darkness of the mountain two immense lions burst forth, roaring and snarling, one white and the other black.

Energy emits from their mouths and eyes as they rush fiercely with unrelenting speed toward the kneeling Zahira. On looking closer, these are the very lions that Zahira met with the lady of the forest many years ago when she was only a child.

As soon as they reach only a few feet of her, she leisurely rises and holds her hand up in a stoping motion calmly stating in a soft but firm tone, "Stop."

On recognition, the cats come to an abrupt halt, reverently moving out of her way to reveal a path inside the tunnel.

She begins to glow radiantly as she walks between the two lions with the three of them entering the cave.

"See," remarks Shamash. "This proves she is of the Light. The lions gave her access to the Koryan."

"You are mistaken, Shamash of Sumeria. The Tanirta lions will accept one of either the pure White or the Blackstar. They will devour all those of mortal decent or of the White or Black Dust, like you and I."

While in the cave, Zahira appears as a zombie. Her eyes are void of pupils and burn a bright yellow.

She approaches the opening to a large lit room.

In its core is a beautiful altar decorated with carvings of warriors and ancient writings written in the ancient language of the Azmarians.

As she walks up the stairs, a deep low humming noise echoes throughout the room.

The two lions calmly sit at the bottom of the stairs and eventually lay down.

Zahira walks toward the altar. Situated above it, hovering in mid air is the spherical energy Koryan, lightening the whole room with intense cosmic energy.

She slowly reaches out to touch the sphere with both her hands. Once making contact the energy from the Koryan rumbles loudly and encases her whole body. She then takes her sword Nazaar and jabs it into the center of the sphere.

The two weapons instantly fuse together. A shattering noise race through the room and exits the tunnel, sending Shamash and the women to the ground.

Energy of various hues encircles her body, bouncing from her, then to the walls and then back to her again until finally entering her body. Her wounds and bruises start to quickly heal.

The Lions rise and walk away, only to vanish into thin air. Zahira walks down from the stairs and exits the mountain, still hypnotized by the energies of the Koryan.

Upon exiting the mountain, she freezes. The mountain then begins to slowly crumble behind her.

"Get her, quickly," yells Tadefi.

Shamash, Tala and Tizirim run and grab hold of Zahira. They run toward the bridge only to find the bridge collapsing away into the sea.

The whole ground begins to crumble into the large canyon. Tadefi makes a chanting call summoning their four winged escorts.

Before they can be crushed, they are rescued by the lionesses and fly safely into the air to the other side.

Upon reaching the other side of the canyon, the lionesses land where Asaryn is waiting for Zahira. Asaryn gently nudges her on the head, awakening her from her daze.

Zahira wakes and is filled with passion and new hope. She then jumps on Asaryn's back announcing, "It is time. Let us return to Tafukt."

As Zahira rides into the distance, Tadefi, Silfa and Tiziri's mouths drop in amazement at the ordeal.

Laughing, Shamash comments, "There is no need to drool over what you have just witnessed women. I am quite sure now you believe."

Once back at the towers of Tafukt, a trial is coming to an end. Queen Thiyya addresses the shackled women.

"You have been found guilty of betrayal and conspiring against the Queen and her guest. You are hereby sentenced to death. It shall take place in the hour of the next moon."

The two women begin to yell, furiously jerking, attempting escape from the Tanazart guards. They are then escorted to the execution chambers.

Upon laying eyes on Zahira, Queen Thiyya and the Tanazart court, including Shamash and Sayda, fall to their knees, prostrating themselves.

"Raise my brothers and sisters; I am only a mortal not a god. Such praise should be given to the true creator of all life." exclaims Zahira. "We are now united in a common goal, reclamation of the once proud lands of Azmaria from the grips of the evil forces of Rathamun. Let us prepare to enter the land as prophesied and restore peace!"

The entire room is filled with cheer as the words of Zahira are accepted. The time has come for the Whitestar to return to the land of Azmaria.

Meanwhile, Zura, on back of a flying lioness, approaches the gates of Zehuma. All seems quiet and still.

"I wonder where all have gone," she asks herself. "I must find Thitila and alert her to the readiness of the women in Tinitra."

As Zura walks deeper into the woods, she notices there is still no activity. She then goes to the home of her cohort, Thitila, to find no one there.

"What is this," she thinks. "Where has everyone gone?"

She goes to the palace of Sayda.

She enters and hears faint voices in the distance.

When she reaches the entrance she witnesses a horrifying sight.

Hoisted in the air by large hands made of the earth are Thitila and the other renegade Zehumians that were awaiting her return. They were all dead.

Zura falls to her knees sick with grief and fear, immediately being apprehended by five soldiers.

Then, from among the elders walks Surra, nephew of Sayda and first in command of the Zehumian armies.

"My sister . . . or shall I say, my enemy. You and your foolish companions have betrayed the order of the Zehumians. Fanatical idiot, now you shall suffer the same fate of your renegade comrades.

"No," screams Zura as the earth starts to grow around her and ravage her, hoisting her into the air with her dead companions.

Sayda travels back to Batheria, to his home in Zehuma. There his plans are in motion to collect his army and return back to Tinitra to assist Zahira. When he arrive his gets word of Zura's betrayal, this causes him untold grief. He leaves his home and is soon found to be missing, with no one aware as to his whereabouts. He is so overcome with grief and disappointment that he retreats into the unknown, and is no longer seen or heard by anyone again.

When Zahira and Shamash get word of Sayda's disappearance they recite the Chant of mourning, taught by the Muhas, in memory of Sayda's great accomplishments.

Zahira and Shamash return to the palace and there to meet them is Barak and Surra. Barak is the second general of the Zehumian armies. Behind them are the fighting men of the Zehumians all adorned in there plated tunics and power wielding scimitar swords. They address Queen Thiyya and the whole court.

"Great queen, with me is Surra, first general and I am Barak, second general over the Zehumian armies. Our forces were sent here by request of Sayda to assist the lost child of Light in her conquest over Rathamun, before his disappearance.

Shamash shouts enthusiastically, "If it is blood you crave then we welcome you with open arms friend."

Looking over at the perplexed expression of the Tanazart queen, Shamash states, "Now . . . if only we were assured of your cravings as well."

Queen Thiyya answers the rhetorical question made by Shamash saying, "At this point . . . the Tanazart will not be able to assist you, Zahira. We must first insure that further attempts to usurp the throne are vanquished. If care is not taken in this regard we could very well be setting ourselves up for further betrayal. I must correct what is here first, before blindly taking my forces out against this threat. I hope you un—"

In a great rage Shamash interrupts the queen.

"What is this that you speak? First you promise to fight to the death, but now your cowardly side rears its ugly head. Your attempts to appear superior to men have indeed failed. You are displaying your inferiority, not being able to even hold out to your own word."

At that moment the Queens captain of the guard Tadefi and three of her soliders quickly come forward and face Shamash with an unwavering stare, she then shouts saying,

"How dare you speak to our Queen with disrespect, you walk on treacherous ground, insolent fool. I alone could slice you from head to toe with one swipe of my dagger. No one questions the wisdom of the queen, especially a sniveling toad like you."

Shamash snarls, "Choose your words wisely woman. You are not the only one here skilled in combat. I am Shamash! Smasher of thousands, and would not dare stand and allow some cow to best me in what I prove most valiant in war. You babbling woman."

"Words wisely? You speak to me about intelligence," growls Tadefi. "The fact that you speak in such a tone to a Tanazart is in itself a lack of yours. Many of you so called warrior men have attempted to bring the Tanazart to their knees, as they so arrogantly thought, but they are now buried deep into the earth. And if you do not cease speaking you will share their fate."

Before Shamash can respond, Zahira place her hand softly on Shamash's shoulder so as to ease his temper.

Queen Thiyya finally intercedes. "Silence! Neither one is to speak another word! Your behavior is childish, so shall I treat you as children?"

Queen Thiyya then turns to address Shamash.

"I am sorry you feel the way you do my friend. But your words do not change what has already been decided upon. If we were to go into battle without even skimming over the surface of my militia, our success could indeed be jepordized, even causing jeapordy to both you and your companions. Betrayal could surely resurface and cause friction within the ranks . . . that is definitely not what we want during this crucial time. The shame of my followers has mounted like floodwaters within me. It must be put to rest. What I have said, is what will be done."

Zahira then states, "I understand . . . we all understand. However, despite our decrease in forces, we will continue our journey to Azmaria."

Finally, Zahira and her mighty forces bid the Tanazart farewell and prepare to leave south for the land of Azmaria.

As they prepare for their departure Shamash approaches Zahira in confidence.

"Why did you remain silent? Why did you not speak up and share your disgust with the sudden removal of their aid? Their reason for pulling their forces out is unacceptable, especially after the sermon given of the aid they would provide by their queen . . . the cowards. And did not the Bahati speak of them joining us in this fight."

"Shamash, it is not for us to interfere in the affairs of others. Although our forces may have declined, we will be successful, regardless. Anyway, I do feel that they will not leave us to face Rathamun alone. They will come to our aid, one way or another. Have faith my brother . . . have faith."

As the days wear on, messengers from the far eastern land of Azal arrive in Tinitra and find there way to Tafukt. They are escorted into the gates by two Tanazart guards.

The travelers consist of six able bodied men, five being hand chosen warriors, students from the school of the Muhas and the one being a young Muhas student himself. They travel with hardy camels fed a rich empowering butter that gave an unusual vigor to the beast. The men are exhausted due to the long trip made through the mountainous lands that takes over two months to make.

The Muhas, Danti, on seeing Zahira after being allowed access by the Tanazart runs over to her eagerly and states,

"Honor is to you, Zahira, the wonderful user of the Whitestar and holder of Koryan," he exclaims. "May you have good health and prosper. We come to you all the way from the land of Azal to deliver a message of utmost importance."

"I remember you," smiles Zahira approaching the young lad rubbing the back of her neck.

"When I was but a girl and brought before the Muhas for questioning, you were the young boy that stood near Ahura. My have you grown and your very appearance speak of the wealth of power that you have attained. It is wonderful to have you here amongst us. Speak my brother."

"And you are more beautiful then ever, a gem in a dark world." He replies, "Ahura, your former mentor, has sent his warmest greetings to you and your companions. However, I bring to you news that requires your listening ear. These are the words of Ahura: 'Zahira may you indeed be the shining star for these lands to gaze upon and may you continue to grow with insight and strength. Our land has already felt the ring of hope with your retrieval of the Koryan, and now we await your triumphant victory over darkness. The enemy you will fight is great and powerful. He is not to be underestimated. Much is to be considered before facing your foe."

Zahira nod her head, acknowledging the statements made by Danti.

He then continues, "Sadly . . . the Muhas also sent dire news, the death of your friend and sister, Salasa."

Zahira's watered eyes open wide, in disbelief. Danti, recognizing her grief walks over to her and grabs hold of her hand.

He continues, "Tribulation in the flesh of the loss of her people and your departure troubled her so that physical and mental illness befell her."

On hearing this, Zahira turns and drops her head. Tears start to run down her cheeks.

Finally, after gaining some control she looks at Danti and asks, "What of Kimoni and Tegene? Have they returned to the land of Azal?"

Looking perplexed and confused, Danti responds, "Why, no. They have not come back to Azal. We have heard not a word from your companions."

Zahira then responds, "Thank you, Danti. Thank you for bringing the warm greetings of the Muhas. Go, now, you must rest a few days and we will equip you with provisions and a map to ensure your safe return. The map will show you the route of safety on your long journey back to Azal."

Danti hastily replies, "My princess, the message that I bring has more to tell. In order for you to succeed against Rathamun this counsel you are to heed. Even though you possess the Koryan now, your opponent's power still might rival that of what you possess. The power of your people still grows within you and will surface correctly when it deems necessary. Rathamun feeds off of all the dark energies of the continent. This has made him unspeakably powerful. But he cannot contain all the energies within him. Only through the use of a catalyst can he use or wield the magnitude of the energies he possess."

"A weapon that can hold such power must be immense," interjects Shamash.

"Not necessarily," replies Zahira. "Such energies can be condensed and contained in a devise like that of a mere cane, or like the very bands you wear that channels your power."

"But, my dear princess," interrupts Danti. "both of you are correct, but Shamash speaks the reality. The catalyst he uses to enhance his power is the temple of Azwrala, the temple of your extinct people Zahira. He has insulated its walls and filled it with all the dark energies he possesses in excess. As long as he remains in the temple, no one can stop his influence over his armies. In order to defeat him even with the power of the Koryan, you must draw him away from his source of extra power, the temple of Azwrala, and only by doing this can you put an end to his existence. This he knows and will protect dearly. However, he will still possess much power, but in limited measures.

"Rathamun has defiled the name of my people and has brought shame to the temple of Azwrala." exclaims Zahira. "I will not rest until he is destroyed."

After speaking with Danti and his companions, Zahira then prepares the young travelers for their lengthy journey back to Azal after their recuperation for five days in Tafukt.

That night in her room, she meditates deeply on the news about Salasa, Kimoni and Tegene. She then falls to her knees and grieves sorely until finally falling fast asleep.

The next morning, she rises and prepares to meet her companions who will assist her on the trip to Azmaria.

They are given many supplies by the Tanazart because their journey back south will indeed be great and long.

CHAPTER 38

The Height of Darkness

"All kneel in the presence of Lord Rathamun," announces Kifo.

Coming from the large doorway, behind the throne steps the iniquitous Rathamun.

He enters the dark palace and sits upon the grand throne. The palace no longer speaks of its grand past of beauty when occupied by the Azmarians, now it is filled with darkness and a red hue of light emanates throughout. Cracks and wholes fill its floors and walls and some of its mighty pillars that once adorned every corner lay broken.

Rathamun himself is covered from head to toe in a long cloak as black as pitch. He possesses a large imposing muscular frame that could be clearly noticed while even enshrouded in his black cloak. Imensley Large gray feathered wings protruded from his back through his cloak. He stands over seven feet in height with glowing red eyes that peer from the darkness of the black hood.

Suddenly, all in attendance, high ranking warriors, counselors, and judges kneel upon one knee acknowledging the dark ruler's supreme presence.

As he sits, he quietly gazes upon all in the large room, with his flashing red eyes passing over them.

Finally, Kifo asks one of the personal scouts of Rathamun, "Have we received word from the messengers?"

"No, my lord."

"Rathamun can feel his enemy approaching. She now possesses the Koryan. Now that she has completed the difficult part of finding it, Rathamun shall now claim from her what rightfully belongs to him. The time of reclamation has come."

Kifo now turns his attention to all the attendees awaiting further instructions.

"The armies of Light are approaching. We shall emerge and give them a greeting made in fire."

Darkness fills the sky above all Azmaria as Rathamun and his forces await Zahira and her army's entrance into the land.

The journey through the middle of Lykanda in route to the Obasi vicinity will take them over twenty five days.

Zahira and Shamash travel with the armies of the Zehumians, three hundred on Zebran backs and thousands on foot.

Still troubled, Shamash approaches Zahira.

"I still do not understand why you did not insist that the Tanazart accompany us."

"Are you unsure of our capabilities? Have you begun to doubt Shamash?"

With pride swelling within him Shamash quickly responds, "Doubt? I am quite sure of my abilities and by no means have I ever doubted the union of our forces. However—"

"As was said before," interrupts Zahira, "I do not believe they will leave us to face Rathamun alone. They will come."

"You are too trusting, Zahira."

"Shamash, even though you say you don't, you do doubt. We are fighting for peace. This is the desire of the Tanazart, as well. That is why I know they will assist us."

"I hope you are correct in your thinking, Zahira."

"If I am wrong and we must meet with death, then our death will not be in vain."

As they enter Obasi it is a chilled night carrying a heavy mist. Obasi is filled with crack roads and caves with sporadic bush and revenes. Soon they begin to hear the faint sounds of moaning in the distance, hovering amongst the hills and mountains.

"We are now in Obasi," exclaims Barak.

Soon they start to hear faint voices in the area warn, "Go back . . . Go back!"

"Did you hear that," asks Zahira.

"Yes, the mist is thick. I can see nothing ahead of us," replies Surra. "We must use caution."

At that moment, a figure clothed in dark rags emerges from the mist before them.

"Go back," the creature cries. The dark figure begins to run toward them, followed by an army of dark figures, who commence yelling, "Go back! Go back! This is the land of a dark god. Go back before death overtakes you."

"We have come to fight the dark forces of Rathamun," boldly replies Barak.

"Go back, I say! You have been warned. Darkness shall prevail. The land is corrupt. Lord Rathamun moves further north, devouring all in his path. We are the last remaining humans of this region. Go back before it's too late!"

Ignoring the warnings, the warriors proceed with their travels.

The strange humans quickly flee back to their cave dwellings.

"What was that all about?" asks Shamash.

"They are refugees, fleeing from Rathamun," replies Surra.

"Their shrewdness may preserve them alive," interjects Zahira.

As they progress further they soon come to a hill, once they reach the top on the other side they witness serpent-men of the Black Dust that start to rise like shoots of grass from the stream that circle the base of the hill.

The serpent-men begin to speak in a tongue unknown to the warriors.

Some start to hiss and crawl up the side of the hill.

"These are the Forgotten Ones," states Surra. "They were chased from the realm of Rathamun, being deemed too weak a species to continue. There deformations proved to be their undoing."

"Then they should not be a problem for us. We are slayers of their enemy," exclaims Shamash.

Surra replies, "They do not care why we have come. They will devour you the first chance given them. The dark and tainted dust of the Blackstar has corrupted their minds."

"How do you know these things?" asks Zahira.

"We once shared the powers of the earth together, thousands of years before they came unto Rathamun. However, they were tainted with darkness. Even though we, too, are of the elements and can sense the origin of all those of the star, they were able to mask their inheritance of Black Dust from us. War broke out when their deceit was discovered.

The Zehumians touched by the White Dust were victorious. Those touched by the Black Dust that did not perish fled. They came to join Rathamun, but were betrayed. They now protect the gates to Azmaria. They became mad and twisted under the hardened hand of Rathamun."

As the creatures reach the top of the hill, they come to a halt. Their eyes glow fire red and they bare their long fangs, hissing and moaning.

"Ready your weapons," yells Barak.

Immediately, the creatures rush toward the warriors, but the warriors are not idle fighters. Hundreds of the deformed creatures are swiftly slaughtered.

Zahira and Shamash race through the creatures, slaying all they pass.

One thousand of the creatures are slain.

Surra then yells to the armies, "Head towards the river."

"The River is teaming with these creatures. It is—" Barak responds.

But Surra urges him anyway, "Forward Barak," interrupts Surra. "This is the best route. It will pull us out of these parts quicker."

The warriors race through the river, which stretches from Obasi into Do'a, right at the border of Azmaria.

Finally they escape the serpent men after galloping for over an hour.

In two days they finally reach a large village deep into Do'a. The tribe in this area is known as the Doata. They have managed to stay safe from many of the creatures of the dust by taking refuge in their homes built into the side of mountains. However, they know of Rathamun's progression northwards and knew that eventual combat was inevitable. The arrival of Zahira and her companions bring hope to the people.

CHAPTER 39

The Calm Before the Storm

In the intervening time during their stay in Do'a, they are housed and entertained by the Doata people. The people are very kind and welcoming. They live in carved out homes in the mountains and have fashioned latter's from one level to the next for moving about freely to different levels. The people dress in desert clothing, and keep their faces wrapped to protect from the scorching sun and sand drenched winds. Their tribal chief is a well known warrior, Zaadan, with a loyal army of over two hundred men.

There is much for Zahira to meditate on, for her entry into Azmaria, only a three days journey will be the most heart wrenching test she will have ever undergone. She overlooks those that accompany her and smiles pleasingly over the large loyal army of Zehumians under generals Surra and Barak. They are dressed in their traditional teal colored light armor and their staffs along with their slender swords, which they use as catalyst to channel their elemental powers. Their Zebran steeds are covered in a light armor to protect their sides and head. The Zehumians spend most of their time practicing their elemental control during the hours of dawn. Shamash himself is also eager for the fight. He lost his parents to Rathamun thus is eager to exact vengeance. Zahira is proud to have such loyal fighters by her side.

During their stay, Zahira finds much time to be alone to meditate, even praying in full prostration over her concerns. She knows that this war will be the determining factor over the condition of the world she knows of, but it is her faith in her purpose which drives her forward with conviction. She finds a quiet stream right outside of the village's boundaries, near the large cliffs and indulges in the silence. Her loyal stallion Asaryn always remains by her side even when she is in deep meditation and prayer. Though there are other women around from the Doata tribe, Zahira does not take company with them.

However, Shamash keeps himself busy with the people of Doata. He visits with the soldiers sharing war stories and spoken legends. There are many poets in the tribe, thus poetry every night is recited by a large fire where they gather to speak of both the horrors of their times and the past days of peace. Shamash muscular form, long hair, braided beard and tall stature draws the attention of many of the young women of the tribe. When telling his stories the young women crowd around in the near distance to hear his powerful and enthusiastic stories.

On their last day before their travel into Amaria, Shamash is caught by the young women and they beg for him that evening to tell them his stories concerning his exploits. He agrees and after that night they are once again elated over his story telling ability.

Zahira passes by shaking her head and briefly laugh under her breath at Shamash boastful and proud behavior.

"Shamash . . . perhaps you should get some rest now . . . seeing we have a long trip ahead of us in the morning."

"Don't worry about me woman," Shamash responds haughtily, "I have more than enough fight for those demons. Perhaps you should be sleep."

Zahira laughs to herself and leaves off to her sleeping quarters.

"She is so . . . harsh, hard . . . and demanding." gripes one of the women.

Shamash responds, "Rightfully so woman. She has been through a lot; you cannot imagine the tests she has undergone in life. Being a woman she has to up her demeanor a bit, she can't be as dainty as you charming ladies. Besides, if her personality bothers you, then stay away from her woman."

The women sneer at Shamash response. One of them states, "If it wasn't for her looks I would think she was a Tanazart."

Shamash rears his head back in loud laughter and reply, "The Tanazart are some tough women, but they have nothing on that white headed Azmarian woman there . . . she is the lioness, the Tanazart are kittens when compared to her."

One of the women reply,

"The Tanazart are tough warriors, what do you mean kittens. They are the slayer of men . . . and have been known for that for centuries."

Shamash reply, "Is that so . . . let me show you the difference between Zahira and those Tanazart you fear so. The Tanazart are rough, tough and full of attitude. They walk about upset with the world everyday of their life, but what they lack is balance woman. Zahira is tough when she needs to be, but she can smooth it all down and be as gentle as a kitten when circumstances call for it. Such balance is what makes her loved and respected . . . . and need I add, trusted."

"If you say so." The woman replies doubtfully.

After that they all retire for the night. A long night of meditation and intense stress overcomes all of them. For once in Azmaria, the balance of life will truly be tested.

CHAPTER 40

The Warring Stars

After a three days journey they finally enter Azmaria. They can see at least a mile away the armies of the Blackstar preparing for Zahira and her comrades entry into Sagala, Azmaria's capital.

The armies of the black dust bang there weapons together and shout in anticipation of Zahira and her companion's entry. The riders of the black armies ride upon the backs of immense rhincerouses with four horns and clad in black shiney armor. The ground warriors are fully armored as well, carrying spears, swords and large shields with protruding spikes. All one can see when looking at their helmets are red glowing eyes that bleed smoke and ash.

A black mist hovers over that part of the land as expressions of lightning and thunder clap in the sky.

The scarf Zahira wears on her head given to her by Romana she tightens closer around her head and neck only revealing her eyes. She inhales and turns to the vast army of Zehumians behind her that stand ready for her command.

"My brothers," she announces, "As we face this great menace, do not shake with fear or anxiety. Righteousness is on our side and will indeed make us victorious.

Many hours pass with both good and evil armies facing one another.

Zahira and Shamash, along with Surra and the Zehumians stand on the higher plains facing Azmaria's capital of Sagala with the armies of Rathamun standing in the lower plains of the land. They all stand in great anticipation for combat.

Surra then encourages his elemental brothers announcing,

"Today marks the day we regain the world, ridding it of the evil that infects its soil. We shall avenge those killed by this great evil. I will die, if need be, in order that all might live under peaceful conditions. Who will die with me for the honor of our earth?"

They shout in agreement, "Aye!"

"In the name of honor, glory and the peaceful existence of all life . . . attack!"

Zahira and the armies with her charge quickly down the hill facing the Blackstar armies. On reaching the black armies they slaughter all they pass by the edge of their swords.

The weapons of the Zehumians, charged with the power of element control, rip apart the very bodies of their victims.

Surra regroups with Zahira and Shamash to fight the countless warriors of Rathamun steadily pouring in from the city.

Though outnumbered, the Zahira and her companions fight an unyielding battle against the dark forces.

Earth attacks are even employed by the Zehumians, ripping up and crushing the enemies.

Rathamun's forces send out their four horned rhino riders, two hundred in number. The large cantankerous beasts, measuring 6 feet at the shoulder and each weighing over 1000lbs, shake the ground as they charge into the Zehumian armies trampeling many and impaling others on their massive 4 foot long horns. The beasts seems almost unstoppable, their hide is thick as rock. Nevertheless, the Zehumians fight courageously, employing their minor earth control to break the footing under the relentless beasts and their riders, turning them over and exposing their unprotected bellies, where Zehumian foot soldiers run in and deliver the death blow.

Zahira and her companions press forward toward the cities of Sagala, an additional one day journey, destroying all evils that dared to stop them, a long excruciating conflict that seem unending.

Once finally in the city, Zahira turns to the armies and shouts,

"Now we reclaim the great city of Sagala, and the mighty temple of Azwrala. I will press forward and continue the conquest—"

But before she can finish, the air grows cold and still and the very heavens begin to darken.

Despite their victories over the armies of the Blackstar, the Blackstar itself cannot be ignored.

Down towards the gates of Azwrala, grandiose energies manifests around the temple.

Three black silhouette figures begin to hover over the armies of Light. The figure in the middle is large and fear inspiring with large gray wings and energy crackling around its person. The only visible feature that can be seen on its dark figure is its two glowing red eyes.

When the three figures come within one hundred feet of their enemies, the middle figure stops while the other two proceed.

When they come within fifty feet of their foes, they slowly lift their hands, pointing in the direction of the Zehumians.

Without warning, an ominous blast is emitted, leveling five hundred Zehumians with one wave.

The armies of Light fearlessly charge toward the figures.

Another blast is emitted, decimating hundreds of warriors again, substantially reducing the army's numbers.

Surra yells to his men, "Hold your attack! This power we face has become greater."

Without warning, millions more of the black dust soldiers spring from the earth, charging at the Zehumians, attacking all they come upon. The odds are staggering.

The Zehumians slowly begin to fall by the edge of the sword.

Zahira, Shamash and Surra fight vigilantly through the armies of darkness, pressing toward the three dark figures in the background that stand motionlessly, as if frozen in time.

The two cloaked figures, once again, raise their hands and emit another devastating blast, leveling more of the Zehumian warriors.

The decimation is great. The fatalities are numerous. Hope seems lost.

Zahira and her companions finally reach the two cloaked figures.

Zahira leaps into the air and plummets at one of the figures with her charged sword Nazaar.

As she begins to engage in combat with her chosen foe, Shamash approaches the other.

"A child is what I left behind. But now a mighty warrior stands before me. It is good to see you, despite the nature of our meeting."

"I don't know you dog," Snarls Shamash, "shut up and take death gracefully."

The strange cloaked man grins sinisterly and responds.

"Is that so . . . my son."

Shamash pulls back, unsure of what to make of his claim. The man then lowers his hood to reveal his face. To Shamash dismay he soon recognizes the dark figure to be his father.

A chill runs up his spine as the unhooded man cautiously moves closer.

Shamash remains silent, staring into his father's eyes unwaveringly.

"Will you say nothing to the man who caused your birth?"

"What is there to say to one who chooses to follow a demon who feed on the innocent?"

"An unfortunate result of war, my son . . . sides had to be chosen, thus I chose the winning side."

"You sicken me," grunts Shamash.

The elusive figure continues saying, "Why do you continue to assist that inferior girl? Are you not Sumerian, the pride of our people was to be found in you boy. Instead you choose to follow a girl like a puppy. You should have had your way with her and be done with her. Instead you allowed that girl to fill your head with false hopes. It is not too late to join us son. We can fight side by side and conquer the menacing rebels. The Blackstar promises are grand, you can have a kingdom and many subjects at your very beckoning, much power and influence in the land . . . and need I add, sensual women, never clothed . . . where you might find appealing to your tastebuds."

"Does not my mother occupy that position of power with you father," screams Shamash. "Why is she not here to join in your attempts to pull me into this den of evil?"

"Your mother was weak, unable to utilize the power of the black dust correctly. Weakness in the kingdom of Rathamun will not be tolerated. She suffered the fate that your sniveling little friends will suffer. And if you chose to remain with them, you also will share their fate. No one will be spared. You my son, are different."

When Shamash hears those words, the blood in his body begins to boil as his eyes turn crimson red eventually encompassing his whole form, bubbling with energy.

Rushing at his father Shamash roars, "If I am to die then I shall certainly take you with me, for I assure you that I do not make idle threats!"

With that a raging combat begins between the two.

Meanwhile, Zahira manages to victoriously defeat the other dark figure and races to assist Shamash.

"Leave woman," screams Shamash. "Go to the temple and continue your battle. This fight is mine."

Zahira ignores Shamash's request and rushes over to assist him, but is knocked backwards by his imposing arm.

In a rage he frantically yells, "I said leave!"

Zahira sees that Shamash is now in his chaotic combat frenzy. She never realized how powerful he is until now.

Reluctantly she leaves, heading over to the temple. Asaryn catches up to her and she grabs hold of his neck and swings onto his back.

Upon reaching the temple, she is very disturbed by the morbid appearance of the temple. The stories of the beauty of Azwrala and its elegance are unfounded here today. Many ruins lay about the vicinity, large stones and pillars lay scattered all around the temple, where once schools and elaborate housing once existed. The solid stone temple stands over 275 feet high with breathe taking dimensions and a chain of buildings connecting, all having golden dome roofs. The walls contain 55,000 cu ft of stone and have a total surface, both inside and out, of 25,000 sq ft. A terrible stench fills the air carried along by a black mist.

She dismounts Asaryn and sends him away from the temple. She then heads up the forty long stairs that lead up to the immense door. The door eerily opens on its own allowing her entrance.

She races through in search of the Blackstar, Rathamun.

Entering the dark palace room she sees large drapes lying on the floor torn and aged. Also tablets and books with ancient Azmarian writings lay scattered about the singed stone floor. Soon she can hear the sound of crackling breath echoing across the empty halls of the edifice.

"Behold, young witch. Today is the day of redemption. You hold the last of the power that I seek. It shall be mine and you will die."

The deep thunderous voice made the floor tremble.

After progressing a bit further across the large palace floor, she comes to an intimidating shadow in the distant corner, sitting upon a lofty throne. She takes out her sword Nazaar and lights up the room with it, which reveals the black figure Rathamun, sitting slouched in the throne in his long black robe.

He rises from off his throne and with one hand rips away the robe revelaing his gargantuing size of rippling muscle. He is clad in a heavy black thorny armor with a helmet that only reveals his blood red eyes. His large powerful wings stretch out from his body and folds back inward.

"Death has become you!"

Without any regard to what he is saying, she races over to him with her charged sword Nazaar held high striking the throned as he swiftly vanishes out of harms way, only to reappear beside her.

He then emits from his palm a bolt of undefined energy that sends her hurling into a broken column. Her protective aura saves her from the impact of the unexpected force.

Rising to her feet, slightly staggering, she gazes wearily upon Rathamun once again.

"Rise, Whitestar, and face me, the very star that makes you tremble."

Rathamun then races toward her with both of his fist reared back to strike, only to collide with her sword, still sending her crashing to the floor, creating a long crater.

A bit dazed but still competent she quickly regains footing and lunges toward her opponent.

Rathamun rears back and slings a massive force of energy, which sends her into the ceiling of the mighty structure.

The blows delivered by Rathamun start to take a mighty toll on Zahira for she has never faced a foe as powerful as he.

Landing on the floor, she quickly rolls out of the way of another blast leaving a larger hole.

"You see, I have become very powerful and once you have been destroyed, I will then possess all power, uniting the stars and their cosmic energies, along with the Koryan to complete my control. It is useless to resist."

Zahira staggers to her feet, keeping a steady unwavering eye on him and keeping her distance, but Rathamun mocks her.

Mustering her strength she races toward him again, charged intensely with the aura of her power.

Once upon him, they begin to engage in intense melee combat.

Rathamun sends charged energy blows with his fist and blocks her attacks, while Zahira sends attacks by means of her charged sword Nazaar, narrowly blocking his blows.

The speed in which both move is awesome, sending streams of residual energies striking every corner of the temple.

Their power soon starts to rip away the very molecules of the edifice and disintegrate much of the statues and interior design.

The two also engage each other in mental bolts and a host of the powers gifted by the power of the stars. Zahira have never been able to display such power and abilities, but now the power of the

Whitestar starts to become more and more evident. The power of Koryan in her sword increases her defense.

Despite her relentless battle she starts to give way under the unrelenting power of the Blackstar. Her power seems yet to display its full capabilities.

Meanwhile, not too far away, all seems hopeless for the warriors of Light; for Rathamun's armies are pressing heavier upon them with their astounding numbers.

The numbers of the Zehumians begins to dwindle significantly.

Barak then screams to Surra amidst the battlefield, "I do not know how much longer we can continue this battle. We must pull back north!"

"If we pull back then they will pursue us towards the north, bringing their evil with them. We must stand firm, be patient for—"

But before Surra can finish, a blinding flash of light quickly streaks the sky, temporarily blinding all those on the battlefield and lighting the entire vicinity.

Surra covers his eyes, and peaks from between his fingers to witness a surprising sight.

Red-winged lionesses mounted by the Tanazart rush onto the battlefield from the sky. Thousands emerge from the sky as if a blanket of flame fell upon the land.

Tadefi leads the women, second ruler of the Tanazart accompanied by the second and third generals Tala and Tiziri.

Tadefi takes her mighty spear and flying towards the general of the dark armies, slays him without so much as stressing her elegant flow.

She then turns and faces all the armies of light announcing, "Fear not my sisters and brothers. This day, the enemy has been delivered into your hands."

The armies of the Tanazart begin to plummet through the land, striking all those by the sword possessing the dark energies. The day grows hopeful once again for the light users.

Only three hundred of the Zehumian warriors remain, but with the assistance of the Tanazart they fight as if they were billions.

Tadefi then asks Surra, "Where is Zahira?"

"The last time I saw her, she and Shamash went towards the temple of Azwrala."

"We must join her; for Rathamun's power could be greater than she expected," exclaims Tadefi.

The two race toward the temple.

As they approach the entrance, they hear thunderous crashing and the sound of energy emitting from within.

"Such destructive forces should surely have brought this building down. How does it still remain standing?"

Tadefi answers, "This edifice was constructed by the Azmarians themselves. Its foundation is strong. But if they continue this, it will eventually fall."

On entering, a dense smoke blurs their vision as they blindly search for the combatants.

Moving forward, they eventually come to the immense room in which the two are fighting.

A smoldering hot aura fills the air.

All of a sudden, a wall collapses revealing the outside.

Out of the smog, Zahira comes soaring backward toward the two onlookers, crashing into the ground.

When the dust clears, her clothing is torn and frayed from the battle, but her scarf, fashioned by Azmarian thread, holds true.

Tadefi grabs hold of Zahira's arm.

"Zahira, rise, your enemy still waits. Focus, the Koryan is within you and your sword, but you must learn to focus its energies properly . . . only you can defeat the Blackstar."

"Indeed," smirk's Rathamun emerging from the thick smog casually wiping the dirt from off his armor. **"Your powers were greatly underestimated, but it only delays your death."**

At that, Rathamun's eyes begin to glow red once again,

"Time to share the fate of your father . . . bastard," Rathamun announces.

A bolt of energy shoots from his eyes.

Tadefi immediately pulls Zahira from the path of the explosive blast.

Surra quickly animates the ground underneath Rathamun, attempting to imprison him in the earth.

When the ground surrounds Rathamun, at once it begins to melt off of him.

Rathamun then faces Surra, **"Foolish creature, did you really believe that a dust user could give me pause . . . even for a second."**

Rathamun sends a sphere of energy, which ingulfs Surra instantly disintegrating him in his tracks.

"No!" screams Tadefi enraged.

She then begins to charge at Rathamun with her power charged spear facing him.

With both hands, he releases a black darkness, which resembles a giant blanket, cocooning her and burying her into the earth.

The harder she struggles, the tighter its grip becomes.

Facing the battle ravaged Zahira, he exclaims, **"Give up! All is lost. Your comrades think they shall emerge victorious. But they shall soon find that their efforts are futile. Armies are encamped in the lands of Odo, Guta'leen in all the region of Mayota awaiting my very command. Their numbers are as the stars of the heavens. And when this pitiful skirmish between you and I has come to an end, I shall call them . . . and they will flood the land as the oceans of the sea. Your maggots will be destroyed, and then we shall journey north and conquer, with the Koryan as my controlling guide and power. All that do not bow to me shall despair . . . prepare to die!"**

Zahira slowly and painfully rises to her feet. She limps toward Rathamun still holding tightly to her sword. He laughs and says frustratingly,

"You still have fight in you girl. Give up and I will make your suffering short and complete, you tapered-minded fool. But if it is conflict you crave to have, then it is a conflict I shall give you."

Unbeknownst to Rathamun, Shamash creeps behind him quietly. Once behind him, he grapples him from the back, with all his might rushing him pass the borders of the temple, which provided the bulk of Rathamun's relentless power.

He then yells, "Now Zahira! Attack swiftly!"

At that moment Zahira charges into Rathamun, glowing with the power of the Koryan emitting from her body and her sword Nazaar.

She then collides into his chest, causing severe damage to his embodiment.

"Arrgh," he yells loudly.

With his catalyst, the temple, not in his reach the blow causes him to falter to the earth.

Zahira then leaps backward.

Rathamun eventually breaks Shamash grip.

Turning around, with his immense hand he grabs Shamash by the face and lifts him into the air.

"Your blind zeal is the creation of your imminent destruction!"

With that he uses great physical force and plunges Shamash into the earth, head first. Shamash lay there immobile.

"No!" Zahira screams in great anguish.

The earth surrounding her begins to rumble. Her eyes bleed a rainbow of energy colors searing through the dust cloud. The Koryan is now fully operative inside her.

Rathamun laughs, arrogantly turning around and walks back to the temple.

Zahira uses a powerful telekinetic force that throws Rathamun to the ground.

She then pummels him with a barrage of cosmic energy varying in its nature and effect.

The earth begins to rumble with pieces ripping away and rising in the atmosphere.

Not letting up, she sends him numerous blows. Not being able to regain footage, he falters under the onslaught.

Tadefi, who is released from her entrapment by Rathamun, joins her in the attack, striking at the behemoth mercilessly with blast from her spear. Every strike topples his attempts to stand. The attacks are unrelenting. He knows he is weakening without the catalyst of the temples walls. The power of the Koryan begins to rip into the very fabric of the Blackstar, connecting as a puzzle and piecing away the black energies within it.

Beaten badly by the domination of the Koryan, Rathamun, in his last attempt for survival manages to emit an effervescence of energy that sends the two hurling away from him.

He then rises to his knees, staggering in an attempt to reach the boundaries of Azwrala temple. But before he can regain reach the temple Zahira charges him again, knocking him off balance and ending with both of them falling into a canyon made with the destruction of their battle behind them.

Tadefi at once summons her winged lioness by a peculiar whistle and quickly proceeds to descend into the canyon to retrieve Zahira. The canyon measuring over forty feet deep is blanketed by black smog. Soon it becomes quiet and no activity can be heard.

Tadefi searches for Zahira diligently, hoping not to find her dead.

After quite some time she notices something shining in a mound of rubble.

She flies down and quickly remove the rubble off the the shining objeft. There lay Zahira, completely still.

Her body is badly battered. It seems as though blood is coming from every inch of her body.

Tadefi checks to see if her assumption is correct. She is wrong. Zahira is alive, but barely.

Tadefi picks Zahira up, places her on the back of her winged lioness and carries her out of the canyon.

She finally lands away from the canyon and places Zahira's limp body on the ground.

After some time elapses, Zahira opens her eyes. At first, her sight is hazy, but little by little she regains full range of vision.

She tries to sit up, but is too weak and broken.

"No, Zahira," laments Tadefi. "You have suffered a great deal. You must rest."

"What happened," Zahira softly asks.

"What happened is that you survived your battle with Rathamun. You accomplished what you have dreamed all your life. You have defeated the Blackstar!"

"Where is Rathamun," Zahira weakly asks. "The battle is not over."

"Rathamun is no longer among the living. His body lies in the canyon below," cries Tadefi with enthusiastic zeal.

Zahira looks into Tadefi's eyes and replies, "He is alive . . . he is alive . . . the Blackstar still lives!"

Zahira tries to get up again, but falls back down.

"You are delirious, Zahira. It is over. There is nothing more to worry about. I will let the others know that we were victorious."

Zahira says not another word. Deep down inside she feels her foe is still among the living.

Zahira staggers back to the Canyon and looks inside. She notices a hand lying beneath rubble and rock.

Zahira and Tadefi immediately head down into the canyon. Tadefi dismounts and remove the rubble from off the figure beneath the debris.

To their amazement, they find a well-formed brown skinned man with white hair laying there dead.

Zahira, still exhausted from the fight takes, a deep sigh and states, "This must be my fathers cousin who was possessed by the Blackstar."

Tadefi then asks, "If he is now dead and returned to his former self, then what came of the dark energies he possessed? Has it fled or been destroyed?"

"This I shall find out." Zahira responds disparagingly.

"By the power of the Whitestar," replies Tadefi. "The Tanazart's sword is with yours!"

After that, the two warriors leave the area and head back to the others.

Zahira looks upon the battle-ravaged field of bodies lying scattered as far as the eye can see.

There, before her, stand the remaining victorious armies of the Zehumians and the Tanazart.

As she smiles, tears start to roll down her cheeks, soon she starts to cry incessantly, softly lamenting, "Where is Shamash . . . where is he?"

"Oh Zahira . . . he fell to Rathamun . . . protecting you. He shall indeed be remembered." Tadefi regretfully responds.

"Of course I shall," declares a faint voice approaching from behind, "but please do not kill me off so quickly."

Zahira pauses momentarily and slowly looks behind her.

There staggering towards her is Shamash, soiled and battered badly.

At once, Zahira runs toward him and embraces him tightly.

Releasing him, she looks into his face and states, "Oh Shamash... I don't know what I would have done—"

But he interrupts her saying, "Did I not tell you woman that I will never leave your side? I am a man of my word."

Zahira smiles and tearfully greets Shamash in the ancient Sabaean greetings of peace, "As-Shlama my brother." And he returns the greeting, "and Alykom Shlama to you my sister."

Zahira wipes the tears from her eyes and looks toward the armies of light that stand before her, anticipating her next orders.

She then shouts, "We shall restore the cities of Sagala to its grand wonders. All the lands of darkness that remain shall witness the power of light as we restore the entire continent to its rightful status, that of righteousness and justice . . . through the power of the Koryan, shall peace reign!"

CHAPTER 41

The Zahira Chronicles

After that, Zahira started a lengthy campaign of righteous warfare against the denizens of the black dust. Her armies swept through the entire continent bringing hope back to a once dark land.

Shamash fought by her side on many exploits and adventures carried throughout the lands.

So did Shamash keep his word and return to Uruk, serving as guard and prince over Sumerias glorious city.

Many wars did Zahira fight against the remaining armies of the Black Dust, restoring light once again to the Continent.

After 15 years of agonizing war, all known remnants of the Black dust were exterminated.

As age befell her, Zahira withdrew to Azmaria, and at its rebuilt temple Azwrala for her remaining days she dwelt as Kandake (queen) over the realm.

Centuries soon passed.

At the end of the era of a once rich and fertile land, history began to be written.

With all powers of the Star extinct, the once shining glorious cities of Sagala eventually became a dune of crystal sand where the great temple of Azwrala once stood.

None may remember that such legends ever existed, the Koryan, the White and Blackstars, but it was written in the forever lost Ged'i that the Blackstar would awaken once again, and would secretly sweep the world, causing mortal man to cry for relief.

In this time of turmoil a hero shall arise, born during a crescent moon, and that said one shall indeed rekindle the name of the Whitestar.

But the future has not yet been revealed, and the story has not yet been told.

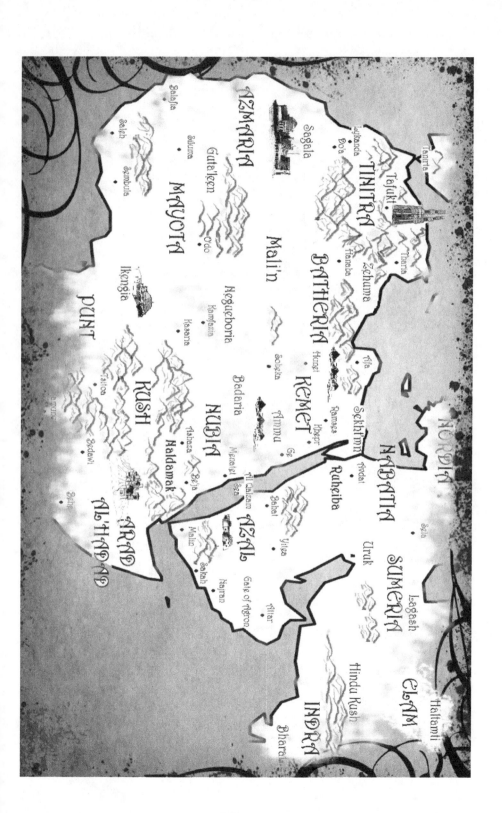